E L KIRK

The Mage Detective

A Death at Ista

This book was professionally typeset on Reedsy.
Find out more at reedsy.com

Contents

1 Map 1

2 Mage City 2

3 Journey 6

4 Disturbance 10

5 A death 16

6 A device 21

7 Guardian 25

8 A Summons 30

9 Debate 36

10 A night of torment 39

11 Home 44

12 The Wind Witch 49

13 Domico 52

14 Ista 56

15 Tilana 62

16 The Investigation Begins 69

17 Examination 75

18 A Table 81

19 The Tintern Pass 87

20 Faskan 93

21 An invitation to dinner 100

22 A Motive? 108

23 Waiting 110

24 Conference with Misco 117

25 Brenta 120

26 Summons 131

27 Tradehome   141

28 Thatcher   145

29 Rumours   148

30 A mad rush   152

31 Portana   158

32 Mage Ripley   163

33 Nimea   174

34 Atos   187

35 The Guild   194

36 Dead end   211

37 War   217

38 Misco   229

39 Fandar   232

40 Return to Tradehome   240

41 The Circle   250

42 Retrieval   258

43 Delivery   271

44 Epilogue   286

1

Map

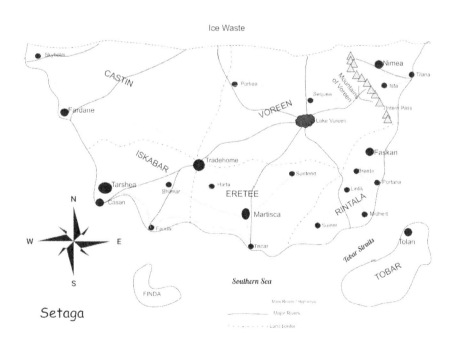

2

Mage City

Tarshea is one of the largest cities in the world of Setaga, and is the capital city of the theocracy of Iskabar, as well as the home city of the Mages. It is also the richest city in the world - primarily because of the influence of the Mages, who use their magic to create Devices that can deliver wonders or power machines that drive the economy of Iskabar, and make it far more technically advanced than its neighbouring Kingdoms.

It is a city of tall, graceful buildings of many shapes and sizes, but always with flowing lines and pleasing on the eye. Only homes are less than three stories tall. There are no warehouses or manufactories in Tarshea, these are located elsewhere in Iskabar, with Tarshea given over to Universities, libraries and offices. There are also many parks and green spaces, providing numerous areas for recreation and contemplation.

Helena loved to walk among the trees of the park - so different from the rundown, not-quite-slums of her home in her native Casan, where she spent her earliest years. Casan was a port town, and there were no green spaces at all until you left the confines of the town wall, and certainly no time or inclination for idleness or relaxation.

Helena was one of only a handful of mages born of a common family with little wealth. Born into a family of Chandlers, she was their second child and six years younger than her brother. However, from the beginning she had shown a lively intelligence and a desire to learn - outstripping her brother before she reached her teens. Her parents were not wealthy and although they had their own shop, it wasn't in the best part of town and only did enough business to survive - rather than thrive. She had therefore worried early about what her future would be, as there was no way that the shop could support both her and a family and her brother and his. But, she had not starved as a child, even though there were no funds to pay for an education or University - although she was talented enough.

That had not stopped Helena, though, and she spent her early teenage years haunting the only public library in Casan and begging for the loan of books from anyone who would lend them to her. But apart from the book learning, she was excellent at reading people and understanding human nature - including the darker emotions that sometimes drove people to actions unlike others. Therefore, when a travelling Mage heard of her in the little town, he visited and assessed her potential.

She was fifteen years old when travelling arrived, and it astounded him at the things she had read - and understood. He offered her the chance to study at the Mage University, and, if she proved to have the spark, become a Mage herself. Helena jumped at the chance, and had never left the University since. Misco became her mentor and guided her through the ways of University life, and later, the magic training to become a Mage herself.

Twenty years on, Helena didn't regret her decision to leave home, although she did occasionally wonder what her life would have been like if not for Misco's offer.

On this bright spring day, with the early promise of the heat of summer to come, Helena was sitting under the branches of a tree in the local park, reading her favourite book. It was a book that dealt with the history of the Kingdoms. Helena loved it not only for the factual content (that desire to learn was still strong), but also because it illustrated so much about human nature and the psychology of how the ruling families thought and acted, how they looked at the world.

A shadow fell over the page and Helena looked up to see Misco standing over her.

"Good morning Helena, are you well?" he asked

"Good morning Misco. Yes, I'm well, thank you, are you?"

"Yes, thank you. I have sought you out to speak to you about something. "

"Yes?" answered Helena, a little worried that she had failed some test or something. It wasn't often that the Head of the Mage order sought anyone out, and Misco's career had come far in the last twenty years.

"I've been thinking that it's about time you undertook a Tour. You have spent your entire adult life here and perhaps it's time you saw some of the world, and undertook duties out in the Kingdoms," he said.

"Are you sure I'm ready? I understand the nature of things well enough, but I still can't make Devices well or consistently, and I'm not even good enough at magic to teach yet."

"Making and managing Devices is important, but it's not all that we do Helena. As you know, we also hear disputes, find new students and carry out investigations when asked, and the latter would suit your gifts well."

"You have known me for over half of my life, Misco, and taught me so much, but I'm really not sure that I am ready to go out into the world yet. I don't think that my abilities are good enough."

"I think they are, and if you don't go soon, you will keep finding more excuses - you should have undertaken your first Tour years ago, and you are already fluent in all the major languages, but keep putting it off - I won't continue to humour you in this. You need to go soon."

"Well, if you're ordering me, then I don't have a choice, do I?" she said, sounding sulky - this had indeed been something that she had been putting off for at least two years already. It was just so daunting. She really didn't feel that she was imposing enough, or skilled in magic enough, to do a good job of whatever was requested of her on a Tour... Much easier to stay here and continue learning.

"No, you don't. I had hoped that you would see that you need to go, and it wouldn't come down to me ordering you, but obviously that hasn't worked. Why don't you prepare? I'd also suggest that you consider who you will appoint as your Guardian. It can take some time to find the right man, as you will have to ensure that you are compatible given he will be both your bodyguard and your confidante for an extended period. There's nothing worse than being forced to spend a lot of time with someone you can barely tolerate... Have you been down to the Squads at all yet?"

"I have spent some time down there - more to study their training and get a feel for their personality types, but I think that there are one or two that might suit me. But I still need to see if they feel the same about me, and whether I would suit them, and therefore whether one of them would wish to come on a Tour with me,"

"Good. Let's assume that one of them will, and does suit, and that you can therefore leave in a week or so then,"

"Yes Misco. I hope you're right that I'm up to this..."

"Helena, of all the student mages that I found on my Tours, you are by far the most talented, despite your trouble with Devices... Perhaps it is time that you believed in yourself and your abilities - you have a gift. Perhaps this Tour will help you realize that," With a smile, Misco turned and walked away.

Well, thought Helena, I guess I'd better spend some time in the Squads and start mapping out a Tour. "I knew that this would come eventually, but I hope I'm ready and don't make a complete fool of myself," she said to herself before closing the book and setting off back to her rooms.

3

Journey

The caravan of waggons snaked along the South Road. Strung out like some dark centipede with scouts riding ahead and soldiers alongside for legs.

It was a bright, dry day with a definite chill in the air but only a little wind - in short, a perfect spring day in the Kingdom of Voreen. The route the caravan was taking was not a well-travelled one at this time of year, although it would become busier with merchants later in the season and throughout the summer and early autumn. It was just a mite too close to the Mountains, and most people preferred to travel by sea when they could, given the long distances between towns and home comforts.

The Mountains of Voreen were a few miles to the right of the road, as you travelled south, and there were things in there that were dangerous to travellers if they were unwary or ventured to close while outside of the Tintern Pass.

The caravan, with its most precious cargo, was heavily guarded and well provisioned, adding to the number of wagons needed, as the journey from Nimea to Faskan was not a short one. It was expected to take about thirty days, providing that the snow wasn't too deep coming through the Pass.

Not for the first time, Kubu wished her Mistress had agreed to sail to Faskan, instead of making one last Progress through her home Kingdom. Making the journey by caravan was not only tedious but also infinitely more risky. She was already bored and frustrated, as they were only five days into the journey and still had a long way to go.

The Royal Family, while not unpopular, had enemies. The order that they had enforced on Voreen over the last thirty years, while allowing the Kingdom to prosper, had made the neighbouring kingdoms of Castin and Eretee nervous. Voreen was already the largest Kingdom, and the coming union with Rintala, through her Mistress' marriage to Prince Lyton, would, eventually, unite the two kingdoms, making Voreen larger still. There were also some, in Voreen itself, who felt that the Princess should not marry a southerner - they were different (although still human) and often viewed the kingdoms of the north as barbarian tribes - how would they view a Princess marrying into the Royal Family?

Kubu sighed quietly, trying to disguise her boredom. Turning her body towards her Mistress she asked, "Are you well my Lady?", more to break the silence than anything else. Her Mistress had been silent for most of the day, when she was normally talkative and vivacious.

"I'm well Kubu," replied Princess Casili. "But I must confess some trepidation regarding the events at the end of our journey."

"But why my Lady?"

"Because although I think I could learn to like Prince Lyton, I've only ever seen him twice. I don't know who he really is, what he's like, or his feelings for me - or whether he even has any… I know I was born to be married off for political alliances, that is the nature of being a Princess, but I had hoped to at least come to know my future Husband before the betrothal. And of course, we're likely to be very different. I have little idea about how southerners live, and I know that many of them view us as inferior…"

Kubu looked appraisingly at Princess Casili. Like all of her family, she was tall, with fair skin, blonde hair and unusual grey eyes. Her heart-shaped face had well-defined cheekbones, a small, straight nose, plump lips and a nicely rounded chin. Being tall, her figure looked quite slim, but Kubu knew, better than anyone, that Princess Casili had curves in all the right places. More than that, though, she was intelligent - loving games of strategy and discussions on history. She was also generous of nature, unpretentious, and good at putting people at their ease.

"Come, Princess, you know you are beautiful and intelligent. Why wouldn't he have feelings for you? You know that Prince Lyton has pressed your father for your hand for the last three years - he wouldn't have done that if he thought us barbarians!"

"Yes, but was he asking for me, or for the chance to marry the heir of Voreen?" replied Casili.

"It might indeed be both, but do you think that he would have been so insistent if you were short, fat, ugly or thick-witted?"

"Perhaps not. And perhaps this is just pre-wedding nerves, but I wish I knew for sure."

"No doubt these worries will be eased when you meet the Prince again," concluded Kubu. Casili just nodded and gave a shrug.

Just then, their carriage, in the long line of waggons, came to a stop. Hileat, the Captain of the Royal Escort, appeared at the side of the carriage. "Your Highness, there appears to have been some sort of disturbance a little way ahead. I would advise stopping here for the night, while my men and I secure the area and ensure the way forward is clear," he suggested.

"Isn't it rather early to be stopping, Captain?" replied Casili, looking troubled.

"Only by an hour, your Highness, and I'd much rather lose an hour than lose lives by riding blindly into potential trouble,"

"Then we'll do as you advise Captain,"

"Thank you, your Highness. If you will just wait in your carriage, I'll arrange for your quarters to be set up."

"Thank you Captain, you are dismissed."

Hileat bowed in the saddle and then turned to ride away, calling orders to deploy his men and set the servants from the waggons scurrying.

The waggons and the carriage pulled off the road, into the open grasslands to the left, and people began climbing down and moving to unpack the tents. The teamsters driving the waggons moved off to their own group - they didn't mix with the palace servants - and collected the dried grass and twigs for their own fires.

The palace servants began with Casili's own tent. It was a large thing, with two chambers, one for sleeping and changing and another for 'entertaining' (as if she'd be doing that out here in the middle of nowhere) and eating. It was also a heavy tent, of double canvas type layers in order to minimise the cold and wet seeping through to her Highness.

Voreen was a cold kingdom, with the top half melting away into the Ice Waste, and even in the southern reaches, the summer wasn't hot, merely warm (ish). Casili also had proper furniture in her tent, rather than a small camp bed, and, of course, multiple chests of clothes and a small chest of jewellery. A smaller, although still relatively luxurious, tent was being set up for Kubu, while most of the rest of the servants would sleep in large communal tents of only one layer. Other servants were also gathering material to feed cook fires, and still more were going through the supplies to decide what to prepare for the evening meal.

Casili watched the surrounding activity. She loved the order of it all - each person knowing exactly what they needed to do, like a well-drilled troop of soldiers on parade, moving like some sort of intricate dance. Still, she was concerned about the early stop. What was the disturbance ahead? Had it been designed to delay them? Was the purpose to ensure that the caravan stopped here? She resolved to discuss it with Captain Hileat when he'd had time to investigate and had deployed his men for the evening.

4

Disturbance

Captain Hileat rode forward with a troop of his best men, including two scouts and trackers. It was one scout that had originally come riding back to tell of an odd disturbance a couple of miles in front of the caravan.

Hileat was a big man, a bigness of build and muscle, rather than fat, and he had the rugged, used look of someone who had spent their whole life outside - in all weathers. His short, dark hair was sprinkled with early grey, and his bright blue eyes had wrinkles at the sides, as if he squinted a lot. His forehead also has its fair share of grooves, where he'd drawn his eyebrows together in concentration.

Although only in his early forties, it was clear that life had not been easy, and stress and worry were familiar companions to him. One of the few Officers in the Royal Guard who had not come from a noble house, he had worked hard to work his way up through the ranks to Captain - leading Princess Casili's guard contingent.

The lead scout, Sergeant Tasco, rode back towards Hileat, stopping just in front and saluting quickly.

"Well Tasco? Report," said Hileat as soon as he had finished his return salute.

"About half a mile ahead, Sir, there is something wrong with the road."

"What do you mean, wrong?"

"Well Sir, I know this road and about now we should see busy farmsteads on the left, and some small woods on the right, and there should be activity from locals in those woods, and the farmsteads should have workers in the fields. But it's silent. No people, no bird noise, nothing. It just feels wrong."

"It's not a Feast day is it?" replied Hileat, thinking that perhaps he'd lost track of the days and the locals were all off at a festival.

"No Sir, not for another few days,"

"OK, let's take it easy then, and we'll send some men into the woods and let's check on those farms." Hileat directed his men, sending two pairs off into the woods and another couple of pairs off to the nearest farms.

"Right Tasco, let's continue along the road for now," he said, motioning to the rest of the troop to continue forward at a cautious walk.

Within half a mile, Hileat also noticed the dead silence, apart from the noise of the horses and creaking of saddles, as his men trailed behind him and Tasco. The silence was strange, as even the small sound of the wind in the trees seemed to have died. The sky overhead remained clear, but it wouldn't be long until dusk, and the brightness of the day seemed to be fading away quickly. Hileat pondered, he should have been able to hear something from his men in the woods - particularly with the absence of the wind sounds in the trees, but it remained silent. He decided to give it another half an hour before calling his men back in.

The minutes and the silence ticked by, with Hileat and Tasco leading the men down the still silent road. Just before the allotted half an hour, Hileat heard a noise. It sounded like people moving through the woods. He held his hand up for a halt, and sat in the middle of the road, listening.

"Get ready," he barked to his troop, sounding loud in the relative silence. He drew his sword and the men likewise drew theirs, with the three archers in the troop knocking arrows, but not yet drawing their bows. They all turned to face towards the woods, and the noises coming from them. There was no way to know if the noises belonged to their men, or something else.

After a tense wait that felt like aeons, but was actually only a few minutes, the sounds resolved themselves into two people travelling through the brush and undergrowth, murmuring. Moments later, two of the guards sent to investigate in the woods came into view. Hileat tried not to let his relieved sigh show and ordered the men to stand down.

"Report," he said sharply. The two guards shared a look, and one rode forward slightly, saluted, and took a deep breath.

"There's a dead Taka in there, Captain. About four hundred metres in. It's not clear what killed it, but the energy wave when it died is probably what frightened off the locals and the wildlife,"

Hileat considered. There weren't many things that could kill a Taka, and at this time of year it should still be in the mountains, hibernating. Did this pose an additional danger for the caravan?

"OK, let's finish the sweep and see if there is anything that shows what happened," he said eventually.

"You two continue through the woods for another mile, then come back to the road and we'll meet you there. The rest of us will continue on. Keep an eye out for the other team in the woods while you're in there."

Hileat, Tasco and the remaining troops continued on along the road. After a further half a mile or so, normal sounds returned - although there was still no sign of other people.

At the end of the mile, they pulled up and waited for the returning men. Tasco approached Hileat and murmured,

"So, what do you think could kill a Taka out here?"

"I don't know… A Mage certainly could, but why would either a Mage, or a Taka be out here - in the middle of nowhere? Why would the Taka not be still asleep in the mountains? I just don't know Tasco. What do you think?"

"I've been pondering, and while it's not usual, it's not unheard of for a Taka to wake early, and at this time of year, there wouldn't be much food in the mountains - perhaps it just came down for something to eat?"

"Yes, but what killed it? That's what is concerning me most. Very few things are more dangerous than a hungry Taka - and I don't want to face any of them - not this trip."

"Perhaps it's nothing, Captain. Whatever it was, it's likely to have moved on by now, and it's unlikely to challenge a caravan such as ours with over a hundred armed men."

Hileat smiled. "Yes, you're right, Tasco. You always knew how to keep me grounded and in the present. Let's see what reports the men come back with."

After about ten minutes, the two patrols sent to check the farmsteads came riding in together. Both reported that the farm folk had heard a loud booming noise and then felt a sort of shock wave that froze everything for a moment. At that point, the men working in the fields had all run for the relative safety of the farmhouse, as well as wanting to check family members were OK.

"They took shelter in the root stores and cellars, and stayed there," concluded one man. The others nodded.

"How long ago was the boom and shock wave?" asked Hileat.

"About four hours ago, Sir. They were arguing about coming out when we found them."

Hileat ordered the men to fall in, and turned to look towards the woods, waiting for those patrols to return. Shortly after, both wood patrols appeared from the woods together. Neither reported seeing anything other than the dead Taka. The second pair had examined the beast to see if there was anything obvious about how it had died.

Takas were odd creatures, a legacy of magic having spawned them. They looked like huge, feathered lizards with long wings. Adults could be up to four metres long in the body, with a further two metres of powerful tail. However, they also had some magic, and could hypnotise their prey and their bite paralysed instantly because of a type of venom in their long top fangs. They were difficult to kill, being fast, wily, and agile - despite their size. But when they died, their magic was released, and they gave off a quick burst of energy that expanded outwards like a shock wave.

"There wasn't anything obvious about what killed it, Captain. No wounds, no evidence of a fight, and nothing disturbed on the ground. There was no sign of anything else even being there, no tracks, nothing."

"Thank you Guardsman. Fall in. We'll all return to the caravan," ordered

Hileat.

They were going to have to hurry to get back before dark.

5

A death

Captain Hileat saluted, turned and left the tent after briefing Princess Casili on the dead Taka. She leaned back in her chair to consider the news. It was a reasonably sturdy chair, especially given that it was designed to be broken down for transportation. Everything in her tent came apart for easy travel, but the chair was standing up well to being taken apart each day. The same could not be said for the table or the bed.

Casili leaned back and pondered what the death of the Taka meant. Was she in danger? Hileat thought not, but you never know, she thought, or was it completely unrelated to her Progress? She wasn't conceited enough to assume that everything had something to do with her, but the nearest town was, according to Hileat, three days away, given how slowly they were moving. This was therefore a relatively lonely point in her journey, so if there were any trouble, it would be tricky to get help quickly.

After some thought, and going round and round in circles in her mind, reaching no conclusion, she decided she was getting nowhere, and she needed to trust Captain Hileat to ensure they remained safe.

Kubu entered the tent carrying a large jug. "Your hot water, Highness, for your wash. Dinner will be ready shortly."

"Thank you Kubu. I think I'll wash and change before dinner and retire early. It's funny, but these days of sitting in a carriage seem to tire more than a full day of activity."

"Yes Princess, it does. Would you like some hot water bottles for the bed?"

"Please. Although it's been a fine day, it has been chilly, and the temperature is already dropping - and we're getting closer to the mountains,"

"Would you like some help to change, my lady?"

"No, I can manage Kubu. You just check on dinner and arrange the hot water bottles, please."

Kubu hurried off to check on dinner and get the hot water bottles, while Casili retired to the sleeping chamber to change. Shortly after, Kubu returned with dinner and found her Mistress sitting at the table looking pensive. As she placed the meal on the table, it rocked, threatening to dump the meal on the floor. Both Kubu and Casili lunged to catch the table. Kubu breathed a sigh of relief when the table steadied.

"Just a moment Princess, and I'll find something to prop up that leg," she said, scanning the tent for something to wedge under a leg that suddenly looked about two centimetres shorter than the others.

"There," said Casili, "use that book that I left on the bed - it looks about the right size."

Kubu grabbed it and wedged it under the offending leg. "That's better, Highness," she said, testing the table. "I'll leave you to eat your meal now, but I'm just outside if you need me."

"Thank you Kubu. I'll call when I'm finished."

Casili ate her meal, still feeling out of sorts and a little pensive. It had been that sort of day. First the worried musings about Prince Lyton and what their marriage would be like, then the disturbance with the dead Taka, and then the table... Perhaps, she thought, I just need a good night's sleep? Tomorrow would be better, and in a couple of days they would arrive in Ista, and she could sleep in a proper bed, and have a nice, long, hot bath. A good soak would be welcome.

After she finished her meal, she called Kubu and prepared for bed. At the last moment, after Kubu had left for the night, she decided to read for a little while. It might distract her and help her drift off.

She retrieved the book from under the table, and when picking it up, noticed a slightly sticky feel to the edge that had been under the table leg. 'Must be something on the bottom of the leg,' she thought distractedly as she climbed into the bed. After arranging the hot water bottles around her feet - they got so cold - and tucking the blankets in around her body, she settled down to read for a while.

Half an hour later, Kubu came in to check on her Mistress, and finding her asleep, blew out the lamp and picked the book up off the floor, then left to tent to seek her own bed.

The following morning, Kubu entered the tent, surprised to find that Casili was not already up, given she was normally an early riser. She entered the sleeping chamber, calling her Mistress' name, but there was no answer. She found Casili still in bed, but breathing heavily and with a flushed, red face, rather like a ripe plum. Moving quickly to the bed, she called her Mistress again, and even went so far as to try to shake her awake. Casili's eyes remained closed, and she was bathed in sweat, while the blankets were thrown off and onto the floor. Kubu tried one last time to rouse Casili to no avail and rushed out of the tent, calling for Captain Hileat.

"What's wrong, Kubu?" he asked, trotting over while still doing up his breastplate.

"It's her Highness. She won't wake and there's something wrong. Do we have anyone in the caravan with some medical knowledge?"

"Not really. We have Harper, who looks after the horses, but I don't think he knows anything about human illnesses."

"We've got to do something." wailed Kubu

"I'll send some men, with spare horses, so that they can change mounts and canter into Ista, but it's going to take them all day to get there and get back with any help."

"That's the best we can do?"

"It is. This is just about the worst place for something to happen. Apart from the local farmers, there's nothing here, and we can't entrust the Princess' health to some farm wife."

"OK, get the men off then, and I'll stay with Casili."

Captain Hileat moved off, calling for his strongest riders and spare mounts. It would mean that the caravan couldn't move until they came back, no longer having enough horses for the remaining troops, but even if Princess Casili woke and felt better, it would be unlikely that they would move today anyway - she'd need time to rest and recover from whatever was wrong. The changes in horses should mean that they would not be ruined and could be ridden tomorrow after a night's rest tonight.

Kubu returned to the tent to check on Casili again, who was still asleep, still labouring to breathe and still hot to the touch. She requested cold water and bathing cloths, to soothe her Mistress, but the cold-compress didn't seem to make any noticeable difference. She kept at it all day, periodically trying to get Casili to take a little water, but nothing helped and Casili remained unresponsive, burning up and breathing with difficulty.

Towards sunset, Princess Casili stopped breathing altogether.

Nothing Kubu could do, including breathing into her Mistress' mouth, could get her breathing again. Princess Casili was dead, and any returning medical help would be too late.

6

A device

Kubu, realising that there would need to be an investigation, left everything in the tent just as it was, touching nothing, but placing a sheet over Casili's cooling body. She left the cold water and compress' lying by the bed and left the tent.

Too upset to sleep or eat, she spent the evening pacing outside the tent, worrying about what had happened, and what had caused Casili's death. It can't have been of natural causes - Casili was too healthy for that - but she had eaten the same food as Kubu, and no strangers had entered the camp. All the servants had been with the royal family for years and were the most trusted retainers. That only left the Teamsters, driving the waggons, but none of them had come near Casili or her tent…

Late that night, they sighted the troops returning to the caravan, accompanied by an older man, who appeared to struggle to stay in his saddle. Hileat rode a short way out to meet them.

"You all did very well to get back here so quickly," he said to them in a deadpan voice, "but unfortunately, it's too late. Princess Casili died a couple of hours ago" The men looked utterly deflated - they had ridden as fast as they dared without killing the horses.

"We went as quickly as we could, Captain," replied Tasco, who had led them. "This is Doctor Vinta. I'm afraid that we nearly killed him with the pace we set. I can't believe that it wasn't enough…"

Doctor Vinta piped up, "It's OK Captain, I certainly understood the need for the pace. I'm just sorry that I'm too late."

"I'd be grateful, Doctor, if you could examine the Princess and advise on what we should do next." said Hileat.

"Of course," the Doctor replied. Hileat dismissed his exhausted troops and turned his horse towards the caravan and Princess Casili's tent. When they arrived, he dismounted and noted Doctor Vinta struggling to stand upright after almost falling off his horse.

"I'm afraid that I ride little, Captain, and I'm getting too old to stay in a saddle for hours at a time," he smiled. After allowing Doctor Vinta a moment to steady himself, Hileat led the way into the tent and Princess Casili's body. Kubu silently trailed behind, red-eyed and looking haggard.

Doctor Vinta paused on the threshold of the sleeping chamber. "You have touched nothing?" he asked them both.

"No, we have touched nothing," they both replied. "I placed the sheet over her, as she'd kicked all the blankets onto the floor," added Kubu.

"Fine. Stay here please - you can observe, but please don't come any further into the room," he said, strolling to the bed, his eyes busy checking around the room.

Pulling back the sheet, he stared at Casili's face, lifting an eyelid and leaning in to sniff her body. He picked up her right hand and then rolled her body onto her side to examine her back and the back of her head.

"There isn't anything obvious," he said. "I assume the Princess was normally fit and well? Was she herself when she went to bed?"

"Yes, she was very fit. She was tired and pensive, but that's not unusual given the circumstances," said Kubu.

"And what about the evening meal? Anything wrong or 'off' about it?"

"No, I ate the same thing, from the same cook, and I'm fine."

"This doesn't look like a natural death. There's something wrong about it, but I'm not sure what caused it. Was she sweating or anything like that?"

"Yes, she was. And she felt like she was burning up and had difficulty breathing. And I couldn't wake her."

"This needs closer investigation by a Mage, I think," concluded Doctor Vinta. "I'd suggest sending for one straight away."

"Thank you Doctor, but it's not my place to order an investigation by a Mage - I will recommend it to the King though."

"Good," replied the Doctor. "I have a Keeping Device that will preserve her current state, in order to provide the time for a Mage to arrive and begin their investigation. I'm sure that the King will agree that a Mage is needed."

"We'll need to move her, bed and all, to a wagon for movement. Do you have one large enough?" he asked.

"Yes, although we'll need to move things around a bit, and store some of the other things in the carriage with you, Kubu." Hileat responded.

"All the other items from inside the tent will need to be stored separately from anyone else's equipment, and will need to be made available to the Mage as well," confirmed the Doctor.

Kubu nodded and left to inform the servants what would need to be done. They would also need to send fast riders back to Nimea to inform the King and Queen of what had happened, and on to Faskan to inform Prince Lyton.

Hileat invited the Doctor to have an evening meal, and spend the night with them, before returning to Ista. The caravan would follow, but would take a few days to reach the Town. The Doctor accepted, thinking that he would need to eat standing up...

7

Guardian

Helena sat at the edge of the Squad training ground, watching some men training. Some were training with knives, either throwing them at targets or fighting hand-to-hand. Others were training on the obstacle course - running, jumping and climbing obstacles, periodically throwing a knife at stationary targets. Still more were riding horses around a bigger, second obstacle course - training themselves and the big, but still agile, horses in the skills they may need on Tours. The last lot were training with swords - mock fights amongst themselves to learn the forms and hone their skills.

Watching the men around her, she pondered their drive to be better - to be the best, to hit the most targets, to do the fastest time. On an intellectual level, she understood that drive - that desire - but had never felt it herself. Did a feeling of being the best really make the risks, and the inevitable injuries, worth it?

"Are you wondering who the best is? Or why do we do it?" said a voice from behind her. She turned and smiled, replying, "The why."

"Ah, well, that differs for each man. For some it's about ensuring that you've learnt enough, have skills enough, to protect - your Mage, your family, your livelihood. The competition to be called the best is what it is for some. For a few, it's about testing themselves, or a way of fighting being smaller, or weaker than others - pushing yourself so that you won't ever be afraid of someone else again."

"And you?" she asked.

"For me, it's the protection of my Mage, and my livelihood. I don't have any family, so this is all I have. I'm Domico, by the way."

"I know. Some of the other men have asked you to show them your techniques in some exercises. I'm Helena."

"I hear you are going on a Tour Helena," he said with a smile. "Are you looking for a Guardian to accompany you?"

"Yes, but it's not just my decision on who that will be, is it?"

"Shall we take a walk?" he offered, stepping to the side of the wide path around the Squad training ground. Helena nodded. She was grateful that Domico had hinted that he would be prepared to consider a Tour with her. She was nervous enough without having to ask someone herself!

They walked around the perimeter of the training grounds. Helena sneaked a few sideways glances at the man walking beside her.

Domico was tall. Helena wasn't that short for a woman, about 5 feet, but Domico towered over her by over a foot. He was also slim - with his height he looked quite thin - but she was sure, from watching the training, and his demonstrations for others, that this masked considerable strength. His hair was also blonde, where she was dark-haired, and had expressive hazel eyes, unlike her own dull brown ones. He was, in fact, such a contrast to her she thought that they probably looked polar opposites.

"This would be your first Tour wouldn't it?" Domico asked.

"Yes, it would, and I do not know what I'll find out there, or whether I'll be up to whatever tasks come my way... I'm quite nervous about it, really."

"So you will need a Guardian who can support and advise, but not take over or dictate." he replied. He pleasantly surprised Helena with both his insight and honesty. Domico also knew something about human nature and psychology.

"It's interesting that you should say that... Do you study human nature?"

"No, but I've been at this for nearly two decades now, and have seen more than one Mage on their first Tour - not all with me, but we talk amongst ourselves, and I see what can go wrong when the pairing isn't quite right,"

"So what, or rather who, do you think I need?"

"I have heard about you, Helena. You are bright and talented, but also don't yet have the confidence and self-belief that a Tour will bring. So I think you need someone with some experience, but who isn't set in his ways, and will support you to take the lead in what you do and how you do it. You need someone who will back you up, but be able to quietly advise behind the scenes without taking control and ordering you around. In short, I think you need me - which is why I sought you out this morning."

"Tell me about yourself, Domico. What's your situation?" She said, latching on to the last part - where he offered to accompany her, and missing the first bit about confidence and self-belief.

"Well, I have no family to speak of. I grew up here in Tarshea with my grandparents, as my mother and father both died when I was only a baby, so my grandparents took me in, and raised me until I was 15. They were good people, servants to one of the more prominent Traders, but didn't have the means to enter me as an apprentice to any trade, and I was not keen to take up the life of a servant, so I came here to learn how to protect and earn my living."

"My grandmother died a couple of years later, and my grandfather about a year after that. I've been doing this for about 17 years now, and in that time have been Guardian to four Mages. We got on well enough and I would have stayed with one of them, but he died of a fever, which no-one seemed able to cure, on a Tour."

"I'm not attached to a Mage at the moment, and have been looking for one that would suit me for the last eighteen months. From what I've heard about you, and your areas of interest and accomplishments, it seems to me that it would be a good fit. Now, it's your turn to tell me about you," he said with a smile.

"Well, I'm not sure what to say… I was born into a Chandler family in Casan and have an older brother, who's now married and has a brood of children. I don't see him and his family often, but my parents still live, and I visit them occasionally, but they're all just too different to me now, and their lives, concerns and interests are so far away from my own that the visits are best kept short…. I've been studying here for about 20 years, and in some ways still think of myself as a student, rather than any sort of teacher, and I'm not great at making Devices…"

"And you think that the making of Devices is important?" asked Domico

"Well, yes, it's mainly what we use our magic for, and they are the reason that we have so much influence…"

"Do you really think so? I've always thought that they were the smallest part of being a Mage, and the influence comes from being knowledgeable, confident and smart - seeing to the core of things, and being able to resolve issues and differences as judges and investigators. Far more of that happens out there in the world than it does here, so maybe you've just not been seeing it as obviously as I do."

"You sound like Misco," Helena laughed, "He's said the same thing to me before - I just assumed he was being kind, given that he's been my mentor for the last twenty years."

"We lowly Guardians have little to do with the Head of the Order, but I'm sure you'll see, on your Tour, that he's right, and that Devices are only one part of being a Mage, and a small part at that,"

They fell into a companionable silence for the next few minutes, continuing to walk the perimeter of the Squad training ground. After a few minutes, Domico said, "Would you like to get something to eat together and talk a bit more about the Tour?"

"Yes, that would be good Domico," she smiled in return.

8

A Summons

King Garrod of Voreen was on his way back to his rooms after what felt like a long day when Thatcher, the Royal Lord Chamberlain, approached him. It was already approaching supper and there remained so much to do before they could leave in two weeks' time for Faskan and the wedding that the King felt quite harassed.

"Your Majesty, Sergeant Tasco and two guards from Princess Casili's escort have been sighted approaching the city."

"I'll meet Sergeant Tasco at the stables - please direct him there, and send for the Queen, Thatcher" he said, turning to go in the other direction. 'This can't be good news, he thought to himself. 'Tasco should be in Ista by now - only something dire would cause him to return. I hope Casili is alright... ' Hurrying his steps, he made for the stables. He knew that getting there before Tasco wouldn't make the man any quicker to arrive, but a sudden dread propelled his feet forward at speed.

Arriving at the stables, he looked around to see if there was any sign of either Tasco or his wife, Queen Irini, arriving, but apart from a couple of servants and stable-boys, all was quiet. He stood still, curbing his impatience and desire to move, aware of the fact that even here, there would be people watching, and he needed to maintain the dignity of the Crown, and not display his nerves for all to see.

It felt like an endless wait, but shortly after, Queen Irini arrived. "What's wrong Garrod? Why are we waiting at the stables?" she asked.

"Sergeant Tasco and a couple of Casili's escort were sighted coming towards the City. It can't be good - they are supposed to be halfway to Faskan by now. I knew we should have put our foot down and told her she must sail with us for the ceremony, but..."

"Portand protect us!" she said, citing the King of the Gods. "I hope she's alright, and it's nothing too bad," but she didn't believe it. There was no way that Captain Hileat would send Sergeant Tasco back for a minor issue.

They both stood there, waiting and nervous. Soon after, Sergeant Tasco came cantering into the stable yard, immediately drawing up his sweating horse and sliding down, straight into a very low bow.

"Don't stand on ceremony, man! Tell me what's wrong" demanded Garrod, showing some nerves despite his best efforts at self restraint. The Queen was quivering beside him, noted Tasco as he straightened up.

"There is no easy way to break this to you both, your Majesties, so I'll just say it," he said, taking a deep breath. "Princess Casili has died."

A small cry escaped the Queen, and she leant on her husband for support, who went white and then recovered to a pasty grey colour.

"How?" was all that he got out, as he felt a huge crushing weight settle on him, and a sensation like a fist squeezing his heart.

31

"We don't know. She was fine when she retired for the night, but in the morning Kubu couldn't wake her and she was flushed and sweating. We brought aid from the local Doctor, but it was too late. He suggested that we'd need a Mage to investigate it, as it clearly wasn't natural, but there had been no strangers in camp, none of the food was contaminated and there was no sign of injury. I'm sorry, Majesty, but there wasn't anything we could do," Tasco concluded, and then bowed his head.

"Where?" was the one word the Queen got out.

"A three days out from Ista, your Majesty. The Doctor had a Keeping Device, so we used it to preserve the Princess and then sent her, and all her things, on to Ista for safe keeping. It would be more secure than the open grasslands near the mountains, and it's closer than coming back here."

"Thank you Tasco, you did well. You may retire now to see to your horse and get some rest, but please report to Thatcher first thing in the morning."

"Yes your Majesty, thank you, and if I may say, I'm so sorry for your loss, it is a loss to the entire Kingdom."

King Garrod nodded and then led his wife, who was clearly in a state of shock, away.

Retiring to their personal rooms, they found Thatcher waiting for them. He had clearly heard the news, as his expression was sombre. News always spread through the Palace faster than a man could run, and the King was yet to figure out how, but on this occasion was glad that he didn't have to say it out loud. "How may I help, your Majesty?" he asked.

"Please cancel our engagements for this evening. We will need some time to be alone - the morning is soon enough to think about what we must do next. Please also send my Queen's Ladies in Waiting to her sitting room, where I am sure she will join them shortly," he answered, knowing that the Queen would want some time alone first, but then would need sympathetic ladies around her.

After Thatcher had left, Queen Irini broke down, no longer able to hold it inside. "Oh Garrod, what has happened to our little girl?" she cried, bursting into tears and folding into herself on the low sofa on which she was sitting.

"I don't know darling, but we are going to find out, and someone will pay for this," he responded in a steely voice, sitting beside her and taking her hand.

"Do you think it was a deliberate act by someone then, not just a fever of some sort?" she asked through her tears

"It could be a fever, but what would have brought it on? The timing of this worries me - we knew that her upcoming marriage would cause some concerns for Castin and Eretee, and not everyone in Rintala was enamoured of the idea of Lyton taking her as his wife. I just don't know if they could have arranged it somehow... I need to speak to Thatcher," he said, suddenly standing and striding out of the room.

After walking out of the room, he made his way towards Thatcher's office.

"We need to summon a Mage, Thatcher. Can you use the Far-Speaking Device to ask Misco for an audience with me, please? We'll also need to dispatch someone to Ista, but I'll hold off on that until I've spoken to Misco... We'll also need to send messages by ship to Prince Lyton. It's unlikely that he's involved, and I'm sure that Captain Hileat would also have sent messages, but he may wish to attend the investigation and funeral, and a fast ship would get there quicker than Hileat's messengers."

"I'll see to it, your Majesty," he replied.

An hour later, the King approached the Far-Speaking Device, a gift of the Mages some years ago.

It was a large blue crystal with a glowing radiance. About three feet tall, and a foot wide, each Device was technically moveable, but given it was surprisingly heavy, it was safer, and easier, to leave it in its own room, mounted on a small granite plinth. Each one was 'Twinned' with another one - allowing two people to speak to each other over long distances. Each colour was also different and showed the 'length' over which people could talk. Blue ones were the rarest, given that they allowed communication over the longest distance.

The Mages had seen that the King of Voreen was seeking to impose control on his sprawling Kingdom, establishing order and reducing the number of bandit gangs that hunted traders and merchants seeking to supply the North. They understood that in aiding him, both through their Devices and their skills, that they could help in creating conditions for the prosperity of the Kingdom, and the wider continent, at the same time as building their influence in the largest Kingdom. Good relations with powerful rulers allowed the stability that the Mage Order sought in order to carry out their research and teaching in relative peace.

The Device pulsed softly like a heartbeat, and, as the King approached the plinth on which it sat, the pulsing grew quicker. Then, out of the air, he heard Misco's voice, speaking in formal Voranian.

"Good evening your Majesty, I want to express how sorry we all are at the events that have taken place."

"Thank you Misco, but how did you know?" asked the King

"Chamberlain Thatcher briefed my secretary when asking for an appointment with me,"

"I assume you are familiar with the issue, and understand why we need an investigation? We need to know what caused my daughter's death, and, if someone was behind it, who that person was."

"Yes. I am going to send you one of my most talented. She is new to Investigations, but is an excellent student of human nature, and understands the darker emotions that drive such actions. She's also fluent in all the major languages, so can follow up on the trail wherever it leads. She will get to the bottom of this, I'm sure. Her name is Helena Hawke."

"Thank you Misco. When can we expect Helena to arrive, and will she be coming here, or should we keep my daughter at Ista?"

"Ista, I would say, that way Helena will be closer to where events occurred. She will arrive in two weeks. Even with a Wind Device, it's a long way for a ship to sail, and she'll need to travel to the port at Casan first."

"Thank you Misco, I will send someone to meet her at Tilana then - I assume that's where she will make landfall?"

"Yes, in two weeks' time. In the meantime, King Garrod, please let me know if there is anything else that I can do to help you through this time."

"I will Misco, and thank you."

They ended the discussion, and the King left to give the orders to dispatch someone to Tilana, and someone else to Ista, in order to inform Hileat and Kubu to remain in Ista for now.

9

Debate

Misco walked quickly down the corridor, towards Helena's set of rooms. He was sure that she was the correct person for the job, but it wouldn't be easy to convince her of that.

He knocked on the door. Although it was late, he was sure that she wouldn't have retired for the night yet - she was probably stewing on finally having to leave and go on a Tour.

Helena opened the door, surprised at who she found waiting in the corridor.

"Misco! What are you doing here at this time of night? Have you changed your mind about me going on a Tour?"

"No, I haven't. May I come in?"

"Sorry, yes, of course," she said, stepping aside.

Misco entered the room, and looking to the chairs, sought one that wasn't piled full of books. Searching in vain, he decided to just move the stack from the chair lying close to the fire. Settling into the comfy chair, he paused and took a deep breath.

"Helena, something has happened, and I'm going to need you to Investigate it,"

"What's happened? Why me?"

"Princess Casili of Voreen has died suddenly, on the way to her wedding, so the timing, if nothing else, is suspicious. I need you to look into it, find the cause, and if someone is responsible, bring them to justice."

"Why me?" she repeated, looking stunned.

"Because you are the right person for the job. You understand human nature, you understand the darker emotions and what they can drive people to, and, because even if you don't believe it, your magic is strong enough to cope with some things you might face while travelling across the continent, plus there is your fluency with the languages of the Kingdoms concerned,"

"I really don't think I can, Misco... This is bound to be complicated, and involves the Kings of at least two kingdoms. I just don't think I can stand up to that."

"Well, you're going to have to. Have you found your Guardian?"

"Yes..."

"Good. I'd suggest you speak to him tonight if you can - you'll need to leave for Ista, in Voreen, tomorrow. You can sail from Casan to Tilana and then take the rest by horse, so make sure you pick a good one out from the stables. Now, I'll leave you to get ready," he said, getting up to leave.

"Misco please! I'm not the right person for this. There must be a more experienced Mage you can send?"

"No, I won't hear anything more about this. It's going to be you, and you're leaving in the morning. I am one hundred percent sure that you can do this," he said, opening the door to leave.

Helena just stood there, stunned.

10

A night of torment

Helena sank into the chair. What was Misco thinking? How could he send her out to investigate this? He was supposed to be her friend! He was supposed to uphold the reputation of the Mage Order - well; he wasn't doing that by sending her out, was he? She was too green and hadn't even had a simple investigation yet!

She couldn't sit still and got up to pace. What was she going to do? Should she go? Could she go? What would happen if she got it wrong, or couldn't figure it out at all? What if her magic failed her, and she didn't survive some encounter with a beast? At least on that one she could take some assurance that she'd have Domico with her… He'd agreed to go on the Tour, but would it be a problem for him if it was now this investigation? She decided to go and ask him - he might think of some way for them to get out of it.

Helena made her way down to the Squads and then realised that she didn't even know which barracks he lived in. Luckily, she saw one of the other Guardians walking across the training grounds.

"Excuse me, but do you know Domico?" she asked him.

"Yes, I do. Why?" he asked.

"Would you mind taking a message to him for me, please? Can you ask him to come out and meet me now? I'm Mage Helena Hawke,"

"Of course Mage Hawke," he said, walking towards the barracks.

Helena, still worried and unsure what to do, paced up and down beside the training grounds. She genuinely didn't know if she could do this, but what would life be like if she disobeyed Misco and didn't go?

A few minutes later, Domico appeared, walking out of the darkness towards her. He saw immediately that all was not well.

"What's wrong Helena?" he asked, looking concerned.

"They have ordered me out to an investigation - leaving in the morning. Are you still OK to come with me?" she asked, hoping that the answer would be 'yes.'

"Of course, it won't take me long to pack, and as I said, I have no family to say farewell to… but that's not the problem is it?" he asked, sensing that there was more to this than a sudden departure

"Princess Casili, of Voreen, is dead - that's the investigation that Misco has ordered me to undertake, and I'm not sure that I'm going to be up to it," she said, looking terrified.

"Look, Helena, I'm sure that Misco would not have offered you up to King Garrod if he thought you couldn't do it. From what you told me this afternoon, he's been your friend for over twenty years, so he wouldn't do that to you, and he certainly wouldn't jeopardise the reputation of the Mage Order. Perhaps you need to trust he knows what he's doing, and that you are up to it?"

"I don't think I can!" she wailed, sounding close to tears

"OK, then what's the other option?" he asked, probing.

"I could disobey him and refuse…"

"And then what would happen?"

"I'd probably be stripped of the Robe and sent home in disgrace."

"And then what?"

"I'd have to find another way to earn a living, I suppose… and somewhere to live - I couldn't move back home. There's no room for me."

"So what would you do to earn a living? Where would you live?"

"I don't know… I don't have any sort of trade, and I only know Tarshea and Casan, so I suppose I'd have to live either here or back home."

"So, which option will you choose? Obedience and undertaking the Investigation, or leaving the Mage Order and trying to support yourself independently?" he asked, knowing what the answer should be, if Helena was being at all rational.

"I guess we're going to need to go aren't we?" she asked

"We are. I'll pack and then send a message to Casan about lodgings and a ship. I suggest that you also go pack. Remember that you'll only have saddle bags, so consider what you really need to take. I know you haven't been on a Tour before, so don't pack everything you own," he said with a smile.

Helena turned to go "Helena," Domico said as she walked away "I am sure that it will be OK, and that you can do this" he said, but, shoulders slumped, she just nodded weakly and walked away.

When she got back to her room, she found that someone had placed a set of saddlebags outside her door. Misco obviously hadn't considered that she might refuse... She took them inside, and started to figure out what she would need to take with her.

A little while later, while she was pondering how many books she could fit in, and whether she could take a couple more if she decided not to take an extra dress or pair of riding trousers, there was a knock at the door.

When she opened it, she found a servant in the hall, with a large bundle in her hands.

"Mage Hawke, the Master requested I give this to you," she stated, handing over the bundle.

Helena took it, thanked the servant and took the bundle into her sitting area, unwrapping it as she went. What would Misco be giving her? She wondered.

Inside the bundle she found a set of the formal Mage robes - incredibly ornate and with silver banding. They were also the formal uniform Mages wore on ceremonial occasions.

She had never purchased her own, given that as she didn't teach, she didn't take part in graduation ceremonies, and little else in University life demanded them. She hadn't realised that she would also need them on a tour, but on reflection, if she was meeting kings and queens, then this would at least act as a uniform and give her the shield and authority of the Order. Misco had been kind to think of it and make sure that she had a set to take with her.

It would mean that she no longer had a choice about taking extra books.

11

Home

Helena and Domico arrived in Casan three days later, after a more hurried departure than either of them originally expected. Domico peeled off to head towards the Docks, while Helena went to find them an inn to stay at for the night. Once settled, she could spend a couple of hours with her family, but getting sorted for the night, and having an evening meal, came first. It had been a mad dash from Tarshea, so some time to rest and relax would be welcome.

Having booked rooms, and stabled the horses, in an inn not too far from the Docks, but not close enough to be bothered by rowdy sailors, she went up to her room. She had only ever stayed in an inn on her way to Tarshea twenty years ago, and it obviously was not in Casan, so this felt new and she had little idea what to expect.

In fact, the Inn was quite cosy, with only three rooms for guests and a small taproom that doubled as a dining room. The rooms were quite small, but still large enough to accommodate a fair sized bed and a small bedside table, with space at the end of the bed for a clothing chest to be placed by the customer.

Helena had packed two of her favourite books, knowing that she would spend some time at sea with little to do but read and talk to Domico, but it was hard to pack any more than that, given the limited space in a set of saddlebags. So she unpacked some clean clothing, had a quick wash and changed, leaving one of her books on the bed for later.

She met Domico in the taproom, who also appeared to have had time to wash and change, as well as enquiring about a ship to Tilana.

"We're in luck," he said. "The Wind Witch is in the harbour and she's one of the fastest ships in the world. The Mages made a deal with her captain a few years ago and fitted a Device, on the basis that we can then use the Ship when needed. So Captain Hartan has agreed to take us and our horses. We can sail in the morning, and weather willing, will be in Tilana in just over a week. It's not the most well-appointed ship in the world, but I think speed is better than luxurious quarters at this point. Is that agreeable?"

"Yes, that will be fine, Domico, thank you," she said, glad that Domico was the one making the arrangements. She wouldn't know where to start. After a pleasant, filling evening meal, Helena left Domico to settle in and went to visit her family.

Arriving at their little chandler shop, she noticed they had already closed for the night, which was unusual given that it was not that late yet. Much of their business came at the end of the normal working day, with people calling in to collect their supplies on their way home from their own work.

Knocking on the main door, Helena wondered if something was wrong. The last letter she had received from her mother was a couple of weeks ago, but all was well then, so she wondered if something had changed.

Her mother, Mishta, came to the door, and smiled when she saw her daughter on the other side of the door.

"Hello darling, we weren't expecting a visit, is everything OK?" she asked, escorting her daughter through to the family living quarters.

"Yes Mum, everything is fine, but I've been summoned to carry out an Investigation in Voreen, and thought I'd call in before we sail in the morning. Is everything OK with you all? I noticed that the shop was closed a little early."

"Oh yes, it's all fine, but your father isn't feeling that well, and Sameer is not back yet from visiting his wife's family. We won't lose much business for closing an hour early."

"What's wrong with Dad?" Helena asked, a little concerned

"Oh not much, just we're both getting on and it's a long day to be on your feet in the shop. I'm sure he'll be fine with a little extra rest. Don't worry, I don't think it's anything more than that," she smiled, and patted Helena on the arm.

"Have you eaten?" Mishta asked

"Yes, thank you. Have you both eaten as well?"

"Not yet. I was just finishing cooking the stew. Are you sure you don't want some? There's plenty…"

"No, it's fine Mum. Why don't you two eat, and I'll join you at the table so that we can talk?"

By this time, they had arrived in the small kitchen attached to the family quarters at the back of the shop. It was quite small, with an old stove, a small table and three chairs, and an old dresser that contained all their crockery and cutlery. Helena settled at the table while her mum called her father from the family room.

Helena's father, Shonti, came shambling through, looking drawn and tired, but broke into a big smile when he saw his daughter sitting at the table. "I thought it might be someone for the shop when I heard the knock," he said "But didn't expect to see you Darling. How are you? Is everything alright?"

"I'm fine Dad, but I was just telling Mum that I've been called to carry out an Investigation in Voreen, so thought I'd call in before we sail."

"This will be your first Investigation won't it?" asked her father

"Yes. I'm quite nervous, to be honest,"

"Ah, I don't think you need to be. You've always been good at that sort of thing - even before you left for Tarshea. Do you remember when Mistress Turat asked you to find out what had happened to her son when he went missing? It didn't take you long, or task your brains much, to find out that he'd left with that merchant, seeking to escape and earn his way as a merchant guard, did it?"

"No dad, it didn't. But this is bound to be much more complicated, and I don't already know all the people involved."

"Oh, I wouldn't worry too much about that," said her mother. "Human nature is broadly the same as you keep telling us - once you understand the various 'types' of personality."

"I know, but I'm still nervous. I just don't want to get it wrong…" Helena said with a frown. "But never mind that. How are you both? How's Sameer and is everything fine with his wife and their family?"

They settled in for a catch up on the family, and a chat about what was

47

happening in their lives, while her parents ate their evening meal. It was a cosy evening, which Helena enjoyed. She loved visiting with her family, but only in short bursts, as after a few hours, they just ran out of things to talk about. So she savoured the evening and tried her best to put aside any thoughts about the coming investigation.

12

The Wind Witch

Early the following morning, Helena woke to someone knocking on her door. She climbed out of the bed and shuffled, still half asleep, to the door. Opening it a crack, she looked out to see Domico stood in the corridor with a wide smile.

"Good morning sleepy," he said. "If we're to sail with the morning tide, you need to be up, and finishing breakfast in the next twenty minutes or so... I assume you do want breakfast?"

"Oh yes, I must have overslept. Sorry. I spent half the night trying to get comfortable in that bed - it certainly looks more comfortable than it actually is... I'll be down in a couple of minutes if that's OK?"

"Yes, fine. I'll settle up with the Innkeeper and get the stable boys to saddle the horses. See you in five minutes."

Helena closed the door and scrambled to dress. She didn't think she had unpacked much from her saddle bags last night, but suddenly it seemed her belongings were strewn all over the room - she really must learn to become more organised in the future.

After a hasty breakfast, they both mounted their horses, their saddle bags already put in place by the accommodating stable boys, and made their way to the docks.

The Wind Witch was a long, broad ship, one of the largest moored to the quayside. It looked huge from the dockside, towering over them and filling the eyes. There was a wide gangplank lowered to the quayside, and Domico led the way. He rode straight up and dismounted on the wide deck, looking around for the Captain.

A short, swarthy man emerged from the cabin in the middle of the ship. He was middle-aged, with bow legs and a powerful build. His short, curly black hair was edged with grey and his short beard was also grey. He came straight towards Domico and Helena, extending his right hand for a quick handshake.

"You made it on time then, Master Domico. I was beginning to worry that we'd miss the morning tide. You must be Mistress Helena?" he said, turning to Helena. "I hope you're both excellent sailors. I really don't want the cabin messed up if you can't hold your food down."

"I'm sure we'll be fine Captain Hartan," said Domico quickly, before Helena could confess to not having sailed before.

"Well, let's hope so. Please keep out of the way of my men, and if you need anything, please see my first mate, Porto. In the meantime, if you can take your bags, we'll get your horses lowered into the hold and get moving before we miss the tide," he said, before turning to call for Mister Porto.

Domico swung his saddlebags down from his horse and motioned for Helena to do the same. Leading the way to the cabin, he said to Helena, "I'm afraid that we're sharing a cabin. This is a trading vessel, rather than a passenger ship, so the accommodations are limited, but the Captain agreed to give us his cabin, as it's the largest one, and he'll take the First Mate's. I hope that's OK?"

Helena was nervous. Apart from the fact that she'd never sailed before, she now found she would be sharing close quarters with Domico... she'd never shared a room with a man before, apart from her brother when they were both little, and that was far, far different. How was she going to get any privacy?

As they entered the cabin, she took a moment to pause and look around. "But there's only one bed," she stated in disbelief.

"Yes, I can set up a camp bed on the floor. It will be tight, and you might end up stepping on me if you get out of your bunk in the middle of the night, but it was that or sleep in the hold, and how can I protect you from there?"

"You think I need protection on the ship?"

"Hopefully not, but it's my job to ensure that you're protected at all times, and I can't do that if I'm not even in the same part of the ship," he said reasonably.

Helena concluded that this Tour, and the Investigation, would, seemingly, put her out of her comfort zone in more than one way.

13

Domico

Spending so much time with Domico was trying for Helena. She had never been forced to spend so much time with one person, and it being with someone that she didn't know that well made it even worse. Even the little things, like being able to pick up on when the other person wanted to talk, or wanted some space, were not things that she had had to learn before.

However, for Domico, this wasn't new at all - he'd done this before, with other Mages, and was therefore familiar with the situation on the Wind Witch.

He tried to put Helena at her ease, and as the days passed, she appeared to grow more comfortable in his presence. On the morning of the third day, she was sitting on the bed, with her legs stretched out along the rather lumpy mattress.

"So tell me Domico, do you prefer being out on Tours, or living in Tarshea with all its home comforts?" she asked

"Oh, I much prefer being on Tours. Getting out and about, seeing the Kingdoms, new people, fresh places, new things. Although I think I've been to most places by now. I get bored just training in Tarshea."

"Why?"

"What's the point of all that training and learning if you're never going to put it to any use? I think that Mages have a great opportunity to travel, and this is the way I get to tag along and see the world for free - while being paid I mean," he said with a smile.

"That said, I know it can be dangerous, some people don't like Mages and would take any opportunity to belittle or harm one, and there's always the odd beast to worry about, therefore I need to stay sharp to make sure that you stay safe. So, a periodic visit back to the training grounds, to catch up with my peers, and learn new techniques is important, but I wouldn't want to be there all the time," he said with a smile.

"I'm not sure that I'm going to enjoy visiting all those new places, meeting new people," she said "After all, I've only ever been to Casan, my home, and Tarshea, so I do not know what people will be like in other places, or whether I'll be able to fit in,"

"You don't need to worry about fitting in - you're not making a home in any of these places. As a Mage you will stand out, anyway. The point is only that you see and gain an understanding of them. That will not only help you in your Investigations, but will also give you an opportunity to seek talent and new recruits for the Mage Order. It will also give you a good opportunity to get to know yourself - what sort of person you are when you're away from the familiar - and to grow your self-confidence," He looked at her with a serious expression "You're going to need to put the doubt and uncertainty behind you - at least in public - and project the image of a confident, knowledgeable Mage. I will help you as much as I can, and I know a lot about the Kingdoms, their peoples, their history - but I can't be the Mage for you, so you are going to need to step up and be decisive..."

"I know, and that's the bit that worries me the most. I'm not confident and I don't know if I can portray confidence, especially with Kings, Queens and Princes!"

"I know it's going to be hard for you... What is it that scares you the most?"

"In this case, that I won't be able to find out how Casili died, and, if it was murder, that I'll be able to figure out who did it and why. The implications, if I get it wrong, could be huge. It could start a war and I'd be responsible for thousands of deaths," she said, staring off into the distance.

"OK, so let's talk about that. If it was murder, then what makes you think you won't be able to figure out who did it?"

"I don't know any of the personalities involved, what their relationships are like, their underlying wants and needs - and I need to understand that to figure out motives and who would be driven to act."

"Yes, but I don't expect that you're expected to solve it on the first day there. Won't there be time for you to get to know the people involved? Isn't that the point of the Investigation? Having some time to figure all of that out?" said Domico, hoping to use his questions to guide Helena's thinking and ease her fears.

"Yes, I suppose so, but how much time will I have? I guess that I'm just concerned that I won't be fast enough to figure it out to prevent a war or something, and I don't want to be responsible for thousands of people dying."

"But what makes you think you would be responsible for that? If the Kings are impatient and declare war anyway, how is that your responsibility? You need to keep in view that you are not responsible for others' actions. If they declare war, then that, and the deaths from it, will not be your fault - it will be theirs. Surely you see that?"

"But if I don't find the individual quickly enough, it will be my fault!" she stated with some heat

"No, it will be the responsibility of whoever murdered Casili, and the responsibility of the Kings concerned - it will be their choice to declare war, not yours. You cannot take the responsibility alone for maintaining peace in the Kingdoms - that is the job of the Kings, not yours. Yours is to find the truth, and only to find the truth, nothing else."

"But…"

"No 'buts' Helena. Come on, when you think about, how can you be held responsible for the actions of a King when someone else has murdered his only daughter and heir? I'm sure if you think about it, you'll see that it's not logical for you to take that burden on yourself. So please, stop worrying about the consequences of the murder. We don't yet know if she even was murdered, but if she was, then your job is to find out how, and who did it," he stated with finality.

Helena looked at him. "I think I'll go get some air," was all she said as she got up to leave the cabin.

Domico remained seated at the small table. He hoped she would take on board what he'd said and leave her doubts behind her. She really would need to show more confidence in herself before they met any of the Kings and Queens…

14

Ista

Ista wasn't a large town, so there was no prospect of everyone in the caravan staying within its walls. The caravan, with all the servants and guards, was just too big.

Captain Hileat had therefore directed the guards to make camp outside the town walls, keeping most of the servants and wagons with them. So it was only himself and Kubu, who rode into town with the wagon carrying Princess Casili and a second one carrying all the belongings from her tent.

The Town itself lay behind substantial twelve foot tall walls made of thick granite blocks. Its proximity to the mountains (and the beasts that made their home in them) meant that very few were comfortable living outside its walls, apart from the few farming families who looked to their own defence.

Once inside the walls, the roads were straight and wide, with most buildings two stories or fewer. It was a moderately wealthy town, being on the main road from the South to Nimea, so boasted two or three good inns for travellers and merchants.

Once inside the walls, the roads were straight and wide, with most buildings two stories or fewer. It was a moderately wealthy town, being on the main road from the South to Nimea, so boasted two or three good inns for travellers and merchants.

Once inside the walls, the roads were straight and wide, with most buildings two stories or fewer. It was a moderately wealthy town, being on the main road from the South to Nimea, and it therefore boasted two or three good inns for travellers and merchants.

Once inside the walls, the roads were straight and wide, with most buildings two stories or fewer. It was a moderately wealthy town, being on the main road from the South to Nimea, and it therefore boasted two or three good inns for travellers and merchants.

Captain Hileat and Kubu headed for the largest, The Mountain Stream. This one also boasted a large stable, big enough to accommodate the two waggons, so it would protect them overnight.

The fast riders that Hileat had dispatched back to Nimea, to inform the King and Queen of the death of their daughter, should already have arrived. It would take another couple of days for the King and Queen's representative to get back to them in Ista - even if they rode quite hard, so he would settle in and see if the King and Queen demanded the caravan return to Nimea. Of course, he may order them to stay here and await the Mage.

The Inn itself was a sprawling L-shaped affair, over two stories with a large ground floor comprising the main taproom, a couple of private dining rooms, the kitchen and a small storeroom. Upstairs, there were four guest rooms and a final room serving as the communal bathroom. The Innkeeper and his family slept in rooms over the adjoining stable block, with a private staircase in the corner of the two arms. A large fence surrounded the Inn, meaning that once in the courtyard, there was security for merchants' wagons, making the Inn popular with traders and nobles alike.

Captain Hileat and Kubu spoke to the Innkeeper about the arrangements for the waggons, and then retired upstairs to bathe before supper.

Once washed and changed, they met again in one of the private dining rooms. The room was one of the smaller ones, being big enough to only seat four people, and therefore had a cosy feel. It had wood-panelled walls, an open fire, and a square table with four chairs around it.

"So, what do we do next, Captain?" asked Kubu, having a desultory poke at the fire with a poker.

"We wait. I'll see the Doctor in the morning, just to check that he got back safely, and retrieve the horse. I will also ask him whether anything else has occurred to him since he left the caravan. He might have some further thoughts on what happened to Princess Casili,"

The server arrived to take their order for food. It was quite a limited selection that was available, but it was still more choice than either of them had while travelling, so after some consideration, they both ordered the beef with cabbage and potatoes.

When it arrived, it was excellent, although neither had much of an appetite and so didn't finish the generous portions. They were both too worried about the death of Casili, and what it might mean - both for the Kingdom, and for their own careers. Normally the King was not a vengeful man, but this was the death of his only daughter and heir, and, as it wasn't clear how she died, he would hold them accountable for it.

They both retired early, pondering their future, and spent a restless night, even with the comfort of proper beds and clean linen.

The following morning, Captain Hileat rode out to see Doctor Vinta. After getting directions from the Innkeeper, he mounted his horse and set off, heeling the directions.

Threading his way through the town, he considered, as he had so much through the night, his future. Even if the King and Queen did not assign the blame for Casili's death to him, it was likely that his future would be limited, to say the very least. So, what would he do now? He really didn't fancy becoming a merchant's guard - that would just lead to spending his life on the road for little pay and even less recognition and respect... Neither did he have the skills to take up any trade... Now he was facing having lost his career, and questioned himself on whether he had wasted his time, and sacrificed any hope of having a family for nothing.

Hileat was a very concerned man.

Arriving at a smart little building, which was where Doctor Vinta both lived and practised, Hileat dismounted and tied his horse to the small fence railing that appeared to surround the house. Knocking on the front door, he hoped the Doctor was in - perhaps he should have asked someone at the Inn to take a message first? A short, pretty maid answered the door. "Yes, Sir?" she said, looking concerned. It wasn't every day that a royal guard came knocking on the door.

"Could I see Doctor Vinta please?" he said, trying not to sound stern, as she looked very nervous.

"He's with a patient just now, but you can come in if you care to wait? I'm sure he won't be too long," she said, standing back from the door and showing he should enter.

He followed her in, and she showed him into a small waiting room with a couple of chairs and a low table. She offered him a chair, but he confirmed he'd prefer to stand - given the armour and breastplate, standing would be easier, although he took off his helmet.

Hileat was normally a patient man, but the last few days had tried him to his limit, so he struggled not to pace. Forcing himself to examine the room, he looked at the paintings that the Doctor had placed on the walls. They were mostly soothing pictures of landscapes and the sea, obviously with the idea to calm nerves for people waiting to see him, or for relatives waiting for a loved one to come out from consulting with him.

After a little while, there was a movement in the corridor, with a small, rotund man being walked to the door by the Doctor himself. He was quite red in the face, had the peculiar waddling gait of the extremely obese and was puffing and wheezing like a leaky bellows.

"You really need to limit what you eat, Master Kern, and get some more exercise, if you wish to improve your health," said the Doctor. "I know Doctor," replied the man, "but I spend so many hours at work, and my wife loves to cook extravagant meals, there just doesn't seem to be enough time for me to take more exercise, and I can't insult her by refusing her food. But I will try," he said, taking his hat from the maid and stepping through the front door.

Doctor Vinta spotted Hileat in the waiting room, and said, "Ah, Captain, would you like to follow me?"

Hileat followed the Doctor into what appeared to be the consulting room. It was bright and airy, with a large window that looked out to the back of the property rather than the street. Tastefully decorated with pale-coloured walls and curtains, with a large desk in one corner, a high divan type bed in the other. A chair stood in front of the desk. Doctor Vinta seated himself behind the desk and motioned for Captain Hileat to sit.

"I just wanted to check that you got back alright, with no ill effects, Doctor, and to ask if anything else occurred to you about the Princess' death since you left the caravan."

"Yes, I'm fine, Captain, and thank you for your concern. One thing that occurred to me was that there may be a quicker way for you to contact the Mages. I heard that one merchant had procured a Far-Speaking Device that is Twinned with one in Tarshea. I don't know if he's in Ista at the moment, but if not, then he will be on his way to Nimea if he's on his usual trading route."

"Thank you Doctor, that may indeed be helpful, but it would be presumptive for me to call one without the approval of the King and Queen."

"Not necessarily. It will take some time for a Mage to reach the Princess, either here or in Nimea, and in the meantime, the memories of the people who they wish to talk to will fade and may be influenced by the conversations they have, and each other's thoughts and theories. The sooner that a Mage is on their way, the better. You can always say that it was on my advice that you contacted them. Surely the King and Queen would see that as efficiency rather than presumption?"

"You may be right, Doctor, but I will have to think about it. I think I'm rather likely to be on thin ice as it is…, and besides, my messengers will have reached Nimea by now, and will probably be on their way back already. So the King may already have requested a Mage,"

15

Tilana

The weather had slowed the Wind Witch, so it actually took a week and a half to make it to Tilana. Even with the aid of a Wind Device that magnified the winds and ensured that it could direct them into the mainsail in the correct strength, there were some days where the wind was just in the wrong direction to be useful. Still, the journey was still at least two weeks quicker than it would have been without the Device.

The time on the ship had been an adjustment period for them both, giving them the time to become accustomed to each other, and to begin to understand each other.

The limited space to escape difficult conversations required a level of honesty that might not have been the case had they had the chance to storm off from arguments and discussions and make themselves scarce... The injunction from Captain Hartan to stay out of his people's way meant that when either of them did venture on deck, they were not out for long, and spent their time scurrying about trying to get out of people's way as the sailors adjusted lines and sails and maintaining the ship.

Still, in that time, they became friends, understanding what made each other tick - what drove them and how they each thought. As well as the minor disagreements, they also had many pleasant conversations and debates about the most esoteric subjects, which they both enjoyed. Therefore, by the time they docked in Tilana, they felt they could rely on each other and understood each other's relative strengths and weaknesses.

"Misco said that a representative of King Garrod would meet us here," Helena told Domico, "So, I guess we'll just disembark and then wait and see who turns up?"

"Yes, but we're on time, so hopefully whoever it is will already be waiting," he replied.

They picked up their saddlebags and left the ship, waiting for their horses to be unloaded. As they waited, a lean man with a wind-burnt face approached them.

"Mage Hawke?" he asked, looking to Helena and speaking in the lower class dialect of Voranian

"Yes, I'm Helena Hawke, and this is my Guardian, Domico," she said, using the same dialect.

"I'm Sergeant Tasco," he said. "King Garrod sent me to meet you and escort you to Ista. I was part of Princess Casili's escort, so if you have questions on the way, hopefully I will be able to answer them. Please, when you're ready, I'll take us to the Inn I've booked for us for this evening. It will be best for you to have some hours on dry land before we set off for Ista."

Once they had unloaded the horses, they all mounted and followed Tasco from the wharf.

The Inn he took them to was one of the smaller ones, away from the docks and on the road that led out of town, making for an easy exit in the morning. Although it was only mid-afternoon, the Inn already had several people seated at the tables in the taproom, which surprised Helena. "It's quite busy already," she said. "Is it likely to get noisy later?" she asked Tasco

"No, this is actually the busiest time for this inn, as most of these are merchants and traders waiting to board ships bound for the southern kingdoms. The next high tide will be in about 2 hours, so by then, most of them will be gone," he informed her. "I chose this inn for that reason, as it's likely that we will actually be the only overnight guests."

"Ah, OK then. I think that I'll put my things in my room and then go for a walk to stretch my legs. Domico, will you be coming with me?"

"Of course," he replied with a smile. "A walk will be just the thing to help me adjust to dry land. Sergeant Tasco, shall we meet back here in about two hours for some supper? You can brief us then if that's agreeable?"

"That will be fine. In the meantime, I'll see about some supplies for the journey," Tasco responded.

Helena and Domico met in the taproom five minutes later. Domico looked at Helena and said, "Is that the warmest coat you have?"

"Yes, why?"

"Yes, why?" she replied.

"We're going to need to find you something warmer. You've never been this far north, and it's still only Spring, so it's going to be cold."

Helena hadn't really noticed the cold on the way to the Inn from the docks, but once she stepped outside she noted the cold, biting wind, her breath turning into a small cloud when she breathed out.

"Is it always this cold?"

"Oh, this is quite mild, as far as I can recall. It's spring, so it's actually quite warm for this far north. In the winter, the snow can get deep, and on a windy day, you get blizzards so bad that you can't see your hand in front of your face. Let's go find you a warmer coat," he said, making sure that his own fur-lined coat was buttoned up all the way to the top and pulling a fur hat onto his head.

They walked a short way down the street, with Helena looking around her with wonder. The Town, as a port, didn't appear to have an outer wall, it just sort of dribbled out into the fields. It was all strange, and wooden buildings dominated, unlike Tarshea and her own native Casan, where buildings were made of stone.

The buildings were long and low, seeming to squat against the ground, with nothing higher than two stories. The buildings therefore gave the appearance of huddling in on each other, with small little walkways between them, rather than wide open roads. Curious, she turned to Domico. "Why are the buildings all made of wood, and why are they so short and squat?"

"It's because of the winters. You'll note that the roofs are all steeply sloped? That's so that the snow slides off, rather than putting too much weight on the roof, and wood is warmer, and easier to heat, than stone. It also flexes a little more in high winds, which is why they aren't more than two stories. This type of architecture just suits the climate better, as does the different type of clothing that the people wear."

Having this pointed out to her, Helena noticed that most people in the street were wearing clothing similar to Domico's - fur-lined coats and thick, woolly jumpers, hats and gloves. Her own coat, which he had thought would be warm enough, seemed no protection at all against the hard, biting wind and her face already felt numb from the cold.

A little way down what appeared to be the main street in the town, there was a shop that looked like it sold clothes, with coats and hats on display outside. Domico pointed it out and motioned for her to enter.

It surprised her to see that inside the shop it was quite a large space - from the front it looked to only be a couple of metres across, but once inside it went back quite some way. It had a long wooden counter down the left-hand side. Like everything else in Tilana, it was a wooden building with a wooden serving counter and long wooden shelves, but they polished everything to a high sheen, and it gave off a lovely warm glow. It surprised Helena just how much warmer it was inside the shop - just getting out of the wind seemed to have made an enormous difference to the temperature.

"Good afternoon my Lord, my Lady. How may I serve you this afternoon?" said a woman from behind the counter in formal Voravian.

"My Lady needs a warmer coat, Mistress. What do you have available?"

"You wish something ready-made?" she asked, with her eyebrows climbing. "Usually I would make something specific to my Lady's measurements,"

"Yes, we need to leave town in the morning, so can't wait for something to be tailored. We just need to find something that is a reasonable fit, please," Domico replied.

This was all new to Helena. She had never considered that someone would have the time, or the funds, to have clothes specifically made for them. All of her clothes growing up were home made by her mother - usually from hand-me-downs from others. Even in Tarshea, she mostly wore the dresses supplied by the University, who provided basic clothing and 'standard' dresses that were often thought of as a sort of Mage everyday type uniform. Of course, she also had her Mage uniform Misco had sent to her the night before they left, but she hadn't thought that it would have been made specifically for her. But she trusted Domico and just smiled at the woman behind the counter.

"If you would step this way, my lady, and remove your coat, I can take some measurements and see what we have available."

Helena did as the woman requested and stood with her arms out to the side. The serving lady stepped forward, with a rolled up tape measure in hand. Smiling, and humming under her breath, she took measurements across Helena's back, from wrist to shoulder, then down from her neck to her knees and then lastly, around the waist and the bust.

"What style would my lady like? Will you be riding in the coat?"

"Yes, we will be in the saddle most of the day, so the coat will need to accommodate that. I'd also like it to have a fur lining, and we'll need a matching hat and gloves," Domico said, before Helena could reply.

"Yes, my Lord, I think I have something that would fit well. I'll just be a moment," she said, bustling off to one shelf. Helena looked at Domico, raising an eyebrow, to which Domico just winked. For some reason, he wanted to take the lead on this, and hadn't wanted to let the serving woman know that she was a Mage, and he her Guardian, accepting the generic titles of 'my lord' and 'my lady'.

The woman came back with a long coat that appeared to have some sort of leather on the outside and fur on the inside. The outside was shiny brown, but felt quite supple and soft to the touch.

"This is one of our newest materials," she said. "The outer layer is water repellent, so should also keep you dry as well as warm. It is quite expensive though, so if you prefer something cheaper…?"

"It doesn't matter," said Domico. "Helena, please try it on, and don't forget the hat and gloves," he said to her.

Helena felt a little nervous, but she wasn't sure why. True, she had never owned anything brand new like this, but it was still only a coat…

When she put it on, she wondered at the feel of it. The warm fur against the side of her face and against her hands, the weight of it on her shoulders, the soft feel of the leather type material on the outside. She pulled on the gloves, marvelling at how soft they felt. Beaming at Domico, she turned in place, with her arms out. "What do you think?" she asked him.

He smiled back. "It looks lovely on you and appears to fit well. Do you like it?"

"Oh yes, this will do just fine," she said. "I think I'll take it, and will keep it on," she said to the serving woman. Domico stepped forward to pay the bill and Helena stepped outside, to just feel the difference to her old coat - which Domico came out with over his arm. "Can't leave this one - you might need it when we return to Tarshea," he laughed.

After a further half an hour of exploring the town, they returned to the Inn for a warm drink and some food. Tasco met them in the taproom, and they settled down to eat and talk about what had happened to Princess Casili's caravan. Tasco told them of the journey, including the dead Taka, and they agreed to meet early the following morning to start the journey to Ista.

16

The Investigation Begins

The journey to Ista was trying for Helena. It took them five days, in punishing, driving, freezing winds that were unusual for Spring. In pleasant weather, it should only have taken two or three days, and they all cursed the winds that delayed them so much.

Helena was thankful for her new coat, hat and gloves, as she knew that she would have frozen to death had she only had her old coat. The journey was through barren fields, with little to see, although the few farms they passed should have had people out planting crops for the summer harvest.

For all that, Voreen was a large kingdom. It was sparsely populated, especially when compared to the Kingdoms of the south, where there was almost always a town or a village to stay in at the end of the day. Instead, the three of them spent most nights in their tents.

Sleeping in a tent on the ground was an unfamiliar experience for Helena, but the novelty soon wore off, and she wished that the journey to Ista was over and she could sleep in a proper bed, and have a long bath. She was sore all over due to long hours in the saddle, and even though Domico gave her a salve for her legs, they felt sore and chapped from long hours of rubbing the saddle. She had ridden before, and was reasonably used to horses, but had never had to spend ten hours a day on top of one, and was tired and sick of smelling of horse - even to her own nose.

Domico and Tasco tried their best to distract her from her pain at the end of each day, and they each took turns cooking the evening meal. Both turned out to be more than competent at producing tasty food from bland rations, but they were all glad when the town walls of Ista came into view towards sunset on the fifth day.

Tasco knew that Captain Hileat and Kubu only had the choice of one or two inns in which they could stay with the wagons, and, luckily, found them quickly at the Mountain Stream Inn. They secured the remaining rooms and Helena retired for a much-needed long soak and a change of clothing. Domico oversaw the unsaddling of the horses and arranged to have dinner in a private dining room with Captain Hileat and Kubu.

An hour later they all found themselves seated in the private dining room, and, once they had ordered their food, Helena turned to Hileat.

"So tell me what happened Captain", she asked in formal Voravian. She'd already had the story from Tasco, but wanted Hileat to tell it in his own words, with his own impressions of what had happened.

Interestingly, he only briefly mentioned the dead Taka, and chose instead to focus on the fact that there were no strangers in the caravan, and none of the Teamsters had been anywhere near Casili's tent or person. Shortly after, their meal arrived, and they began to eat.

"Where did the Teamsters come from? Who hired them?" Helena asked after finishing her mouthful. Domico continued to eat, looking thoughtful.

Captain Hileat finished chewing what looked to be a quite tough piece of pork and took a drink of his wine to clear his mouth. "They were all known drivers of some merchants based in Nimea. Each of them had worked for their merchant for at least a year, and the merchants swore they were trustworthy. Besides, they wouldn't have had the opportunity to do anything to Casili," he concluded.

"Tell me about the routine of the caravan. What did the average day look like?"

"We woke about dawn, and we changed the guard patrols while breakfast was being served. The cooks were probably up first - apart from the last watch of the night patrol - and they saw the troops fed before the changing of the guard. Then Kubu would enter her Highness' tent with breakfast and to help her dress for the day. Once everyone had eaten, we packed away the tents and supplies and got on the road."

"We normally travelled for about four hours and would then halt for a brief lunch break. They would take this cold, and we would normally take about half an hour - during which the Princess and Kubu could get out of the carriage and stretch their legs. We'd then travel for about another three hours and would then stop for the night."

"The setting up of the tents usually took an hour or so, and then it would be up to the cooks to serve the evening meal. Sometimes the Princess would summon me to talk over the day and how far we'd come, for example, and therefore how many more days to the next town."

He stopped and turned to Kubu. "Do you want to talk about your routine?" he asked. Until this point, Kubu had remained silent, focussed on her meal and hardly acknowledging anything that anyone had said.

"There isn't a great deal to add… Once the Princess had eaten her evening meal, we would normally sit and talk for a while and then she might read for a while once she had retired to bed. She was normally an early riser, so didn't stay up late, and all the travelling was fatiguing, so she usually just changed and had her evening meal before retiring."

"And that last night? Was anything different?"

"Not really. She had been quite pensive all day, and a bit out of sorts, but she had dinner as usual and retired to bed. I checked on her about half an hour later and noticed that she had fallen asleep while reading, so I picked up the book and blew out the lamp before seeking my own tent. There was a minor incident with the table, but I don't think that's significant."

"What happened with the table?"

"It was just wobbly that night. I don't know if it was just because it was being taken apart too much, as it had never been particularly sturdy, but it threatened to tip her Highness' dinner on to the floor that night and we had to wedge it up with a book. Perhaps it was just that the ground was more uneven in that spot…"

"I assume that nothing else happened that night? Then tell me about what happened in the morning," Helena said after Kubu and Hileat both shook their heads at the first question.

"I went to help her Highness dress just after dawn the following morning, but she was still in bed. That was unusual for her, as she was normally an early riser and up before I got to her."

"I went into the sleeping chamber, calling her name and saying 'Good morning', but she didn't wake. I got closer to the bed and noticed that she was wheezing and seemed quite flushed. She was also sweating a lot, despite having kicked off all the blankets. I even tried to shake her awake, but it didn't work."

"At that point, I went for Captain Hileat. He sent some men to come into Ista and get a Doctor. We knew that would take a whole day, but there wasn't any other choice - we didn't have anyone with us who had any medical knowledge. I stayed with the Princess all day, trying to keep her cool with cold compresses and trying to get her to take a little water, but she died anyway..." she trailed off as she started to cry quietly.

"You loved your Mistress?" Helena said gently

"Yes, I did. She was kind, generous and intelligent, and not mean or bossy. I loved her a lot, and don't know why she died - it's just not right!" she wailed.

"The symptoms sound nothing like natural causes, so I understand why the Doctor advised asking us to look into it. Let's retire for the night, and tomorrow I would like to see her and have a look at the things that were in her tent if that's OK?"

Captain Hileat and Kubu nodded, and they both left the dining room. That seemed to act as a signal for the servers, who came back into the room to clear the table and feed the fire. Once they had left, Helena turned to Domico.

"What do you think?" she asked

"Too early to tell, I think, but you're correct. This isn't a natural death. The question is, how did she die, and who made it happen?" he said with a serious expression on his face.

"That, Domico, is stating the obvious. Does anything strike you as odd about that last day?"

"The dead Taka is odd. What could have caused its death? Did that have anything to do with the Princess' death?"

"And the table?" she asked him, staring at him as if trying to tell him something.

"I don't know. Camp furniture can be unreliable given how often it's taken apart, but it's odd that it should so suddenly become wobbly. I think we need to see it."

"Exactly!" she said with a pleased smile. "Now, do you have any of that salve left?"

17

Examination

The following morning, Helena started early, breakfasting alone. She waited impatiently for Domico to come into the taproom. He appeared a few minutes later, coming in from the street.

"I didn't know you'd already gone out," she said

"Yes, I ate a little while ago and thought it would be good to call on Doctor Vinta - his impressions might be useful."

"Good idea," she said. "Now, let's go see the Princess."

They left the taproom together, moving across the courtyard to the large stables. Inside there were several horses, including their own, and a couple of high walled, covered waggons. Domico looked in the first one, which appeared to carry all the Princess' belongings, including a very bulky canvas package that could only be the tent. In the second, there was a faint shimmering shield sitting over the bed of the waggon. "It's this one," he said to Helena.

Domico asked the stable boys to pull the waggon out into the light of the courtyard, so that they could have the daylight to examine everything.

Helena walked over to the wagon, taking out of her belt pouch a small green crystal. The Keeping Device that had preserved the Princess needed to be removed so that she could climb into the wagon. Pressing the crystal to the shimmering shield, there was a small popping sound, and it melted away from the point at which she touched it. Domico took her hand to help her up into the wagon bed and then climbed up beside her.

Princess Casili was still laid in her bed, complete with the bedding and the sheet that Kubu had laid over her. Helena pulled back the sheet and inspected the Princess.

It was obvious that she had died a few hours before the Keeping Device was used on her, as she was a waxy grey colour and her eyes had already lost their colour and filmed over, although they had originally been light in shade. Her hair was matted, with some areas darker than the pale, uniform blond that it would have been in life. There was a faint lemon type odour, but it was unclear if that belonged to her linen or was a symptom of something else. Helena pulled the sheet back further, so that she could examine the Princess' hands. The long, slender fingers were hooked like claws, as if the Princess had been trying to grab at something in death, and her fingernail beds had turned a dazzling red.

"Ah," said Helena with a small sigh of satisfaction. "I think I know what killed her. What time is the Doctor joining us?"

"He should be here any minute, really. He said he'd only be a few minutes behind me."

"Then let's wait for him before we restore the Keeping Device," she said, climbing down from the wagon.

A minute or two later, a tall, painfully thin gentleman with silver hair walked into the courtyard. He was well-dressed, with a smart, long blue coat over dark trousers and good boots. Domico smiled and walked over with his hand out for a handshake.

"Hello again, Doctor, thank you for coming. May I introduce Mage Helena Hawke? Helena, this is Doctor Vinta,"

The Doctor smiled at Helena, offering a small bow. "Delighted to meet you Mage Hawke," "And you Doctor, thank you so much for coming. I'd really appreciate your thoughts on what caused Princess Casili's death, and your impressions at the time."

Doctor Vinta replied, "Of course. I'm more than happy to help. I am a loyal subject of Voreen, and appreciate the stability that the Royal Family have brought to the Kingdom, so it is my duty to help."

Helena climbed back into the wagon, motioning for the Doctor to follow. When they both stood at the side of the bed, she pulled back the sheet and turned to the Doctor.

"Would you care to examine her again, Doctor? I'd be interested in your observations."

"My original examination showed that there were no obvious injuries, so I won't repeat that," he said, bending over. "But the light in the tent wasn't bright, as it was evening, so it's helpful that we now have daylight." He ran his eyes over the Princess' body, noting the claw-like hands and the red nail beds.

"Ah, I'm thinking that the dead Taka is suddenly relevant," he said, straightening up. "I think that Taka venom leaves hands and nails like that… Is it just me, or can you also smell lemons?"

"No, we both smelt the lemons as well, but wondered if it was the linens?"

"I didn't smell lemons in my original examination, so that's new. Does that also happen with Taka venom?"

"Some have reported it, but we have found few people after being bitten by a Taka. Despite the stories, Taka attacks are rare, and when they do happen, people tend to get eaten, so there's little evidence left to examine, but I have heard of it before," said Helena.

"So we conclude that somehow she came into contact with Taka venom then?" asked the Doctor.

"Yes, I think we do. But the question is how, and who put it there?" concluded Helena.

"Well, thank you Doctor, we appreciate the help," said Domico as the Doctor and Helena climbed back down from the wagon.

Helena walked to the front of the waggon to retrieve the Keeping Device. "Do you need this back, Doctor? I have one of my own if you need to hold on to this one."

"Yes please. I rarely need to use one, but they are expensive, so I'd like to keep hold of it if you don't need it," he said, taking something that looked like a round orange stone back from Helena. He put it in his coat pocket and looked at them both. "Would you like to share a drink?" he said shyly. "I'm partial to a hot Choo about this time of day."

Choo was a type of tree bark that was steeped in hot water. It contained stimulants that provided a burst of energy to the drinker.

Domico stepped forward and replied, "Yes, Doctor, that would be lovely.

Let's step into the Inn and we can order a cup" Helena wasn't inclined to agree, although she did like Choo. She wanted to get on and examine the belongings of the Princess before she stopped for a break.

However, seeing the look on Domico's face, she pasted on a smile and led the way into the Inn, after licking the Keeping Device to activate it and placing it in the wagon's front to reactivate the shimmering shield.

Following the Choo and a friendly chat about the Doctor, his life and the events in the small town, the Doctor left the Inn and Helena turned to Domico. "Why did you accept the offer of a drink?" she said "I wanted to get on and start examining her belongings, but instead we've wasted half an hour of daylight."

"We did not waste it, I think... It would have been useful if Doctor Vinta had any other observations, and it's better to understand him, and this place, now, rather than stumble later. And don't forget, the Investigation is one thing, but you also have a role in seeking any promising students. Talking to prominent members of any town is sometimes the best way to seek them out."

"I'm sorry Domico, I've just got this Investigation at the front of my mind... I know how important it is, and the likely ramifications now we've concluded that it wasn't a natural death. I just wasn't thinking about the other duties of a Tour..."

"I know Helena, and it's fine, but you need to remember that a Mage is not at the beck and call of anyone who wants an Investigation - you are responsible for your own choices and actions, and should ensure that you are seen to be taking those other duties as seriously as the Investigation." Domico smiled to take the sting out of the words, and to try to not make it feel like a lecture, but Helena worried what else she was neglecting while focusing on the Investigation.

They went back outside and asked the stable boys to take Casili's wagon back into the stables and bring out the first one.

18

A Table

Domico climbed up into the wagon bed. "It's the table you want to look at first, right?" he called down.

"Yes please, but Domico, please put your gloves on before you touch anything."

"Ah, yes, thanks for the reminder" he pulled some soft woollen gloves out of his pocket and put them on. The things were packed closely together, in order to get them all, and the tent, into one wagon, so it took some rummaging to find a small table. It also appeared that everything had just been piled in, with nothing being broken down properly for transportation, but perhaps that was for the best given that the servants did not know what had caused the death.

He moved the things around enough to free the table, and pulled it out of the pile, moving it to the back. He then jumped down and grabbed the table, placing it on the floor in front of Helena. As he placed it down, they both noticed that one leg was shorter than the others. Helena frowned.

"Domico, could you please take that leg off, and one other, and see if it really is shorter, or whether it's just the cobbles it's sitting on?"

Domico pulled out the offending leg, and the one in the opposite corner and laid them on the ground, side by side. One was indeed shorter than the other, but only by a little.

"I'm sure that those legs would have started off at the same length, so what do you think happened?" she asked him. He picked up the leg to inspect it, peering at both ends.

"One end has been cut off and not sanded again," he said "Look, you can see the difference to the other legs… But it's also sticky on this end, not much, and whatever it was has mostly dried, but it still feels a little tacky and seems to be darker than the other ends…"

"That might be Taka venom, so be careful… But why would the Princess be touching the bottom of a table leg?" asked Helena. "I'll need to test this, and make sure it is what we think it is, and you can talk to Kubu and find out more about the minor incident of the table."

"In the meantime, let's leave everything else where it is and get the wagon back in the stables."

Helena put on her own gloves, this time made of cotton, and took the table leg from Domico, disappearing back into the Inn to go to her room for some privacy. Domico spoke to one of the stable boys and followed her in.

He joined her in her room a couple of minutes later and stationed himself in front of the door. He knew that while she was working her magic, she would be absolutely vulnerable, and while very few people knew that there was a Mage in Town, and even fewer knew who she was, he was taking no chances.

Helena placed the table leg on the bed and removed her coat and gloves.

Centring herself, she took a deep breath and closed her eyes. Forming the picture of a small circle in her mind, she focussed the centre of that circle on the end of the table leg.

Drawing on her inner spark, visualising what she wanted to do, she opened her eyes, imagining the particles of liquid being forced out of the wood. She brought her hands up in front of her and motioned as if drawing out of the leg the substance on the end. This resulted in a small globe of black liquid forming at the end of the leg, which she then motioned over to the wash bowl on the small table. The small globule floated across the room and settled into the bowl, holding its shape as a perfect sphere.

Drawing on her inner spark, visualising what she wanted to do, she opened her eyes, imagining the particles of liquid being forced out of the wood. She brought her hands up in front of her and motioned as if drawing out of the leg the substance on the end. This resulted in a small globe of black liquid forming at the end of the leg, which she then motioned over to the wash bowl on the small table. The small globule floated across the room and settled into the bowl, holding its shape as a perfect sphere.

Helena then stepped up to the bowl and again, motioning with her hands, made a small circling motion that caused the globe of liquid to spin. It gained speed, going faster and faster and then suddenly separated into two, as if someone had cut it down the middle. Inside of the black sphere, there was a small centre globule of green liquid.

Helena breathed out. "So, it is Taka venom," she said to Domico. "That answers the what, but not the who or the most important part of the how…"

"Is it at all likely that a Princess would touch the end of a table leg?" asked Domico

"No, but you'll recall that Kubu said they had jammed a book under it to steady the table, so that Her Highness' food wasn't dumped on the floor... So, did Casili then pick up the book, and was there some venom on that as a result?"

"We need to find that book," concluded Domico. "I'll go look in the wagon, as it should be in there somewhere. You'll talk to Kubu?"

Helena nodded. "Can you ask the Innkeeper to dispose of that?" she asked, pointing to the washbasin, with the black and green liquid now spotting the bowl. "It will need to be boiled before anyone can use it safely."

Domico nodded and put his gloves back on before picking up the bowl and leaving the room.

About half an hour later, he knocked on the door. Helena opened it to see him standing in the hall with a small book in his gloved hands. She opened the door wider and motioned him to enter.

"Well?" she asked.

"It looks as if it had something on it. It's dried out now, but there is a slightly discoloured square and the impression of something square having rested on it. If we compare it to the size of the end of the table leg, I think it will match."

"It looks as if it had something on it. It's dried out now, but there is a slightly discoloured square and the impression of something square having rested on it. If we compare it to the size of the end of the table leg, I think it will match."

They did that, and it was a match.

"So, we can conclude that someone placed Taka venom onto the bottom of a deliberately shortened table leg, assuming that they would prop it up with something that Casili would then handle later... Wouldn't that be quite chancy, though?" mused Helena

"Possibly not. You've stayed in a tent - there isn't anything surplus that you don't need or use every day, so the chances of them finding something to wedge the leg that is never touched again, or only touched by the servants, is quite slim. Plus, when you consider the type of person who everyone said Casili was, she was far more likely to fetch something for herself than to send Kubu or a servant to get it."

"Yes, you're right. When I checked with Kubu, she said that Casili had been reading in bed, and that she'd picked the book up off the floor when she checked on her and blew out the lamp."

"So, we now have a choice... We can head to where it happened and see if we can glean anything from the dead Taka - although it's been about three weeks now, so the chances of finding anything are slim - or we can head to either Faskan to see Prince Lyton, or to Nimea to see King Garrod and Queen Irini..." said Helena

"What's your preference?"

"Faskan I think. Few people knew Casili would travel overland rather than by ship, but Prince Lyton was one of them, and Faskan would also be closer if we need to visit the Kingdoms of Eretee or Castin. I doubt that King Garrod or his Queen know more than they already said to Misco. The dead Taka will still be there, but if the guards couldn't tell what killed it at the time, I'm not sure that we'll be able to tell now..."

"What route do you wish to go? We can either ride and go through the Tintern Pass in the Mountains of Voreen, or we can go back to Tilana and sail. The latter would probably be quicker, but only by a few days," Domico asked.

"Ah, so a choice of either more pain, or pain *and* boredom on a ship," Helena said with a smile. "I think we'll ride as I'm hoping to get used to that saddle…
"

19

The Tintern Pass

They spent that night at the Mountain Stream inn in Ista, taking time to secure the supplies for the week-long trek down to Faskan.

Helena spoke to Captain Hileat, Sergeant Tasco and Kubu, informing them of how Casili had died. She also suggested that they make their way back to Nimea with the wagons and news, and informed the King that she would travel on to Faskan to speak with Prince Lyton and see whether it would be necessary to venture on to Eretee and Castin.

"I will ask for permission to use the Far-Speaking Device in Faskan to update King Garrod, but in the meantime, could you please look into the background of each of the teamsters from the caravan," she asked Hileat, just before they were due to leave.

"Of course Mage Hawke. I will see to it personally and will provide any updates to the King's Chamberlain."

"Thank you, Captain," she responded, before turning away.

Early the following morning they left Ista travelling south east towards the mountains and the Tintern Pass. This time it was just the two of them, so they reduced the need for multiple pack animals and share a tent, given that the tents were the bulkiest and heaviest thing for them to carry. After sharing a cabin on the Wind Witch, this no longer made Helena nervous, and she felt comfortable sharing with Domico.

As they travelled along the South Road, they occasionally came across merchants travelling north, seeking to bring the early spring supplies to northern Voreen and gaining a substantial profit from being the first to arrive with the new year's early provisions. However, the merchants were few and far between, and it was generally just the two of them.

The terrain, as they travelled south east, slowly changed from open grasslands into fields and farms. Running a couple of miles out from the mountains, but parallel to them, they felt like constant companions, and Helena moved from feeling dwarfed by their immense height, to seeing them as unchanging, familiar friends.

Three days after their departure from Ista, they entered the foothills leading to the Tintern Pass. The Pass itself was a winding path between two of the higher peaks, where a smaller mountain had eroded and worn down, creating a path that, although still high and reasonably steep in places, was wide and navigable for a wagon or cart.

They had made camp early the previous night, wanting to get an early start, as, if they were lucky, they could make it through the Pass in one day, cutting out the need to spend a night camped somewhere on its high, twisting road.

Skipping their usual hot breakfast, they broke camp while it was still dark, setting off just as soon as it was light enough to see the start of the path. Domico took the lead, making sure that his sword on his back, and the knives strapped to his arms and ankles, were free of obstruction and available should they be needed.

The Pass actually acted as the border between Voreen and Rintala, and while the King of Voreen had worked hard to stamp out the bandit gangs that had roamed the country, the Pass was still no place for the unwary, and occasionally harboured the odd desperate gang of thieves and highwaymen.

They rode in single file, so talk was limited, with the two packhorses strung out behind Helena. This was probably just as well, as Helena felt quite nervous, knowing the dangers of the Pass, and would otherwise have been inclined to talk to hide her nerves and distract herself. Unfortunately, this would also have distracted Domico, and he was aware he needed to be vigilant.

They were almost through the Pass when they heard something moving above them. Whatever it was, it made no effort to be quiet, so it was unlikely to be a gang of bandits, but that meant that it was potentially even worse. There were more than a few beasts living in the mountains, including Taka.

Domico halted, and put a hand up for Helena to stop, staying behind him, and looked up, trying to see over the top of a ledge about three metres above them. The angle of the ledge, and the sun, meant that there was a significant blind spot, so he nudged his horse forward to get a better view. As he did so, he glimpsed a large blue coloured beak, shining in the sun. So, they were dealing with a Roc... Rocs were similar to over-grown, blue eagles and stood at about a metre high. They were not normally very smart, unlike their more normal sized cousins, and while their talons and beaks could pose a danger, they were normally wary of people.

Domico motioned for Helena to ride past, with the packhorses, while he watched the Roc for any sign of aggressiveness or attack. He could hear a chirping noise from the ledge and assumed that this was a nest with a chick inside it. Therefore, as long as they moved on quickly, and made no threatening gesture, they should be safe, he thought to himself.

Just as Helena was about to ride clear, a dirty, dishevelled man stepped out from behind a large boulder at the side of the path. He looked like his last wash was whenever it had last rained, and his matted beard and hair showed it had been some time since he was last near civilised society.

"Give me all your money and jewels," he said in a raspy voice "Or my friends will shoot you both full of arrows and then we'll take them anyway," at which point he pulled a long dagger out of a sheath at his side.

The dagger itself was about thirty centimetres long, and pitted with rust with small nibbles taken out the sides of the blade. It looked, somehow, far more menacing than a brand new, shiny dagger.

Helena paused. Ordinarily this wouldn't be a problem, as Domico could defend them both easily from one man, but he had said something about companions in the Pass with bows... Also, Domico was distracted by the Roc... Helena considered trying to use her magic to freeze him in place, but that wouldn't work on any companions that she couldn't even see.

'What about a shield?' she thought to herself - that may be possible, but she wasn't sure if she could manage one large enough to cover herself, Domico, and both the pack horses.

Her moment of indecision cost her - the man raised his hand as if to signal to others in the Pass, but just then, a small, shiny knife came spinning, end over end, past her head, sinking into the man's chest.

"Ride!" shouted Domico, urging his horse into a canter through the pass. Helena reacted and booted her horse into action. Cantering along the steep trail she looked back, but there didn't appear to be any arrows coming in their direction, and no-one else was visible in the Pass, other than Domico, herself and the dead man. Domico did not stop to retrieve his knife.

A tense few minutes later, they were both past, cantering along the path to put some distance behind them. Domico had nudged his horse in front, and rode with his eyes busy, scanning everywhere for further potential hiding places. After a little while, Domico slowed his horse and motioned for Helena to slow and they both came to a stop, the pack horses breathing hard and sweating behind them.

"What was that?" asked Helena,

"A lone bandit, I'd think. I guessed he was bluffing about companions with bows, as there weren't many places they could have hidden at that point, and the Roc was taking the most viable spot. Even a desperate bandit wouldn't share a ledge with a Roc. I think he picked that spot hoping that anyone coming through would focus on the Roc until it was too late."

"Do you mean the blue bird thing?" she asked, having seen nothing like it before.

"Yes, that was a Roc, on its nest with a chick, I think. They aren't usually dangerous to people, but with a chick you can never be sure. I do not know why it chose a ledge in the middle of the Pass for its nest - they are usually much higher, on ledges that are inaccessible to other beasts in the mountains. As a result, you don't see them very often."

"Is it likely to come after us?"

"No. It might have attacked if it thought we were threatening its nest, but it won't seek us out. Besides, the dead bandit will provide meals for the next few days for it and its chick, so it's got no reason to hunt us down."

"How much longer to the other side of the Pass?" she asked, thinking that they had travelled all day, with no break, and she'd dearly like to get out of the Pass…

"About another hour and we should start getting back down to the foothills, with perhaps another half an hour after that to the plains. But we can pick up the pace a little and make it sooner if you'd like?"

"Yes please, I'd like to get down and walk for a bit, but I'll wait until we're out of the Pass for that, I think."

The pair picked up the pace to a wary trot and continued on, seeing nothing else to bother them. At the plains, after coming out of the foothills, they gladly pulled off the road a little way and made camp in the woods at the side of the road.

Three more days of travel would put them in Faskan, but they were now almost in the kingdom of Rintala.

20

Faskan

Rintala, being on this side of the Mountains of Voreen, and far enough south from the Ice Waste to be reasonably warm, suffered from neither freezing winters nor baking summers, remaining temperate most of the year. As a result, the extensive farmlands were rich and profitable, able to grow and harvest crops throughout most of the year. Indeed, the entire economy of Rintala was based on agriculture and farming. More than self-sufficient, it exported thousands of tons of grain and wheat, as well as hundreds of thousands of cattle, sheep and pigs, into the northern kingdoms of both Voreen and Castin.

This gave the landscape an ordered look, with most land divided into neat parcels, enclosed by fences, walls and hedges. Everything generally went in straight lines, including the roads, and, where possible, rivers, providing straight irrigation ditches.

Helena almost felt that she'd returned to civilization from the frozen, wild lands of the North.

It was approaching dusk when Helena and Domico came in sight of the high walls of Faskan. It was a big city, the capital of the Kingdom of Rintala, and the seat of the royal family. King Fanton and Queen Darla had been in power for over forty years, and were slowly handing the reins over to their son, Prince Lyton. He himself was approaching his thirtieth year, and many in the city felt it was time for the King and Queen to step down and formally crown the Prince.

The capital itself, however, was the exception to the straight, ordered structure of the fields and villages, being ancient and mostly developed before agriculture became the driver of the economy.

Instead, the City had been built for defence, where straight lines and wide roads were a potential problem, and instead they tended to curve and twist around buildings that were themselves curved. There were more than a few buildings that were entirely round, giving those that were over one story the look of towers, with very few having any windows on the ground floor, and those that did, they were narrow things that functioned more as archery gaps, rather than wide windows to let in light.

It fascinated Helena. "I wonder how they find furniture that fits?" she said to Domico.

"Well, you'll soon find out," he said with a chuckle. "Are we going straight to the palace, and are we expecting to stay there?" he asked her.

"Not sure. What do you think would work best? I don't mind announcing who I am, but I don't want to be bogged down in formal dinners and events, and I do not know how the Rintalans view Mages. However, access to Prince Lyton and his family would be easier if we stayed in the Palace..."

"Hmm, their view of Mages is mixed. They appreciate what you can do, but would generally prefer that you do it far away from them... How about we go to the Palace first, and see if they invite us to stay? If they do, then we can always stay a day or two and move into the City if it gets too much?" he suggested.

"Yes, my mighty Guardian," she said with a smile. "Lead the way."

Domico had visited the City before, and was basically familiar with the route to the Palace, but it was getting darker and it had been a few years since he was last here. After a couple of wrong turns, he at last found the correct street that led to the Palace. "These streets are disorientating," he said to Helena as an attempt to justify getting lost.

"I think that's rather the point," she observed dryly. "I've never seen architecture like this. It's fascinating how you can't just plot a straight path from a to b... It feels rather like a maze. I'm glad you're here. I'd be completely lost on my own," she smiled in forgiveness.

"Well, we're nearly there now, but please, don't leave the Palace without me, or it might take days to find you!" he said with a chuckle.

They approached what must be the largest building in the City, and, as like all the others, it had a curving wall, and from the angle of the curve, Helena estimated it must be at least a couple of miles from one edge of the circle to the other. So was this a wall, or was the building truly that big?

In front of them were a couple of soldiers, guarding what looked to be a small gate, next to a large arched opening that looked to be sealed by strong wooden gates, bounded in iron. That must be the ceremonial entrance, she thought to herself. The smaller gate to the left must be the everyday one, and much easier to guard...

They both dismounted and Domico approached the guards speaking High Rintalan, "It is my honour to present Mage Helena Hawke. I am her Guardian, Domico. Would you please let your superiors know that we're here and would appreciate an audience with the King?"

One guard looked to the other and nodded, with the second one turning smartly and marching through the small gate and disappearing inside. They waited in silence, as the guard didn't appear inclined to talk. The appearance of a Mage often did that.

A few minutes later, the gate opened, and an officer stepped out, the original guard trailing behind him.

"Good evening Mage Hawke, Guardian Domico. I am Lieutenant Flint. If you will follow me, I will take you inside."

He turned smartly and disappeared through the gate. Helena and Domico had no choice but to follow suit. Although the gate was small, it was, thankfully, tall and wide enough to admit the horses - just, given the bulky saddle bags. Lieutenant Flint gestured to the guard, saying "Look after the horses. Make sure they are watered and fed," leading Helena and Domico away.

"That doesn't sound promising. I guess we're not staying then…" Domico whispered to Helena.

Once through the gate, Helena noticed that the large round building was actually a ring, about three metres deep, with stairs periodically climbing up to a second story that gave access to a wide walkway that appeared to continue all the way around the ring itself. This meant that the building was actually a wall, with space for guards to muster, fight, and defend the royal compound, but the ground floor also had rooms - accommodation, maybe?

Inside the compound, there were several buildings. The horses were being led off to what was clearly a large stable to the left of the path they were now walking along. Straight ahead was a large white building that, while slightly curved, was nowhere near as pronounced as some of those in the wider city. It was to this building that the Lieutenant appeared to be taking them.

It appeared to be of three stories, with hundreds of small, quite narrow windows and a wide double door at the top of a few wide steps.

As they were approaching, the wide doors opened, and a man stepped out to wait at the top of the steps for their approach. As they mounted the steps, the man bowed to Helena and then turned, and bowed, slightly less, to Domico.

"Welcome to Faskan, Mage Hawke. I am the King's Chamberlain - Lord Justar. If you will follow me, I'll take you to the Royal Family. I am afraid that they are giving an audience at the moment, but it should be over soon." He turned to the Lieutenant, "Thank you Lieutenant Flint, I will take it from here." The Lieutenant nodded and stepped back before turning to walk away.

He led the way into the building. "I'm afraid that we can't offer you any accommodation at this time. The whole compound is full of noble guests who had come for the wedding, but I'm sure you will find good accommodation in the City," he said. It surprised Helena to find that the Rintalan language had, in practice, developed so that the speed of the word delivery indicated the status of the speaker - the higher the rank of speaker, the slower the speech. This should mean that if she were to have any problems following someone's words, they were likely to be from the poorest of people, rather than the nobles or merchants.

From the walk inside the building, it was clear that it repeated the curve from the outer wall. Their corridor was slightly curved and the doors to the rooms were also slightly curved, carrying on the odd angles. Helena still wondered how they would manage furniture, as unless it was also curved, nothing would fit against the walls...

After walking for about ten minutes, during which Helena estimated that they had travelled parallel to the outer wall of the building, and gone about a third of the way round, the Chamberlain opened a door on the right-hand wall of the corridor, and motioned for them to enter.

They walked into what looked like a large audience chamber that already held about fifty people. They entered from the back of the chamber, while everyone else was facing the front, where the Royal Family were seated on a raised platform that sat about half a metre higher than the main floor. The Chamberlain escorted them forward, through the crowd of people, halting a couple of metres from the platform.

"Mage Helena Hawke and Guardian Domico, your Majesties" he intoned. The murmuring conversation that had been going on in the room suddenly stopped, with everyone turning to look at Helena and Domico.

Helena felt nervous, suddenly very conscious of her travel stained clothing and the pervading smell of horse that seemed to cover them, but she slowly walked forward towards the raised platform. She then performed a small courtesy, not deep enough to imply servitude, but more than adequate to show respect. Domico bowed beside her, also not deep, but enough.

"Thank you for receiving us, your Majesty," she said directly to the King, more than aware that it was her place to speak first.

"You are welcome to Rintala, Mage Hawke," said the King in a deep voice. "We will retire presently, and would appreciate it if you could join us," he said, more as a statement rather than a question.

"We would be honoured, your Majesty." she replied. Curtseying again, she and Domico then moved to the side of the room to see what else would occur in the audience. However, it appeared that the audience was over, as the King stood and announced "Thank you all for coming, please excuse us as we must retire now", at which point, his wife, the Queen, and his son, the Prince stood up and walked out a door that was concealed towards the back of the platform. The Chamberlain motioned for Helena and Domico to follow.

21

An invitation to dinner

Helena and Domico went through the door, and she was surprised to find herself in a small square room. The squareness came as a bit of a shock after all the curves and circles. Perhaps only the outer rooms were curved? Helena mused and then realised that she really needed to get a grip and move on from focusing on the architecture and focus on what she needed to know here.

The room contained a tall wardrobe, in which the King, Queen and Prince already had servants hanging their ceremonial robes. Aside from that, there was a small table with some refreshments and a couple of armchairs. The King, once the servants had left, turned to Helena and Domico and said,

"Thank you for coming. I assumed you would want to speak to us following the death of my Son's fiancé. What can we help you with?"

"Firstly, I'd like to know how many people knew that Princess Casili was travelling overland, rather than coming by sea, your Majesty,"

"Well, we certainly did. Lyton, did you tell anyone?"

"Just a couple of friends, but it wasn't exactly a secret, so they could have told others," he replied in a rather bored tone.

Helena looked, for the first time, properly at Lyton. Domico had told her that Lyton was a popular figure in the kingdom, being athletic and good looking. He excelled at hunting and sports, and had a wide circle of influential friends. He was tall, with short, curly, dark hair and deep brown eyes, with a long nose and a smiling mouth. Perhaps it was just how he stood, but Helena got the feeling that he was always on the move, ready to take action, and used to being the centre of attention.

"I will need to speak to these friends, your Highness, if you don't mind. It was definitely a planned murder - she didn't die of natural causes..." Helena started to say, but was interrupted by the King.

"Really? We thought that there must have been an accident of some sort. The message to us was just that she had died... We had assumed that you were just looking into it as a formality. Who would want to murder Casili? She was a lovely girl, popular with the people and didn't, as far as we know, have any enemies."

Helena turned to look at the King and Queen. The Queen had collapsed into the chair, looking extremely shocked, while King Fanton had gone pale and looked like he also needed to sit down. Prince Lyton, on the other hand, showed no reaction to the news.

"I appreciate that this must be a shock, and I'm sorry that I broke the news in such a blunt fashion. I had thought that you would already know, as even before I examined her, we understood it to be a sudden, unlikely death. Perhaps we should leave you, and we can talk tomorrow?" Helena offered.

"Yes, perhaps that would be best," said the King. "I'm afraid that we don't have any spare rooms for you at this time, but we would be grateful if you could join us for dinner. It's a formal affair, I'm afraid, as we are due to be entertaining some of the more prominent nobles this evening. They will serve dinner in two hours. In the meantime, I'll ask Justar to escort you out."

Helena nodded and curtseyed while Domico bowed, and they turned and left the room - back into the main audience chamber, where the Chamberlain Justar was waiting for them. He escorted them out of the chamber and then back along the way that they came. At the top of the steps outside the main door, Lieutenant Flint was waiting for them. As he escorted them across the grounds, one soldier came trotting up with their horses - including the pack animals.

Once outside the compound, Helena turned to Domico

"So, any idea where we can stay? I think it will need to be close by, as otherwise we won't have time to wash and change to get back before Dinner..."

"I think that there's an Inn just down this street," he said, turning to ride down a different street from the one they arrived from. About three hundred metres down there was a large Inn. Domico dismounted and disappeared inside, leaving Helena with the horses.

A few minutes later, he came back out. "They do have a couple of rooms, but they aren't their best, and they are expensive," he said. "What do you think?"

"Let's just take them anyway Domico, it's late, I'm tired, I need a bath, and we still have a formal dinner to get through,"

"OK, the entrance to the courtyard and stables is around the back," he said, leading his horse around the side of the building.

They showed Helena to a rather poky room that was only big enough for the bed, a single chair and the washstand.

"If you want a bath Mistress," said the maid who showed her up to the room "then it's in the cellar, but you'll need your man to stand at the door as there ain't no lock," she said before leaving.

Helena sighed and unpacked her formal robes. Once she had a clean dress draped over her arm, she stepped out into the corridor and found Domico waiting for her.

"I'm guessing the maid told you the same thing she told me," she said to him. "Do you want to go first and I'll stand guard on the door and then you can stand guard for me?"

"Let's do it the other way round, as I'm guessing it's going to be difficult to get two lots of hot water, and I don't mind it being cooler," he said with a smile.

Once they had gone down to the cellar, Helena was pleasantly surprised. Based on the impression given by the maid, she was expecting something dark and dismal, with no privacy and very little in the way of amenities, but in reality, it wasn't that bad.

Yes, it was a cellar, but there were lots of lamps around the place, giving it a warm, inviting feel, and although the door didn't have a lock, it had a wedge that could be placed on the floor inside, stopping the door from being pushed open.

There were also two enormous bathtubs and a huge hearth with a big fire, with many large pots of water heating.

"This is better than I expected." she said to Domico

"Yes, me too. But I'll still wait in the corridor for you to go first."

Helena didn't take long over her bath - aware that there was little time before they needed to be back at the Palace - so she washed quickly, but took the time to properly wash her hair, to get rid of the smell of horse.

Swapping places with Domico, she waited for him to finish before they both returned upstairs to dress formally for the Dinner.

She wanted people here to know who she was, as that would ensure some level of cooperation and might make people less likely to lie or avoid her. The reputation of the Mage order could be helpful in some ways.

She therefore chose her formal dress, the uniform of the Mages. It comprised a long black under-dress, with wide sleeves that had silver banding on the cuffs and ornate silver embroidery on the bodice and skirt. She then placed an over-skirt on top, which was cut away at the front, providing a second layer on the sides and back. This overskirt also had silver banding and was matched by an ornate yoke that went as a second layer over her shoulders and a tooled black leather belt that had silver chasing to match the design of the dress.

Overall, it looked quite impressive, but was bulky and impractical and therefore reserved for formal occasions. She had never worn formal dress before, as most of her time at the Mage order had been taken up with study and a little teaching, but Misco had presented her with this, just before her departure on the Tour. She guessed she would need to get used to wearing it from now on…

A short while later they stepped out of the Inn, having decided to walk to the Palace given it was only a few hundred metres away.

"The King and Queen seemed genuinely shocked," noted Domico after

Helena asked him his thoughts on the family's reaction to the news they brought. "But I wasn't sure about the Prince - he showed no reaction at all as far as I could see, but possibly it just hadn't sunk in yet?"

"Yes, they seemed to be shocked, and I wasn't sure about Lyton either. So either the King and Queen are good at dissembling, or they are not responsible, and we'll need to see more of Lyton to be able to make a judgement I think," said Helena. "We'll know when I talk to them properly in the morning," she said, and just as they arrived back at the small gate to the Palace.

They served the Dinner in the main dining hall, in which the King and Queen welcomed the highest nobles in Rintala, as well as the merchant kings - those whose exports to neighbouring Kingdoms numbered in the millions. The room was a long, relatively narrow one, with a long table down the centre, with a short one placed at the top to give a T shape.

The Royal Family sat on the top table. The nobles then ranged down the long leg of the T and finally the merchants down towards the end of the table. This was clearly a case of them being invited, and therefore honoured, but not being placed over the traditional support of the noble families. Though, Helena found herself and Domico sat opposite each other and less than a dozen places down from the top table.

The room was reasonably hot, and Helena's heavy outfit made her feel as if she was being slow roasted - fortunately she was on the side of the table furthest from the fire, but Domico must have been near to melting point in his formal attire. His outfit comprised garments similar to her own, but where hers was black with silver, his was grey with black banding, and with the obvious change of trousers and tunic rather than a dress.

However, he still had the matching yoke and the addition of a much more ornate belt that was tailored to carry a sword and scabbard.

Helena found herself seated next to Lord Santu, the Baron of Brenta, one of Prince Lyton's closest friends. Helena was keen to engage him in conversation, to understand more about Lyton and how he had felt about the marriage to Casili.

At first, he appeared quite reticent, obviously wary about saying too much to her. He obviously wasn't fooled about the power of a Mage to discern what people were thinking, unlike many people, and neither was he intimidated into sharing more than he would have done with anyone else.

However, Helena persevered, pulling his attention back to her when it looked as though he wanted to turn to his other neighbouring guests.

"So, Lord Santu, how long have you been friends with Prince Lyton?" she had asked him shortly after the initial introductions.

"Almost my whole life. We've been friends since we were both about five years old, I think," he said, tucking into a roast quail dish.

"What sort of person is he?" she asked, probing.

"He's an exceptional hunter, and excellent sportsman - always wins the archery contests - and intelligent. He's easygoing, and popular with the common people."

"And how did they feel about his upcoming marriage, do you think?"

"Well, I think most people were in favour of it. He's approaching thirty, and many people felt it was time for him to settle down and start producing heirs. He hasn't had any significant relationships yet, and I think some people had given up on him."

"And what did people think of Princess Casili?"

"That's a bit more difficult… I think some thought she would be a good match, but others, not so much. She might be from the neighbouring Kingdom, but her upbringing would be quite different, with a different outlook and priorities. Voreen differs greatly from Rintala, and while it is geographically bigger, it has a smaller population, a different climate and a very different economy. What would she know about ruling here? Or what we need? Our economy, traditions and interests? The Prince is a light-hearted soul, and I have heard that Princess Casili was very serious and quite the opposite of him…"

"You sound as though you didn't approve of the marriage," she stated, staring at him intently

"No, it's not that at all, but you asked me what I thought people thought of the match. I'm his best friend, I just wanted him to be happy," said Lord Santu, moving his gaze to the Prince, who was currently laughing at something someone sitting close to him had said.

Helena leaned forward slightly to look closer at Prince Lyton. He appeared to be happy, and not at all in mourning for the woman he was supposed to be marrying in a few weeks. Were there any feelings there or not? She wondered.

Baron Santu turned away with obvious relief and engaged in conversation with the person on his other side. Without being rude, Helena had no opportunity to engage him in conversation again, and it appeared that the guest on her other side was giving her the cold shoulder, as he didn't once turn in her direction or even introduce himself. So Helena just sat in silence, pondering her next move.

22

A Motive?

The following morning, Helena and Domico shared breakfast in a private dining room at their inn, in order to discuss the events and conversations from last night's dinner.

"So, Domico, did you hear anything last night that might give us a direction in which to make enquiries?" Helena asked him.

"Not really. I did some fishing about how people felt about Casili, and from the people I spoke to, she seemed liked… Not loved, certainly, but liked I think… I think most people didn't know her, and hadn't met her, but I didn't get the feeling that there was any resentment. No one even once mentioned the word 'barbarian', but then, they were mostly nobles and favoured merchants, so their opinions might not reflect the general population."

"I heard something similar, but perhaps my informant was a bit more forthcoming. Evidently, people felt it was time for the Prince to settle down, but perhaps not with a foreign Princess who knew nothing about Rintala, her traditions or people. Does that chime with what you heard?"

"Not really. Perhaps people were being cagey with me, or your informant knew more than mine?"

"I'm not sure. There was something there though, so we'll keep that as a line to look into. Anything else?"

"I noticed the Prince didn't seem particularly sad at dinner... Was that an act - to seem normal and OK - or do you think he didn't really care for her?"

"I wondered the same. He certainly looked to be enjoying himself at some points last night, so perhaps we need to keep that in mind and see how he is with us today."

"OK, well, when you're ready, let's go back to the Palace and see if we can get an audience with King Fanton and Queen Darla. Do you want to see them together with Prince Lyton, or should we meet him separately?"

"Separately, I think," concluded Helena after a moment, laying her napkin aside and standing up.

23

Waiting

Once they were admitted to the Palace, they were shown to a small room and asked to wait. After about an hour, the door opened to admit Lord Chamberlain Justar.

"I'm afraid that the King and Queen won't be able to meet with you today, Mage Hawke," he said after the barest of greetings.

"Their day is already full of appointments that cannot be put off until later. However, if you return tomorrow, I am sure that I can arrange some time for you to speak to them."

Helena looked at Domico in disappointment. Domico looked ready to say something about having been kept waiting for an hour, but Helena didn't want a scene, so quickly replied,

"Thank you, Lord Chamberlain. I would appreciate it if you could try to find some time in their Majesties day tomorrow. We will return in the morning," and she got up and left the room, Domico trailing behind.

Domico held his tongue until they were back in the street on the way to their inn. "Why did you just accept that? We've been kept waiting for an hour and then just brushed off like some lowly trader - it's not acceptable!"

"And what would you have me do? I can't force my way in, and arguing with the Lord Chamberlain will not do us any favours. We will see the Royal family tomorrow."

"And if they find another excuse tomorrow?"

"We'll deal with it then, but I'm sure there won't be any need," said Helena, hoping deep in her bones that she was right, and they would grant her an audience with the family.

Domico fumed in silence. He was sure that Helena needed to exert herself more, and be more confident in pushing her way through obnoxious servants - no matter what their position.

The following day, they repeated their journey back to the Palace and were once again put into the same waiting room. Domico started to pace almost as soon as the door was closed by their escort. Once again, they were left waiting for over an hour before a servant came and informed them that they could not see the family today and this time it wasn't even the Lord Chamberlain who came to tell them.

This pattern continued for three days, with Domico getting angrier each day and Helena feeling smaller and smaller, losing more and more confidence and retreating into herself - she couldn't even face arguing with Domico, and she knew he was fuming.

On the fourth day, after waiting for over two hours, Lord Chamberlain Justar appeared.

"My apologies, Mage Hawke, but I have been trying to arrange some time for you with the King and Queen, and it has taken quite a bit of work. However, I have arranged for you to have a short audience with them this afternoon. You may either wait here or return in about three hours?"

"Thank you Lord Chamberlain, we will return in three hours," she blurted, before Domico could mutter something about waiting all day, and not even being offered refreshments or lunch.

After returning to the Inn, and having some lunch and Choo, they made their way back to the Palace - again.

This time, upon entry, they were admitted to a smaller audience chamber, different from the one the family held their audience on that first night. This one was smaller, and didn't have a raised platform at one end, just a series of chairs arranged around a large, open fire.

After the cold of Voreen, it already felt comfortable to Helena, but the fire was lit anyway, and gave off quite a bit of warmth.

The King and Queen were already seated, so when Helena and Domico entered the room, the King directed them to a couple of chairs further away from the fire and his (and his Queen's) seats.

"Now, Mage Hawke, how can we help you?" asked the King impatiently, once Helena and Domico had made their courtesy and bow and seated themselves.

"Your Majesty, we would like to know how you felt about Princess Casili's upcoming marriage to your son," she stated.

"We were both in favour of it, of course…" the King said, with a note of derision "…as if we'd allow it if we were not! It's time the boy settled down, and while we might have preferred a southern Princess, there are none of a marriageable age, and I won't have him wedding a noble who doesn't bring me any new alliances. Casili was therefore a good choice, and would have meant an alliance with Voreen," he stated. The Queen stayed silent, but it was clear from her expression that she agreed with what the King had said.

"And how did Prince Lyton himself feel about the match?" asked Helena

"He was in favour of it. Of course, it wouldn't have mattered if he wasn't - he'll do as he's told - and he knows we think he needs to settle down and start producing some heirs."

At this point the Queen added "He knows that I'd like to have grandchildren, and soon, so that I can enjoy them before I get too old to be tired out by them," she smiled, possibly thinking about the grandchildren that she had expected from the match.

"And how about the noble families? Did any of them object to the match?" Helena asked, trying to get a feel for the sentiment among the nobles, who'd been ruled out from arranging an alliance with the royal family themselves.

"None of them objected," stated the King flatly. "Frankly, I think you're barking up the wrong tree here in Rintala. Her death certainly had nothing to do with my family, and none of the nobles would have gained anything by it. I'd suggest that you look to Castin or Eretee for the culprit," he said, rising from his chair. The Queen rose with him and they both stalked out of the room.

"Now what?" said Domico to Helena, once the royal couple had left. "We still haven't spoken to Lyton."

"We'll need to ask Justar, I suppose," said Helena with a definite lack of enthusiasm.

Waiting outside the room for them was the Lord Chamberlain.

"Lord Justar, when will we be able to speak to Prince Lyton?" asked Helena timidly.

"I'm afraid that Prince Lyton is not here. He has retired to Brenta, the estates of Baron Santu," he stated in a flat voice.

Had Prince Lyton deliberately removed himself so that they couldn't question him? Is that what the delays had been about?

"I see," said Helena, "when did the Prince leave?"

"Two days ago Mage Hawke," he replied, with just a suspicion of a smirk in his voice.

"Thank you for all your help, Lord Chamberlain," said Domico, with a slight edge of sarcasm to his voice, taking Helena's arm and guiding her towards the exit of the Palace.

"What now?" asked Helena when they were once again in the street outside the Palace compound

"If you want to question Lyton, then we're going to need to go to Brenta," Domico stated

"I know, but we didn't even get to use the King's Far-Speaking Device, so we can't update King Garrod or Misco. Do you know if there is another one in the City?"

"There might be one at the offices of the Merchant's Guild, but we're unlikely to have any privacy there," stated Domico doubtfully.

"It doesn't matter. I need to update them, and that means we'll need to visit the Merchant's Guild before we can go anywhere."

"All right, let's go there now," said Domico, striding off. Helena had to walk fast to catch up with him.

"Are you angry with me?" she asked him once she's caught up

"Not really, it's just that they have played us for fools and I don't like it," he said with some heat.

"I know, but there's not a great deal we can do about that at the moment, is there?" she said, trying to sound reasonable and as if it wasn't such a big deal.

"Let's not talk about it now," he said shortly.

After some considerable twisting and turning through the City, they came to a white, round building that looked like a tall, slender tower. It was one of the highest buildings in Faskan, and sat in the City's south, perhaps a couple of miles from the palace.

Domico entered the large reception room and asked to speak to the First Merchant. A small, wiry man, with a sort of faded look, got up from behind the desk in the reception room and scurried off. The fact that Domico and Helena were wearing their ceremonial robes (as they had been every day while seeking an audience with the King and Queen) may have added to his obvious nervousness.

A short time later, a short, rotund man in ornate robes with wide bands of gold thread showing various pictures of animals and crops arrived. He squinted at their robes and then placed on his nose a pair of wire-rimmed looking glasses.

"How may I assist the Mage Order?" he asked in a formal tone.

"Ah, First Merchant, do you have a Far-Speaking Device?" asked Domico

"Yes, we do, Guardian. We have two of them. One is twinned to a Device in Tarshea and another is twinned to a Device in Tradehome."

That they had a Device twinned with one in Tradehome wasn't surprising, given that Tradehome was literally the centre of the trading world, and comprised a year-round market for all types of trade. However, also having one that was twinned with Tarshea was a bit of a surprise. He must have interpreted their surprise on this point, as he then said,

"We often have to ask the assistance of the Mage Order ourselves, especially regarding Investigations when valuable goods have been stolen or gone missing. We therefore twinned our Device with one in the Mage Order itself, in the Chief Clerk's office," he said, sounding proud of their association with the Mages directly.

"We would like to use this Device to contact Tarshea. Please, First Merchant." said Helena.

"Of course, if you will follow me," he stated. He turned and walked out of the room and to a set of stairs. Going up five flights was obviously arduous for him, and he was perspiring heavily by the time they got to what appeared to be the top of the tower. After recovering his breath slightly, he managed to wheeze out, "I will leave you to it. The blue Device is twinned with Tarshea" and stepped back out of the room.

24

Conference with Misco

Helena stepped up to the crystal, placing the fingers of her right hand to her lips, then placed them on to the surface of the crystal, towards the top.

Like all Mage-build Devices that were designed for use by non-Mages, saliva activated it. Helena could have used her magic to activate it, but this way was quicker, easier, and for Helena, more reliable, as she still wasn't confident in her abilities. Domico frowned behind her.

"You should have used your magic," he stated flatly. "Using it more often will make you quicker, and stronger, at using it in the future."

"Possibly, but it didn't occur to me to use it - this is quicker for now," she stated defensively.

The crystal pulsed, with the pulses slowly speeding up. After a few moments, a voice came through from the other side.

"How may we help you First Merchant" came the voice of the Chief Clerk.

"Good afternoon Tepo, it's me, Helena. Would you please ask Misco to step into the room? I have an update for him on the Investigation."

"One moment, Mage Hawke," he said.

Two minutes later, Misco's voice said, "Hello Helena, you have an update?"

"Yes Misco. I can confirm that Princess Casili was murdered. Someone deliberately ensured that she came into contact with Taka venom."

"How would someone get hold of Taka venom?" he asked, puzzled.

"The caravan came across a dead Taka, so that must have been the source of the venom, but I don't yet know how it was killed."

"And how did they ensure the Princess came into contact with it?"

"A piece of her furniture was doctored with it, a table, in fact. With the leg shortened and then venom placed on the end, so that she was forced to prop it up with something that she then handled - a book."

"And who did it?" he asked

"That we don't know yet, but we have spoken to King Fanton and Queen Darla, and I don't think they were responsible. They seemed genuinely shocked by the news that it was murder."

"And Prince Lyton?"

"We have not managed to speak to him yet. It would appear that he left Faskan after our arrival, and has decamped to Brenta. We intend to follow so that we can question him there."

"Good. It's unlikely to be him, but he may have some thoughts on it."

"King Fanton suggested we look to Castin and Eretee," she stated, wanting his thoughts on that avenue.

"It is possible that one of those kingdoms is behind it. They are both nervous about an alliance between Voreen and Rintala, and a merger through the marriage's children. We need to be very careful here, Helena. If it is one of them, then war could be on the cards. I'll liaise with King Garrod and try to stop anything precipitate, but you need to get a move on and come to some conclusions soon."

"Are you sure someone else wouldn't be better doing this, Misco? King Fanton and his staff kept us kicking our heels for four days before we managed to question them!"

"No, you're in place now, and we can't afford further delays in getting someone else there. Besides, you're already making progress... In terms of King Fanton, you need to understand that you have the right to demand an audience with anyone - including Kings - and start throwing the weight of the Mage Order around."

"I'll try Misco," she said, with a heavy note in her voice.

"Good. Try to keep me updated, and I'll update Garrod," he concluded, and the crystal went dark.

25

Brenta

The journey to Brenta took them two days. This was a well-populated part of the Kingdom, and they travelled along wide, established, safe roads. They passed a few small villages and many farms, making a living from selling their produce directly to the City. The people were open and friendly, and they found a pleasant inn to stay at overnight. It felt a very different journey from their time travelling to Ista, or even to Faskan, through the mountains of Voreen.

The estate of the Baron was large, with a small town situated a couple of miles from the house itself.

Helena and Domico had a minor disagreement when they arrived, as Domico wanted Helena to use her status to demand rooms in the castle, whereas Helena was much more inclined to stay at the only Inn in the town and seek an audience early the following morning. In the end, Domico let it go, and followed Helena's inclination, although he believed, and had pointed out, that demanding accommodation would have set the tone, showing that she out-ranked him and meant business and was not about to be fobbed off.

So, they both settled into the small inn and took their evening meal in silence.

Domico was still mulling over the argument, and was pondering other ways that he could try to get Helena to use the power of her station, while Helena was anxious about approaching the Prince in the morning. After the stilted silence over the evening meal, neither was inclined to linger, and they both retired to their rooms early.

The following morning, Domico and Helena breakfasted together, and then set off for the estate.

"So, how are you going to tackle this, Helena?" he asked

"What do you mean?" she replied, distracted by her inner thoughts on what she needed to ask Prince Lyton

"Are you going to demand an audience, or are we just going to politely wait until they condescend to see us?" he said pointedly

"I'll be polite, and just ask. I'm sure they will agree to see us, seeing as we've travelled all this way," she said, rather naively Domico thought.

"And if they don't? Are we going to spend some days kicking our heels here too?" he said rather sourly.

"No. If they refuse, then I will demand an audience," she said, picking up on the hint he was trying to give her, although secretly hoping that she wouldn't need to.

They arrived at the tall, open gates of the manor house and trotted their horses through. The gates led to a long path, bordered by mature trees, all in full bud. Summer had already arrived in this part of the continent, and the trees provided a long shaded path for the last half a mile to the house itself. It was still reasonably early, but was getting warmer, so the shade was welcome.

They slowed the horses to a walk and took the last half a mile in silence, each thinking about the coming conversation. Domico hoped Helena would exert her authority, and demand some answers, showing some backbone and not allowing them to be fobbed off. Helena, meanwhile, was thinking about what she needed to know, and how Prince Lyton's apparent lack of sadness at the death of his betrothed might hint at a motive.

As they approached the house, they both inspected it as it emerged from the tree-lined path. It was a large, square, stone building, over two stories, and with many wide, glazed windows facing out onto the path and the wider fields that surrounded it on all sides. It was obviously quite old, as the wind and rain had rounded the stones, and it lacked the sharp corners and joins that would have shown recent additions. A small hedge portioned off some land to their left as they rode in, possibly indicating a formal garden or maze and off to the right and running parallel to the main house, was a long low building made of wood - Helena took that to be the stables or some sort of storage building.

They rode up to the main doors and dismounted. Domico gave Helena his reins and strode over to the door, banging the side of his fist against it twice. He stood back to wait for a response.

A minute or so later, the door opened to reveal a tall, well-built man dressed in some sort of livery. He was wearing black trousers and a black tunic, with a small hawk in red stitching over the left breast. There was also red piping around the cuffs of the sleeves and in a red fabric stripe down the outside of each leg of the trousers.

"Yes?" he said, when he had fully opened the door

"Mage Helena Hawke to see Baron Santu and Prince Lyton," stated Domico flatly. The servant noted the steely gaze, and assumed, correctly, that this was not someone to trifle with.

"Yes Sir. If you will give me a moment, I will arrange for someone to take your horses to the stable." he stepped back inside and closed the door.

Helena looked to Domico, and would have said something if the door had not opened again, almost immediately. The servant stood wide of the door, and another man stepped out, dressed in the same livery, and came to take the reins of both the horses.

"If you will step this way," said the first man, "The Baron and the Prince are still at breakfast, so if you will just wait in here, I'm sure that they will be with you shortly," he said, directing them into an elegantly furnished room on their left, that looked out over the gardens and the path they had just ridden up. With that, he turned and left the room, closing the door behind him.

Helena looked around. The Baron obviously had wealth, as the room was decorated in a costly fashion, with blue silk window hangings, polished wooden floors, and pale yellow paint on the walls. There were also comfortable furnishings, in the shape of deeply upholstered chairs and settees, with small occasional tables with expensive inlays forming the hawk motif that seemed to be part of the Baron's crest. A large, unlit fire dominated one wall of the room, with an impressive carved marble mantle surrounding it. Helena was thankful that it was unlit, as she was already getting quite warm, despite the early hour.

After a wait of about ten minutes, the Baron came striding into the room. He wore a plain brown tunic and trousers, but she noted a gold brooch, in the shape of a hawk in flight, on his right shoulder.

"Mage Hawke, how good of you to come and visit me," he said with a smile. Helena noted it didn't reach his eyes, which stared at her coldly.

"I didn't come to visit you, Baron Santu," she stated flatly. "I came to interview

Prince Lyton and understand that he's staying here?"

"Ah, yes, he is. But I'm afraid that he is in no condition to meet with you. He is distraught at the news of his fiancée, that is why he retired from the court."

"I'm afraid I must insist, Baron Santu." she replied

"Or what?" he stated belligerently.

"Or it will force me to use my skills to ensure an audience," she stated.

Domico noted she was trying to project confidence, but he didn't really believe it - possibly because he knew her too well, but he hoped the Baron had not noted that, as Domico was unsure what he would do if Santu called her bluff…

Baron Santu stared at her, and under his gaze she squared her shoulders and stood a little taller, meeting his gaze directly. After a moment, he backed off, "If you will wait here, I will speak to the Prince," he stated, sounding worried, then he turned and strode out of the room.

Domico wandered over to her. "Well done," he whispered, not wishing any passing servants to overhear.

"Let's hope it's done the trick," she whispered back.

A short while later, the Baron came back into the room, followed by Prince Lyton. Santu walked over to the chairs and stood in front of one, waiting for the Prince to sit, and, once he had, the Baron seated himself. Neither of them gave permission for Helena and Domico to sit and join them.

Helena took a long look at the Prince. He didn't look visibly upset, and there was no evidence of suffering, such as dark circles under the eyes, or a weariness in his posture. Was he really suffering or was it a pose?

"Prince Lyton, please tell me about your relationship with Princess Casili," she said, her voice sounding loud in the silent room. Neither Baron Santu nor the Prince had said a word since entering. The Prince hadn't even greeted her.

"What is there to tell - we were to be wed," he stated with some heat

"How well did you know her?"

"Not well. I think we'd met on three occasions, never alone, and never for more than a few minutes at some state event or other. I hardly even knew her,"

"But you wanted to marry her?"

"Wanted is a strong word," he said. "I needed to settle down, and my father was opposed to me marrying a noble from Rintala. The only woman of marriageable age, of a sufficiently noble family, was therefore Casili, so she was really the only choice,"

"Did you love her?" Helena asked, knowing it was a stupid question, but wanting to see the reaction.

"Love her?" sneered the Prince. "Don't you understand? Princes do not marry for love, they marry for alliances, and father was clear he wanted an alliance with another Kingdom, so an internal marriage would have gained him nothing... Besides which, I didn't know her, so how could I have loved her? She was pretty enough, in a northern sort of way, and I had heard that she was bright and could hold a conversation, so I was, at least, not dreading the prospect of her becoming my wife, but you expect too much if you think it was love."

"So you're not heartbroken at her death? Then why retire here and leave the court?" she asked him

"I'm upset that she's dead, of course," he stated, although he didn't sound it, so Helena didn't really believe him, "but I came here to escape the court - I was supposed to be getting married in a few weeks, the court is full of nobles, visiting for the wedding. I didn't want to stay and be an object of speculation until they all went home. So I came here. Santu is my best friend, and this has always felt like a second home."

"And what will happen to you now? Regarding marriage, I mean,"

"I've got a reprieve. I don't particularly want to marry anyone, and as I said, Casili was the only choice outside of Rintala, so either my father relents, and allows a marriage to a lady of Rintalan nobility, or we wait and see if the noble daughters of Castin or Eretee are suitable in a year or two,"

"Why don't you want to marry? Are you not bothered about an heir? What about the succession?" stated Helena in disbelief. It was one of the primary duties of the royal family to ensure continuity and stability - and an heir was a necessary requirement for that.

"I've got a few cousins on my mother's side that I'm sure could be named heir - not that it's any of your business," he stated tartly and showing signs of anger "Now, unless you have questions relating to Casili's death, then this interview is over!"

"No, thank you for your time, Prince Lyton. I'm sure I know where to find you should I have any more questions later," Helena stated.

Prince Lyton stood up and marched from the room. Baron Santu slowly rose and said to Helena, "Producing an heir is a sore point for him, Mage Hawke. I'd steer clear of that type of question in the future if I were you." and then he too left the room.

"I guess we'll see ourselves out then," said Domico, and he took Helena's arm and escorted her out to the door. They found a groom, waiting with their horses outside, mounted and rode back down the long path towards the town.

"Now what?" asked Domico once they had passed through the enormous gates to the estate.

"I'm not sure. I think there's more to this than Prince Lyton suggested, and why is the production of an heir a sore point?" she answered

"Perhaps you need to see and hear what they are discussing now?" Domico suggested.

"I can try. Let's pull off the path and find a pool of water," she answered. They pulled off the path into a small wood that appeared to border the estate. They had heard running water on the way to the house, so Helena hoped that there was a small stream or river running through the woods - such was normally the case. After about fifteen minutes of searching, Domico spotted a small, narrow stream running parallel to the path, about three hundred metres away from the road.

"Here," he said to Helena

"Now we just need a way to get it to pool, or find a pond or something," she said. They followed the stream for about half a mile, and then came to a spot where it bent around a large tree. Some of the roots had created a small puddle of water away from the main flow. Obviously, when the stream had been higher, earlier in the spring, some of it had flowed over the roots and made this small pool that had then been cut off as the water level lowered. It wasn't deep, and looked like it would be gone in a few weeks, but for now, it would serve.

Helena and Domico dismounted, and Domico tied the reins to a branch on the other side of the tree to the pool.

"What will be your focus?" Domico asked

"The hawk brooch Santu was wearing." She said "Let's hope he's still wearing it,"

Helena stared into the pool, concentrating on the water, in her mind's eye, she summoned up the image of the hawk brooch, and projected it into the pool, forcing the water to form around it, leaving a small indentation in the hawk's shape. To Domico's eyes, it looked like the water just suddenly flowed around something hawk-shaped in the water, but nothing was there... Domico stood up and scanned the woods. Helena would be totally engaged with what she was seeing and hearing, so wanted to ensure that she remained safe while working her magic. He took a couple of steps away from her and the horses and then continued to scan the woods for anyone approaching.

Meanwhile, Helena was engrossed in the pool. She had forced the water to take the shape of the hawk and was now using her magic to form a bridge between this impression and the hawk on Santu's shoulder. After a few moments, the pool changed, and she was looking at an image that mirrored the view from the brooch. Sound slowly increased in volume until she could hear what was being said.

"... Mage!" said Prince Lyton's voice. "Why would she want to know about the heir? It's none of her business anyway, and certainly nothing to do with that bloody northern barbarian woman's death!"

"I know, my Prince…" said the voice of Santu "… but we could not refuse her interview, and it would have looked suspicious if you had not answered her questions,"

"How much do you think she knows? Or has guessed?" came the Prince's voice, with a note of anguish.

"Not enough to solve it, obviously…" responded Santu "… or she wouldn't be here, fishing. To be honest though, quite apart from Casili's death, people are going to be wondering why you haven't married, or ever had a serious relationship with one of our noble daughters if you don't settle down soon. Tongues will always wag, and you've gotten away with it until now, because people have seen you as young, but that will change soon, so you are going to have to take a wife."

"Santu, we have discussed this before, when my engagement was announced, you know I don't want to - the very thought of being with a woman makes my skin crawl, I just can't face it,"

"Well, we're going to have to do something - soon,"

Helena gasped at the implications of what she had just heard and lost concentration. The image in the pool disappeared, and the sound faded away. She tried to concentrate on the image again, but it just kept slipping away from her, as her thoughts swirled and intruded. She just couldn't find the concentration.

She tried one of the mental exercises taught to novice mages, and while it calmed her, it didn't bring the focus needed to establish contact again.

She sighed and stood up, wobbling slightly. The focus and energy needed to create the link always left her slightly disoriented and a little weak. This was true, to some extent, for all Mages - hence the need for a Guardian - but she always felt, wrongly, that it affected her more than others. She still had to come to terms with the fact that this was normal, and all Mages suffered this after-effect - she just wasn't as good as some others at hiding it yet.

Domico saw her stand and moved over to take her arm and help her on to her horse.

"Well?" he asked, having been a couple of steps away meant he had neither seen the image nor heard the conversation.

"It was at the edge of my range, so it was a strain to make the link, but I managed it, and heard something very informative…" she said to him "… but I am not sure what to make of it, and I don't know whether or not it gives us a motive. Let me think about it for a while,"

They travelled back to Brenta in silence.

26

Summons

When they got back to their inn in Brenta, Domico took the horses to the stable while Helena retired to her room.

The conversation that she had overheard through the pool certainly seemed to point at Prince Lyton having a motive to kill his intended bride, but was it strong enough? Would he really go that far to achieve what was, at best, a temporary reprieve from marriage? It risked plunging both his own nation, and Voreen, into a war, as King Garrod would suffer no one taking the life of his daughter, especially someone who had seemed keen to cement an alliance with him.

Helena felt that she needed more information, which could only be supplied by either Garrod himself, or Misco. She could travel back to Faskan and use the Far-Speaking device to contact Misco, or she could try an element of magic that she had not attempted before, and try speaking to Misco through mind-contact. It was powerful magic, requiring the initiating Mage to establish a mind link, and over this distance, that would be incredibly difficult. It would also open her thoughts to Misco, and given the turmoil she felt about her abilities, it wasn't something she took lightly. She knew what Domico would advise, but didn't know if he knew enough about the toll it would take on her to temper his opinion.

She heard a knock on her door, and knew it would be Domico, come to talk about what she had seen and heard, and what they were going to do next.

Opening the door, with a sense of defeat, she admitted him to the room.

"Well? You've had some time to think about it… what happened?"

"I heard something that I wish I hadn't - that's what. Prince Lyton can't bear the thought of being with a woman…" Domico, who hadn't yet sat down, looked like he was about to fall over in shock.

"Well, that's certainly a motive," he breathed. "Is it because he doesn't feel that way about women, or he doesn't feel that way about anyone?"

"I don't know. There seems to be something odd about the relationship with Santu. They are certainly close, but it was Santu himself who was telling Lyton that he must marry and produce an heir - that people would start to talk if he didn't. So is Santu concerned about the succession, the Prince, or his own reputation?"

"Santu isn't married either, and is about the same age as Lyton. Could they be lovers, do you think?"

"It's not unheard of. Even though it is illegal, people have been circumspect and discreet and done it, anyway. It would explain the relationship possibly, but then why would Santu be telling the Prince he must marry if that's the case?"

"To protect his reputation, and to draw attention away from them both,"

"Yes, you could be right, but then why would either of them murder her?

Why now, when they have obviously agreed to the marriage, and are just weeks away?"

"Perhaps one of them just couldn't face the reality?"

"The conversation didn't sound like that though - Santu was telling Lyton that he must marry soon, so they are only postponing the inevitable, not changing anything,"

"We need to do some more digging into their relationship, I think, and also find out how the proposal to Casili came about - was it forced on Lyton, or did he voluntarily ask?"

"I don't think that King Fanton will just tell me that, and I can't see the Queen telling me either - she seems to be mourning her lost grandchildren rather than focussing on Casili," retorted Helena.

"So what do you want to do?" he asked her. Helena turned away from him and gazed out of the poorly glazed window.

"I was thinking about that when you came in… I can either speak to Misco or we can speak to King Garrod - we still need to find out what they have found out about the Teamsters in that caravan. But, if I'm to speak to Misco, I have a couple of choices on how…"

"You mean either travelling back to Faskan and using the Far-Speaking device?"

"That's one option. The other is to try and establish a mind link. But, I've never tried it before, and it's a vast distance, and it will take me a while to recover, if I can even do it," she said. She turned to look at him "I don't know if I have the ability, or the strength to reach so far… It would take us two days to get back to Faskan, but if I attempt the mind link, and fail, it will equally take me a couple of days to recover my strength, and we'd need to go back to Faskan anyway, so it won't save any time,"

"It would if we need to travel in the other direction, though. If we need to travel on to Eretee or Castin, then we'd be going two days in the opposite direction. Look, I know it will take a lot, and I also know that you are not that confident in your magic. You've hardly used it at all since we left Tarshea, but I believe in your abilities. Misco believes in your abilities, so how about you believing in yourself?" he said. This was the second time he'd said something similar, but this time he wasn't smiling - he looked very serious indeed.

Helena paused, considering it. She could always try it, she thought to herself. It wouldn't kill her, and perhaps she would be strong enough, and she certainly knew Misco well enough to be able to try...

She nodded to Domico. "I'll try," she said.

"Now?" he asked

"Now," she replied, steeling her resolve.

Helena seated herself on the floor, glad that this room was considerably larger than the one she had stayed at in Faskan, crossing her legs and tucking her heels close to her body and fanning the skirts of her dress out in front of her. Domico crossed over to the door and threw the bolt, then stood with his back resting against it and staring at Helena.

Helena meanwhile had closed her eyes and sought to find that calm centre of herself. She didn't need to close her eyes to use magic, but Helena always found it easier to start that way.

Once she had found that calm centre, she sent her thoughts outward, focussing on Misco, the sense of his presence, the way he tilted his head when speaking to her, how he stood and folded his hands... At the same time, she silently called his name in her mind.

"Misco... Misco... Misco," she repeated, straining to push her thoughts all the way to Tarshea.

Misco was sitting at his desk, working on a communication that was to be sent out to all the Mages currently undertaking Tours. He suddenly felt someone calling his name, felt it, rather than heard it... It sounded like Helena, but was very, very faint. He put his quill down and sat back in his chair.

"Helena?" he said in his mind, while calling up an image of her, and pushing his thoughts outward to meet hers and strengthen the contact.

Helena was so relieved she let out a deep breath that she hadn't realised she had been holding.

"Misco! I'm so glad I reached you. I wasn't sure I'd be strong enough."

"You're stronger than you think, Helena," he said silently. "What have you found out?"

"Something odd. Prince Lyton can't bear to be with a woman," she said, replaying the conversation seen through the pool in her mind's eye. Misco saw, and heard, the result of the eavesdropping.

"Ah, some had wondered about that," he said. "Is this the motive that you were looking for?" he asked

"I'm not sure. Something about it still feels missing. I need to understand whether he volunteered for the match, or whether they forced it upon him.

Do you know, or is it something you can find out?"

"I know already. King Fanton had heard of the rumours of his son, and insisted that Lyton marry. Casili was really the only eligible candidate, but it took her father three years to agree to the match - I think he also wondered about Lyton, but that's only my speculation. And after all, there weren't so many eligible candidates for Casili either,"

"Ah," said Helena "Were there any no other suitors for Casili then?"

"Not serious ones. There were a couple of minor nobles from Voreen, but they weren't significant enough for her father to put off an alliance with Rintala… Look, King Garrod has demanded a conference at Tradehome. He wants to look the other Kings in the eye - particularly those from Castin and Eretee - and ask who did this. He is getting impatient for progress. I will leave to travel there tomorrow. I suggest you meet us all there. All the Kings and Queens will be present, and Lyton possibly as well. It will make it easier to question them," he said, sounding weary.

"I will Misco. Are you alright?" she asked him, sensing a deep tiredness.

"Yes, I'm fine, but there is a lot to do before I leave tomorrow… So, unless there is something else…?"

"No, and thank you Misco" she said silently before letting go of the sense of him. As soon as she let go, her body slumped in position, and a throbbing, sharp pain started in her head. She gasped from the sudden pain and would have toppled over if Domico hadn't rushed over to her and held her upright. He slowly helped her up and onto her bed.

"Are you OK?" he asked her

"Not really, that took a lot out of me, and I feel like my head is about to fall off…" she said weakly. Each time she took a breath, her head throbbed, and she had black spots dancing in front of her eyes. Trying to take shallow breaths only seemed to make the spots worse, so she accepted the pain and breathed deeply.

"I'm not surprised, that was a long way to reach… Did you make contact with Misco?" he asked, as he removed her boots.

"Yes. We need to travel to Tradehome" was all she got out, past the pain in her head.

"Right, well, you get into bed, and I'll arrange for cold compresses and, later, dinner to be brought to you. Do you want me to stay in here with you?" he asked.

"Yes, please," she said, trying not to cry.

"Right. You get into bed, and I'll be right back," he said, turning to leave the room.

Helena rested for the rest of that day, and all the next. By the day after, the pains in her head had reduced to a dull ache, and while she still had some spots before her eyes, they were only occasional and she wanted to get started on the journey to Tradehome.

Domico tried to make it as easy for her as possible, choosing the most travelled routes, rather than cutting across country, so instead of travelling due west, they travelled south west to Lintik and then Northwest to Suntend, a small city in Eretee. From there, the road was almost due west, and was filled with traders, merchants and caravans, with an easily reachable Inn to stay at each night.

Despite that, it was still a long, tiring journey, and Helena was exhausted by the time they settled in to an Inn each night. The journey took them two weeks, although they could have done it in less had they been willing to push the horses and themselves.

Tradehome was situated at the point where the Kingdoms of Voreen, Eretee, Iskabar and Castin met, and acted as a sort of agreed no-man's-land. Each Kingdom, including Rintala, which didn't actually border Tradehome, provided men to police and guard the permanent trade fair that met there, and took a fixed percentage of the profits, and there were border points on each road out of the fair, where goods coming into each Kingdom were declared and taxed. But the fair, and the town itself, didn't formally belong to any Kingdom. This made it the natural meeting point when Kings wanted to meet on neutral ground.

Domico guided Helena to one of the larger inns in the town, and they settled into their spacious, well-appointed suite of rooms.

"Where do the Kings stay when they come here?" asked Helena as they unpacked their saddlebags.

"Each Kingdom has a small castle - I suppose you could call it an embassy - in the centre of the town, where their factors and trade masters live. They stay there when they come here, as the Inns are not well enough appointed for them and their entourages," smiled Domico.

Helena looked around the suite. It comprised a central room that fed onto the main hallway and was the only entrance to the suite, and then leading off from that at each side was a bedroom, a dressing room and a small private bathroom, giving the suite a total of seven rooms. Some of these rooms might be small, like the dressing room, but it was still more space than Helena was used to in her own rooms at the Mage Order.

"I don't think I'll ever get used to this," she said to Domico "one night you're sleeping in a tiny little cell, with little more than a bed, and the next you're staying somewhere like this, with a whole suite of rooms that are for your use alone."

"Yes, it is a contrast, but for me, it doesn't matter if the rooms are small, as long as the bed is good. I've often ended up putting the sleeping mat on the floor, especially when the bed is lumpy, or doesn't look like they have aired it in months," he smiled.

"Hah! I never even thought of that, and I may have slept better on the floor in some places we've stayed at - that Inn in Faskan springs to mind!"

"I did sleep on the floor there - hence my increasing grumpiness in the delays in getting in to see King Fanton."

"Ahh, it all makes sense now," she smiled. "Do you know where Misco will probably stay?"

"Here probably. I enquired when we arrived, but he's not here yet, so let's take tonight off, have a good meal and relax for a while," he suggested.

"Good plan. I'm looking forward to a long hot soak, but first, some decent food I think!" she smiled, and they went down to dinner.

Over Dinner, Helena became more and more withdrawn, a marked change from her cheery mood in their suite.

"Something wrong?" asked Domico, after he's noticed her staring into space for a few minutes

"I'm worried. We've been at this for over a month now, and we're not really any further forward than when we left Ista... I'll need to report to Misco soon, and I don't really have anything to say. We have a plausible motive -

but it's weak, we have a method - but it's odd and not straightforward, and a possible suspect - but that relies on the weak motive. I'm just worried that we're not getting anywhere, despite having travelled more than halfway across the continent…"

"It is progress, Helena. Despite the method being odd, we have found it - the Taka venom - and can prove that Casili was murdered. That's progress in itself, surely?"

"Not enough. I just don't think that I can do this. I might be good at understanding people when I know them, and can observe them for months, but this snap judgement, based on a few minutes' conversation, is probably beyond me…"

"Don't think like that, Helena. You are getting there, and even using your magic is coming along, isn't it?"

"Well, possibly, but I haven't tried to do a lot with it yet, have I?"

"You made the mind link with Misco, didn't you? That was a very long way to reach, but you managed it," he said, trying to get her to see her achievement for what it was. "Very few Mages could reach so far."

"Yes, I suppose I did," she replied, but still didn't smile, and resumed her staring into space.

27

Tradehome

Misco arrived the following day and immediately sent for Helena and Domico. They settled into his sitting room, as his suite looked much like theirs, but with only one bedroom, dressing room and bathroom off the main room.

"Have you discovered anything else since we had the mind link?" he asked. They both shook their heads.

"No Misco, the mind link took so much out of Helena that it took a couple of days to recover, and then we came straight here," said Domico. Helena stayed silent and looked miserable.

"Right. So... Garrod is getting impatient, and he's accusing Castin and Eretee of seeking to sabotage the wedding, preventing an alliance between Voreen and Rintala. They are both protesting their innocence, but he doesn't believe them. The rhetoric is ramping up, and I fear that if we don't find something soon, there may be war. King Garrod is not about to be placated unless we find the truth, and can give him the guilty party."

"So what do you want us to do?" asked Helena. "I don't know where else to look, or who else to speak to. I'm lost, Misco… I knew you should have given this to someone else!"

"I want you to go out and find who did it. Look at it from another angle if you can't move forward from this one… How did someone get the Taka out of the mountains? How did they kill it? How did they get the venom onto the table leg? Come on, Helena - you know you need to answer these questions. Look for the 'how', and see if that gives us the 'who'," he said, sounding exasperated.

Helena nodded, looking downcast, muttering to herself about the obvious questions that she had failed to even think about.

"King Garrod is not a patient man. His primary solution to any problem is a force or arms - look at how he stamped out the bandit gangs - so unless you make progress soon, I can only stay his arm for so long before he will declare war on someone - likely either Castin or Eretee, and that would be disastrous. So, speak to the Kings and Queens, their servants, their bloody horses if you have to, but find out who did this!" exclaimed Misco.

Helena had never seen him so worried, or so short-tempered, so, once again, she nodded and bolted from the room.

Domico rose, nodded to Misco, and left after her. He found her pacing in the corridor.

"What am I going to do, Domico? I don't even know where to start!" she said, eyes shining with tears.

"Before we left Ista, you asked Captain Hileat to ask King Garrod to look into the Teamsters, didn't you?"

"Yes?"

"So we can start there. Let's go and ask Garrod what he found out, or, more likely, who he asked to look into it."

"Right, let's do that then," she said, but with a notable lack of enthusiasm.

They left the Inn and proceeded to the castle of the Voreen royal family in Tradehome. When they arrived, they knocked on the impressive, iron bound wooden door - large enough to admit two riders side by side - and waited.

A minute later, a smaller door, inset into the larger one, opened to show a royal guardsman.

"Yes?"

"Mage Hawke to see King Garrod," replied Domico

"Please wait," he said, disappearing inside. Shortly after, Thatcher, the Vorainian Royal Chamberlain, appeared at the door.

"Ah, Mage Hawke, please step this way," he said as he retreated through the door. Helena and Domico stepped into the castle after him. He escorted them through the castle, down a corridor lit with torches that had turned the grey stones black with soot. It all felt very imposing to Helena, and she seemed to shrink into herself with each turning.

By the time that they reached the King, Helena was, once again, beset with self-doubt - who was she to question a King? What made her good enough to find the person who had murdered this man's daughter?

Her curtsey was low, and long, as she struggled in her mind to form appropriate questions.

"Mage Hawke, have you discovered anything else since you spoke to Misco from Brenta?" King Garrod asked with a note of impatience in his voice.

"Not yet, your Majesty. I was hoping to discover whether you had found anything out about the Teamsters that drove your daughter's caravan."

"Bah!" he shouted. "It has been over six weeks since my daughter was murdered, and you seem incapable of finding out why or who did it. I am loosing faith that you, or the Mage Order will get to the bottom of this, so it seems I must take my own action… I ordered Thatcher to look into the Teamsters - you are free to talk to him, but bother me no more unless, and until, you have some solid news for me. You are dismissed," he concluded.

Helena and Domico left the room in silence.

"Even my coming here has not helped matters," she said to Domico. "It sounds like I've made it worse… Do you think he now means to accuse the other Kings?"

"Yes Helena, I fear he does, but perhaps Misco can reign him in a bit, for a little longer anyway…"

"How long do you think we have?"

"Perhaps six weeks at most - it would take that long to get word back to Nimea and start to mobilise his army, should he choose war - we need to find Thatcher, and quickly,"

They turned down the long corridor, seeking to find the Royal Chamberlain.

28

Thatcher

It felt like they had been wandering the corridors of the castle for an age before they found a servant to direct them to Thatcher, but eventually they found him in a small study-like room near the main gate.

"Chamberlain Thatcher, we need to talk to you about what you have found out about the Teamsters," stated Helena as she entered the small room. Domico entered behind her, and suddenly the small room felt very crowded, but she wasn't about to send Domico away, or suggest moving somewhere else.

"Of course, Mage Hawke. What would you like to know?"

"Everything. Where did they come from? Have any of them got any links to the other kingdoms? How long have they been employed? Did any of them leave the caravan after Princess Casili died?"

"I have had my agents looking into it. As far as we have been able to find out so far, all of them have been employed by known and trusted merchants of Nimea for at least a year. Some of them are not from Voreen, so may have family elsewhere, but that's not unusual for a teamster - they tend to move about a lot, and work for several merchants over the years. None of them left the caravan before it returned, with Captain Hileat, to Nimea, although a couple have left since. But again, that's not unusual, really. Why? Do you believe that one of them may have been responsible?"

"It's possible. They are the ones most likely to have had access to the Princess' belongings while on the road, as Captain Hileat had already stated that there were no strangers in the camp that day - or in the days before she died," explained Helena. "Where are they now?"

"A few are here, with us in Tradehome, but the rest will be in Nimea, or out on their masters trading routes I would imagine,"

"Can I please have a list of who they were, their employers, and, if you know it, their current locations?"

"Yes, of course. I can use the Far-Speaking device here in Tradehome to speak to my agents in Nimea, and we'll see if they can track down the whereabouts of those not here with us. It will take a little time. Would you return here tomorrow?"

"Thank you Chamberlain Thatcher, we will see you tomorrow," concluded Helena and left the room, Domico, once again, trailing behind.

"Now what?" he asked once they were outside of the castle

"Now, we need to think about what could kill a Taka, and therefore how someone could have got hold of some of its venom," stated Helena.

"Any ideas on how we do that?" he asked

"I think we need to talk to another Mage, and perhaps find out if any of the traders here in Tradehome have heard of anything... If anyone has heard of a way to kill Takas, then they might know," she stated.

"Let's go back to the Inn, and I'll nose around a bit," suggested Domico. Helena nodded and let him lead the way.

29

Rumours

Helena was tired of waiting. Domico had been gone for hours, and she had been pacing their sitting room for most of them. Now she was not only sick of waiting, and dwelling on the deadline they now seemed to have, but also exhausted from walking what felt like miles up and down their little set of rooms…

Just when she had decided that she should go out and look for him, the door opened and in he walked!

"My God Domico, I was about to start looking for you!" she said, before he'd even closed the door.

"I think I must have talked to just about every merchant in the fair," he said, closing the door and trudging over to sink into the settee. "Most of them looked at me like I was some sort of spy from their competitors, and the rest just assumed that I wanted to waste their time…"

"But did you manage to find anything?" she asked desperately.

"Yes, as you would guess, with the last merchant that I spoke to. He was friendlier than most and actually offered me a drink. Over that glass of wine, he confided he had heard that a Mage had made, and sold, a device that emitted a certain note, that not only paralysed a Taka, but could kill it if the person using it was close enough. He hadn't seen the device himself, but he had heard that it was sold to someone from Tobar a few months ago,"

"An assassin?" she gasped. Tobar was the home island of the Assassins, although a few regular people were also rumoured to live there, supplying the assassins with food, services and goods. However, no-one who wasn't invited had ever set foot on the island, and those that had been there, neither broadcast that fact nor told others of what they saw.

"He didn't think so, he thought it was more likely to have been sold to a merchant who traded there - something like that would fetch a high price in Tobar, so perhaps the merchant was just thinking of the profit someone would make from it,"

"So, we either need to find the Mage, or the merchant... I don't suppose your friendly informant knew any more than that?"

"Not that he was telling. Would Misco know anything about the Mage?"

"He might, but I'm sure he would have mentioned it already if he knew someone had invented a device that could kill a Taka," she replied, frowning.

"Let's ask, anyway. You never know, and it will only take a minute," suggested Domico.

Helena rose and left the room to pay a visit to Misco's suite. Luckily, the Mage was in.

"Helena, what do you want to see me about?" he asked, once she had taken a seat in his room.

"Domico has picked up some information that a Mage has developed, and sold, a device that can kill a Taka. Have you heard anything like that?" she asked him.

"No, but I do know that one of our Order has been working on something secret, that he has refused to share or talk about for the last year or so... I do not know if it's the same thing though... It could be I suppose, but what I don't understand is why he wouldn't share his discovery with us all..."

"Who is it?"

"Mage Ripley."

"And do you know where he is now?"

"The last contact I had from him was from Portana, but that was six months ago. He may have moved on by now,"

"Well, it's the best lead we've got, so we'll go to Portana,"

"We're running out of time, Helena. I can only stay King Garrod's hand for another week or two. After that, he's going to mobilise his army. I do not know who he will declare war on. I don't even know if he knows that himself, but you'll need to travel fast if you're going to get to Portana in less than three weeks..."

"I know Misco. We'll cut across country and change horses when we can - hopefully we can do it in less than ten days that way."

"Well, be careful then - the lands between here and Portana are settled, but that doesn't mean that there won't be danger," he said, looking worried.

"I will be careful, but speed is what we need now, so we don't have time to stick to the roads… I'll keep in touch when I can, hopefully without the need for a mind-link,"

"I'll be here," he said as she rose and left the room.

"Portana," she said to Domico as soon as she entered their suite. "We'll need to cut overland, and get there as soon as possible,"

"We'll leave tomorrow then, after we've got the information on the Teamsters from Chamberlain Thatcher," Domico said. "I'll arrange the supplies."

30

A mad rush

The journey cross-country to Portana was not an easy one. To reduce the baggage, Domico and Helena had once again made the decision that they would share a tent, as the extra space that was given could then be given over to carry extra grain for the horses. Keeping them fit so that they could run for longer was paramount. There would also be few places to stay, and so fewer places to buy additional supplies.

Domico taught Helena all the little ways to conserve her horses energy, walking up hills then cantering down the other side, trotting a mile, then cantering a further mile, then dismounting to walk a mile so that they walked one mile every three, and feeding them generous amounts of grain each night, after walking them for the last mile to cool them down. All these little tricks meant they could cover about sixty miles a day, but Helena was still anxious.

She had become a reasonable rider over the last few weeks, but this was also about her own fitness and endurance, and that hadn't been something that she had had to worry about before, and she found she was constantly sore and tired. It gave her a new appreciation of just how fit Domico was, how much he knew about travelling, how good he was at navigating, and understanding the distances involved, and how much she relied on him.

She had become a reasonable rider over the last few weeks, but this was also about her own fitness and endurance, and that hadn't been something that she had had to worry about before, and she found that she was constantly sore and tired. It gave her a new appreciation of just how fit Domico was, how much he knew about travelling, how good he was at navigating, and understanding the distances involved, and how much she relied on him.

On their sixth day out from Tradehome, while they were leading the horses for a stretch, Helena saw a small shimmering, like when the air is distorted above a heat source, between themselves and the next grove of trees. She paused to look, and Domico, walking in front, looked back and noticed that she had stopped.

"What's wrong?" he asked

"Nothing - I'm just wondering what that is. It looks like the heat is shimmering, but it's not that warm today, and I can't see anything that would make it…"

He looked to where she pointed. "I can't see anything. Are you sure?" he asked.

"Yes, it's just there, between us and the trees," she said, bemused that he couldn't see it.

He looked again, but still couldn't see it - everything looked normal to him.

"Well, I can't see it, but we'd better get on," he said, paying it no mind.

They both mounted again and started to trot their horses towards the trees. As they grew closer, the shimmering grew more obvious to Helena, but

Domico still confessed to not seeing anything.

Suddenly the shimmering disappeared, with a small popping sound that sounded loud in the silence. In its place was a large, four-legged creature that looked like a grey cat, but was the size of a horse, with impressive claws almost six inches long.

"Tontcat!" Domico shouted, drawing his sword and trying to reign in his suddenly rearing horse. Both horses were rearing, snorting and neighing wildly, and in the panic, the lead rein for the two packhorses snapped, and they both galloped off a short distance before turning to face the monster. Tontcats, while being the same size as a horse, had formidable claws and teeth, and being carnivorous, would hunt anything, including horses, given the chance.

Domico tried to spur his horse towards the Tontcat, but it refused to move in that direction, trying to turn and run, despite Domico using all his skills to try and move it towards the beast. Helena also had her hands full with her mount, as it was trying to rear up, throw her off and follow the pack horses.

The Tontcat sprang, seeking to cover the few hundred metres between it and the horses before they could flee out of range. It was fast, covering the ground in only a few seconds and closing with Domico and his mount quickly. As it brought up a paw to slash at Domico, he raised his sword and inflicted a cut across its pads, finally bringing the horse around to face the beast.

The Tontcat circled, narrowing its eyes and looking for an opening while Domico danced his horse around, keeping it facing the Tontcat. Helena had finally managed to calm her mount, although it shivered and snorted and tried to prance backwards and move away.

Domico stared at the Tontcat, waiting for the bunching of muscles that showed it would pounce again, but it continued to circle, waiting for Domico to be distracted. One slash with those claws would be all it would take to kill - either a horse or a person - and Tontcats could be patient.

Helena tried to centre herself, but couldn't force herself to close her eyes, scared that the beast would focus on her in a minute. Her thoughts chasing each other, she fought to find that tiny centre of calm within herself. Eventually, she found it, and once more, pictured a circle in her mind and then opening her eyes, tried to centre it on the Tontcat.

That it was constantly moving wasn't helpful, and Helena felt like she was constantly chasing it, trying to aim at a moving target. A growing sense of panic also meant that Helena was in danger of losing her focus. However, she persevered, and trying to anticipate the movements of the Tontcat, waited for it to pace into her circle. As soon as it did, she envisaged the air turning solid within that circle, pinning the beast in place. It was as if it suddenly turned to stone - it couldn't move, as the surrounding air had literally solidified.

Domico dismounted, dragging his horse over to Helena and handing her the reins

"Hold him, while I take care of it," he said, a note of anger in his voice.

"You cannot do anything," she told him. "The surrounding air is now solid, so you won't be able to push your sword through it, just the same as it can't push itself through it,"

"So what do we do?" he asked her, "You can't sit here and look at it forever!"

"We won't need to. It also can't breathe - the air is too solid to allow its ribcage to open. It will die within minutes," she said sadly.

"You can't feel sorry for it, surely?"

"Yes, I can, and I do. It's my magic that has killed it."

"But it was trying to kill us," he said

"I know, but it's probably just looking for food. Look, I know it's not rational, and I know it would have killed me in a heartbeat, but I still feel bad about using magic to kill something. OK?"

"OK Helena," he said, mounting his horse again.

"Will you be OK if I get the pack horses?"

"Yes, I'll just give it a couple of more minutes before I let go."

Domico rode off to collect the two packhorses, and Helena tried to stem the tears that were about to start. Domico was right. This shouldn't be something that she should feel bad about - she had saved their lives by doing what she did - but that didn't stop her tears.

After a few minutes, Domico returned, and Helena let go of her focus. The Tontcat slumped to the floor, dead.

"Is that how Mages also kill Taka?" Domico asked after they had ridden on.

"Yes, I would think so," she said in a subdued tone. "You see, when I focus on something, I imagine all the tiny particles and atoms doing something else... So in this case, I imagined that the air particles were suddenly packed together so tightly that they couldn't move, they formed a solid mass... When I did the eavesdropping trick, I imagined that the impression of the brooch in the water was actually attached to the one that Baron Santu was wearing, and that therefore it could pick up the vibrations of sound, and 'see' the image in front of it… Do you understand?"

"Sort of… So when you do magic, you actually change how something behaves, at the lowest, most tiny, atomic, level?"

"Yes, basically,"

"So why are you not confident in your magic then?" he asked, curious.

"Because I haven't really used it much, and while I know and understand the theory, the practical side of it sometimes doesn't work for me - perhaps my will, my ability to use my imagination to change things, isn't strong enough. Perhaps that's why I have so much trouble creating Devices…" she trailed off.

"Well, you're certainly getting some practice now," he smiled, and kicked his horse into a trot, leaving the dead Tontcat behind.

31

Portana

The rest of the journey to Portana was uneventful, and they arrived, tired (and for Helena) sore, eleven days after they left Tradehome.

Portana was the major port city for the whole of Rintala, and was therefore large, crowded and noisy. Helena had never seen such a place. While she had grown up in a port city, Casan was nowhere near as busy or crowded, and the architecture was vastly different. Casan was mostly built of stone - thick sandstone blocks that gave the town a golden colour that felt welcoming. Portana, however, while also made of stone, was built of a type of dark grey stone that hadn't weathered at all as far as she could see, and was all sharp edges and left Helena feeling small and unwelcome. The buildings were packed close together, as if jostling for space, with narrow, dark walkways between. The only exceptions to this seemed to be a few large boulevards that ran from the warehouse district directly to the docks, presumably so that large waggons and carts could navigate them with full loads.

Neither did the people seem particularly friendly, each more than prepared to jostle her and Domico out of their way, seemingly in a hurry to reach their destination.

After such a struggle to get there, Helena felt weary and was suffering from sensory overload, with all jostling, shouting, and arguing, the variety of colourful clothing and goods and animals seemingly everywhere she looked. There were also porters scurrying about, carrying large bales of materials, and cages full of small animals like chickens and ducks. She just wanted to find somewhere to stay and get off the streets.

Domico guided them to an inn that looked respectable, with a wide frontage onto a relatively quiet street. He nodded for Helena to enter while he took the horses to a livery yard across the street.

Inside was a large taproom, with many round tables that were far enough away from each other to afford their occupants a little privacy. Along the walls were small booths, each one looking like a little room with one wall - the one separating it from the taproom - missing, with wooden partitions that reached all the way to the ceiling separating each one from its neighbours. Helena loitered, looking about her while waiting for Domico to arrive. After a few moments, he appeared with his, and Helena's, saddlebags slung over his shoulders.

Domico looked at Helena, and then strode past her, indicating that she should follow, so she fell into step, just behind him, and followed him to the bar.

"We need a couple of rooms," he said to the large woman behind the bar. She turned to look at him, and Helena studied her. So far, at all the Inns they had stayed at, the barkeepers had been men - often large men, with evidence that they were no strangers to fighting. However, although the woman was big, it wasn't all muscle, and while she had heavily muscled arms and large hands, she wore at least one ring on each finger, which Helena assumed would hurt their wearer in any fist fighting. She had a mass of blond curly hair that had been cut into a short bob, and deep blue eyes that regarded them both keenly.

"How long for?" she replied

"A couple of days, possibly up to a week," replied Domico

"I want to see your gold first," she stated flatly. Helena couldn't really blame her - they both looked like they needed a bath and clean clothes - it had been a hard eleven days.

Domico reached into his tunic and brought out his money pouch. "How much?" he asked

"A gold mark each - that will buy you rooms for up to a week, and two meals a day." He handed over two gold marks, noting that her eyes were weighing the pouch, and how much might be left in it.

"This way," she said, stepping out from behind the bar "Margie!" she called, "Look after this lot while I see these people to their rooms," a small, willowy woman stepped out from what must have been a room behind the bar, and stepped over to a customer waving their empty tankard at her.

"I'm Mistress Dorka," she said to them, leading them along a narrow passage to the side of the bar, turning to look at them expectantly.

"Master Domico and Mistress Helena," replied Domico, not sharing anything more.

Mistress Dorka, gathering that this was all she was going to get, pointed them to a set of stairs. "Up there, second floor," she said. As they started up, they heard her heavy step behind them. Once on the landing on the second floor, they paused, waiting for her to catch up. She stepped up the last step and then moved past them, along another narrow, dark corridor. After passing a couple of doors, she paused and took a set of keys out of her apron.

Handing one key over to Domico, she said, "You can have this room," and she handed another key to Helena. "And you can have the one next door. They do have an adjoining door, but it can be bolted from either side, should you wish. Dinner is available from dusk to ten of the clock, and breakfast is available during the hour after dawn. If you want hot water for washing, let me know, and if you need anything else, I'm usually in the bar." and with that, she turned to go. They both murmured their thanks, and then separated to enter their rooms, Domico handing over Helena's saddle bags.

Helena was pleasantly surprised when she entered the room. It was quite spacious, and had room enough not only for the large bed but also a free-standing bath, just off to one side of a large, unlit fireplace. There was also an extensive wardrobe for clothing and a washstand in front of a wide window. A large, comfortable looking chair completed the room, also sitting off to one side of the fireplace and opposite the bath. Having a bath in her bedroom wasn't something that Helena had come across before, but the arrangement struck her as convenient, and it certainly meant better privacy than a shared room with one or more baths somewhere else in the building.

She took her saddle bags over to the wardrobe and unpacked, hanging her dresses and formal robes so that some of the creases would fall out. After a few moments, there was a knock at a door that was to one side of the fireplace. Going over to it, she noticed a large bolt that was placed at shoulder height - unbolting the door. She opened it a fraction, wanting to check that it was indeed Domico on the other side. It was, so she opened the door wider and nodded for him to enter.

"It would appear that the rooms are better than I expected," he said, noting Helena's room. "Mine mirrors this one, but I'll need to investigate to find out where the privy is," he said with a smile.

"I thought that I'd go out and ask around, see if anyone knows Mage Ripley, and whether he's still here," he said to her as she resumed unpacking her bags.

"Yes, that would be helpful. Do you want me to come with you?" she asked. He noted the reluctance in her tone, and decided that it might be better if she stayed here, at the Inn, for now, until she got more used to the crowds and noise outside.

"No, it's fine. I'll just have a little nose about. Why don't you stay here and get some rest, and we can meet for dinner in a couple of hours?"

She looked at him gratefully. "Thank you Domico. If you don't mind, I will. I'll just have a long soak and an hour's sleep, and I'll feel much better able to face the chaos out there after that."

"OK, I'll leave you to it then. Bolt the door after me, and I'll ask Mistress Dorka to send up the hot water for you. I'll see you later," and he turned and left, through the dividing door into his own room. Helena once more bolted it, and sat on the bed to await the hot water.

32

Mage Ripley

Domico wandered down one of the narrow, dark streets, towards the docks area. He was looking for one of the many street children that infested the port town. If anyone knew about a Mage in the city, he reasoned, it would be the street children, who made a meagre living running errands, doing odd jobs, and if all else failed, stealing minor items from unwary travellers and merchants.

He's been walking the town for over half an hour, and hadn't seen a single one yet - what was going on? Normally they were everywhere you looked... But he was sure he'd find some loitering around the docks.

He arrived at the bustling docks just as the tide was turning, with many of the ships going about the business of casting off, preparing to leave for destinations scattered across the continent.

Spying a group of children sitting at the end of the wharf, he checked his purse was secure inside his tunic, and removed a small silver coin in readiness - he had no wish for them to see where he kept his purse when he offered to pay for the information.

"I'm looking for a Mage," he said when he was close to the group. It comprised about six children, who looked to range from the age of about ten to fifteen. All were ragged, with clothing that hadn't been washed in weeks, possibly months, and all in obvious need of a bath and food. Two of the younger ones appeared to be girls, with the rest being boys. It was unlikely that the girls would stay with the band once they reached puberty, having other ways to make a living by that stage.

One of the older boys stepped forward.

"I can take you to a Mage, Sir," he said, looking shifty

"So there is one here, in Portana, then?"

"Yes Sir, he makes Devices for trade with the merchants. He's got a small shop," he answered. Domico pondered, why would a Mage open a shop? Yes, Devices were made for trade, but they were not normally privately sold, instead being traded with local guilds, who then rented them out to members, thus providing the guild with income... This was getting strange - did the child seek to fool him with some sort of charlatan? Domico decided to see where the child led him and decide from there.

"OK, lead the way, and I will give you this," he said, flourishing the silver coin. He noticed that the other boys refused to look at the one offering to lead him.

The boy set off at a brisk walk, down a street that led to the seedier part of the town.

"Why wouldn't the other boys look at you when you offered to take me to the Mage?" he asked the boy.

"Because they fear the Mage," the boy sneered. "They think he will turn them into toads or something if they look at him wrong."

"But not you?"

"I know Mages can't do that," he said, trying to sound manly and grown up, "Besides, I don't actually have to go into the shop, do I?" he said, showing that he didn't quite believe his own rationalisation.

"No, you don't, I suppose," replied Domico.

They walked for about ten minutes, getting further away from both the docks and the more respectable parts of the town, with the buildings around them getting smaller, dirtier, and more run-down as they progressed. Just as Domico was about to ask if it was much further, the boy stopped and pointed at a small building that looked out of place. It wasn't so much that it was in better repair than those around it, more that it looked somehow cleaner. There was also actual glass in the windows, whereas many other buildings in the street had old bits of canvas nailed to the window frames, or were boarded up altogether.

"The Mage sells his Devices from there, Sir," said the boy, "although he's probably closed for the day now."

"Thank you," said Domico, handing over the coin. The boy took the coin and ran off - probably back to his companions on the docks.

Domico decided to take a slow walk past the building and see if he could see anything inside. He thrust his hands into his pockets and walked slowly along the middle of the street, turning to look at each building as if he was just examining the surrounding buildings. When he was parallel to the Mage's building he stopped, and turned, looking back down the street he had just walked up - trying to make it look like he wasn't interested in the Mage's building at all, and then slowly turned and looked directly at

165

the glazed windows. It was odd that any building in this part of town had actual glass; he thought. It was possibly only the reputation of the Mage that stopped people from breaking and removing the glass.

He ambled over to the building, as if interested in the glass, and sought to peer in. Unfortunately, there were heavy drapes on the other side of the glass, in a dark colour - either very dark grey or black, preventing anyone from seeing into the shop. Domico didn't think it wise to try the door, so ambled on, down past the shop and into the next street. From there, he navigated his way back to the main part of the town, and then to the Inn where they were staying. He could find his way back to the shop in the morning with Helena.

He ambled over to the building, as if interested in the glass, and sought to peer in. Unfortunately, there were heavy drapes on the other side of the glass, in a dark colour - either very dark grey or black, preventing anyone from seeing into the shop. Domico didn't think it wise to try the door, so ambled on, down past the shop and into the next street. From there, he navigated his way back to the main part of the town, and then to the Inn where they were staying. He could find his way back to the shop in the morning with Helena.

The following morning, they both set off from the Inn, Domico escorting Helena by the arm, and taking care to take the less busy streets. She was looking around her with a mix of wonder and wariness - she still wasn't used to the press of people, their loud shouting and calling, and the chaos of porters, street children, animals in cages and belligerent, swaggering sailors and merchants. Things grew quieter and less crowded the further they got towards the poor part of town, but the looks became more pointed and hostile.

Domico had filled Helena in on what he found out the night before, and, as they arrived at the shop, Helena said, "But wouldn't he do more business in a better part of the town?"

"Yes, most likely, so I don't know why he's set up here. Perhaps the rents are cheaper?"

"Or perhaps he's up to no good and doesn't want to be easily found?" she responded

"But we found him easily enough, so I doubt it's that," he replied.

Helena squared her shoulders and opened the door after a brief knock.

Inside it was dark, as the heavy drapes not only prevented people from seeing inside but also cut out most of the light, so it took a few moments for their eyes to adjust.

"Good morning," said a gravelly voice from in front of them somewhere.

After a moment, they could see that in front of them was a counter that ran the width of the shop, with a tall, long- haired, bearded man standing behind it. Both the beard and the long hair were white - giving him a look of being elderly, although the face and hands appeared strong and unlined, and the voice, while gravelly, was full and strong.

"Good morning," said Helena "We are seeking Mage Ripley,"

"And what do you want with a Mage?" he said, sounding aggressive.

"I am Mage Hawke," said Helena, "and I need to speak to Mage Ripley on an urgent matter."

"Urgent? Then you had better step this way, but your man must stay here,"

Helena looked to Domico. She did need to speak to Ripley, but didn't like the thought of doing so alone, and she knew Domico would not be happy with her going somewhere without him - who knew what else was going on in this building?

"No," she said "He will come with me, or we will leave now, and I will report to Mage Misco that Mage Ripley was unhelpful in meeting with us," It was a bluff, as Helena didn't know if she could contact Misco, or that he could help, or even whether Ripley would care…

"Wait here," the bearded man said, and disappeared through a door, that until that moment, neither of them had spotted in the dim recesses of the shop.

They shared a look, and Domico opened his mouth to speak, but before he could, Helena shook her head and pointed upwards. So they waited in silence.

A few minutes later, the bearded man returned, looking angry.

"You may both go up. Top of the stairs," he said, his tone clearly showing that he was not happy, but had been overruled by someone else - Mage Ripley, perhaps?

He lifted a portion of the counter, and waved them through, and then opened the door that he had previously disappeared through for them.

At the top of the stairs, they found a small room that looked like they had set it up as some sort of workroom, with a large, tall table taking up most of the space. Around the walls were shelves and cupboards that seemed to be crammed with all sorts of things, from springs and cogs through to rocks and crystals.

The table itself was covered in parts of Devices. Small Far-Speaking Devices, designed to cover short distances, commonplace Devices to preserve foods, similar to the ones that preserved Princess Casili, and Devices to encourage crops to grow, were all being built or repaired on the table. From the looks of it, Mage Ripley was receiving a lot of work.

He himself stood at the far end of the table. Helena remembered seeing him around the Mage Order building in Tarshea. He was of middle years, but they didn't look to have been kind to him. Only slightly taller than her, being short for a man, he was also of a slender build. His short red hair needed a comb, as it looked like he'd been running his hands through it, leaving it sticking up at the front. His green eyes were hooded, with the folds of the eyelid drooping, almost as if he was on the verge of going to sleep, and the eyes themselves were bloodshot, with dark circles underneath.

"Mage Ripley," Helena said, when it was clear that he had no intention of welcoming them to his shop.

"Mage Hawke," he replied.

"I am investigating a murder on behalf of the Order, and I need to know if you have developed a device that can kill a Taka," she said without preamble.

"And if I have?" he replied with a note of insolence.

"Have you?" she demanded

"As it happens, I have. It emits a note of such pitch that the sound vibrations can alter the rhythm of the heart."

"But then, why doesn't it kill the user?"

"It is designed in such a way as the sound can be directed - so you can affect something in front of you, but the sound doesn't affect your heartbeat. Clever, eh?" he said, sounding proud of himself.

"So it's a killing Device then? How responsible is that?" she asked, angry that someone would develop something solely designed to kill. "This could kill hundreds! Thousands!" she said, getting increasingly wound up at the prospect of such an indiscriminate thing being available to purchase by just anybody.

"Well, it should be used to stun only, but I suppose someone could use it to kill… but that's not really my problem. Who was killed?" he asked, sounding only slightly curious, while he removed a hip flask and drank deeply from it.

"I think your Device was used to kill a Taka," said Helena. She disapproved of the hip flask, suspecting what was in it, as alcohol and magic didn't mix well.

"Well, what are you worried about that for? They are monsters, after all!"

"Yes, but then someone milked it for its venom and then used the venom to murder someone,"

"That's certainly a lot of effort to murder someone. Much safer and easier to stick a knife or a sword in someone, isn't it? Or, to use the Device on them rather than on the Taka?" he said, sounding bored. He took another long drink from the flask.

Domico wandered over and gestured to ask for the flask. Mage Ripley considered, and then, begrudgingly, handed it over. Domico sniffed it and shook his head.

"You know Mage Ripley that drink and magic don't work well together, and it's very early in the day to be starting, don't you think?" Domico asked him.

"It's none of your concern, though, is it?" he asked, sneering at Domico.

Helena jumped in. "It is mine, though. I could report this to Misco, and they would recall you to Tarshea. How would your 'business' cope, then?" she asked.

"You assume I would actually cooperate and return, though, don't you? Who are you, a junior Mage, who's never been out in the world, to judge me?"

"So you would disobey and become a renegade magician?" she asked, disbelieving that anyone would turn their back on the Order.

"If it came to that choice, yes! The Order doesn't own me, and I can do what I like. I make my own living here, and Misco doesn't have any right to prevent that,"

"He can, and will, if he thinks you are bringing the Order into disrepute. He'll hunt you down and have every Mage in the Order looking for you. You wouldn't last long under those circumstances." She took a deep breath to calm herself. This wasn't getting them any further with their investigation. "But this is getting us nowhere... I am here as a representative of the Order, so you will cooperate, or face the consequences. Now, who did you sell the Device to, and was there only one?"

Mage Ripley's shoulders slumped, and the bravado he was putting on slipped away in the face of Helen's determination. "I've only sold one, yes, it was a prototype, and I sold it to a merchant,"

"Do you have the technical specification for it?"

"Why?"

"I want it, to see if there is some way to block it - I don't want it turned on people, and without that specification, you won't be able to make any more in a hurry. In fact, I'd advise against making any more at all,"

"Why should I hand it over to you?"

"Because if you don't, Misco will find out, today, what you are up to here, and I'm sure he will take steps - steps that you won't like, or that would leave you with your little business here,"

Ripley stalked over to one of the shelves and opened a small drawer that was concealed by rolls of parchment. He flipped through some drawings, diagrams, and technical specifications, and drew one out of the small pile. He thrust it at Domico, saying, "Here, take it!"

"And the Merchant?" questioned Helena. "Did he trade with Tobar and the Assassins?"

"The Guild of Death? No, not that I know of. He said he was based in Nimea and wanted something to protect himself as he took the route through the Mountains,"

"His name?"

"I'm not sure that I recall... it was over a year ago,"

"Remember it. Now!" said Helena, losing patience.

Mage Ripley looked up and closed his eyes, as if trying to recall the exchange.

"Atos, I think. Merchant Greig Atos,"

"Thank you. I would suggest that you cut down on the drinking quite a lot.

You're already looking a bit seedy, and how many merchants will trust a drunken Mage?"

"More than you might think, but I'll take it under consideration," he said. "Now, if you would both please leave, I have work to be getting on with. I trust that Misco will be kept out of this?"

"I can't promise that, as I will need to tell him about the Device, and we will need to find a way to counter or neutralise it, but I won't volunteer anything about the drinking unless he asks," she said, turning to go. Domico close on her heels.

33

Nimea

Back in their Inn, Domico and Helena settled into a booth in the taproom to talk.

"So, what's next?" asked Domico.

"Have you got that list of Merchants that the teamsters worked for?" Helena replied.

"Yes, it's here," he said, fishing a piece of parchment out of his coat.

"Is there a Greig Atos on the list?"

"No, but there is a Tomas Atos,"

"Does it say where he's based?"

"Yes - Nimea,"

"I don't think we have time to travel to Nimea, do we?"

"Possibly. If we can find a fast ship, that can sail up the river from Tilana… It would be very tight, though."

"Right, you head to the docks, and see if there is a ship that is fast enough, going to Nimea, and I'll try to contact Misco and give him an update. It might be enough to curb King Garrod's impatience and buy us a little more time," she said, rising to go up to her room. Domico nodded, stood and left the Inn.

Helena had just finished speaking to Misco, through the mind link, when there was a knock at her door. She rose from the chair and wobbled over to the door. Domico stood on the other side.

"We've done something good in a past life… the Wind Witch is in the harbour and Captain Hartan is amenable to a trip up to Nimea. If the weather is kind, then we can make it two or three days," he said. "We can sail on the midnight tide,"

He noticed Helena didn't look well, was holding on to the door frame for support and her eyes were tight with pain.

"The headache again?"

"Yes," she whispered, not daring to nod or speak any louder.

"Right. You rest, I'll pack and arrange for some supper before we leave," he said, coming into the room.

He packed with efficiency while Helena laid on the bed with her eyes closed.

"You stay here," he said quietly, "while I arrange for some food and a cold compress for your head," and he slipped out of the room.

A few minutes later he was back, and unbolted the connecting door, so that he could enter his room and pack his things as well.

A short time later, while he was sitting in front of the fire in Helena's room, the food arrived. It wasn't anything fancy, just a stew, but he thought that the meat was beef and there were some satisfying dumplings to round it out. Domico ate all of his, and most of the bread, to mop up the remaining gravy, but Helena only managed a few mouthfuls.

"I know it hurts to eat Helena, but you need to try, as it's going to be very plain fare on the ship for the next couple of days," he said, coaxing her to try and eat a little more. After she had eaten about half, he stopped pushing her and suggested that she try to sleep for a couple of hours.

Domico woke her about an hour before midnight.

"It's time," he said, as she opened her eyes. "How do you feel?"

"A little better. Perhaps it gets easier with practice," she said, rolling off the bed with a groan.

"Do you need help getting downstairs?" he asked, loaded with both of their saddlebags.

"No, I can manage. You go ahead, and I'll meet you outside."

"OK, but if Mistress Dorka asks, I've already settled the bill, so don't let her get any more money out of you," he said with a smile, sweeping out of the room.

Helena made it down the stairs in one piece and left the Inn. Mistress Dorka was busy serving people in the taproom and just nodded as Helena went past. Perhaps she's more honest than she looks, thought Helena.

Domico was waiting outside with both horses. "Here, I'll give you a leg up," he offered. Gingerly, Helena climbed into the saddle, looking like she might vomit any moment.

"It's not far," he said, glad that they would be there within a few minutes.

It was reasonably quiet on the streets at this time of night, although occasional voices could be heard from inns and taverns as they passed them. Only a short time later, Domico motioned for Helena to dismount and she came out of her haze to realise that they were standing next to the ship, with one sailor standing by to take the horses. She almost fell rather than dismounting, and Domico, again laden with the saddlebags, rushed to her side to hold her up and steer her up the gangplank and into the Captain's quarters.

Helena fell, rather than sat, on to the bed, and then went back to sleep almost immediately. She slept right through the reminder of the night, and all the following morning, while Domico came and went around her.

When she awoke, she felt much better, and when Domico suggested some food, she smiled and agreed that she was hungry.

"How's the head?" he asked when he came back in, noting that she was sitting on the bed, and had washed her face and combed her hair while he was out.

"Much better. I think that it really must get easier each time you use the mind link. It hasn't taken as long to recover this time, has it?"

"No, it hasn't. I was almost expecting you to sleep the whole way," he said with a smile.

"How close are we?" she asked

"Actually, we'll arrive in Tilana this evening, and should be able to sail up the river to Nimea by sunset tomorrow. The Captain says that the Device won't help much in the river, but we've saved quite a lot of time anyway since Portana. Now, what did Misco say?" he asked, having waited until now to find out how things stood at Tradehome.

"It's not good... King Garrod grows more angry and erratic, and even with the news that the Device was sold to a Vorainian merchant, Misco isn't confident that he can rein him back for much longer. Misco believes that King Garrod has decided that it was Castin's plotting that killed Casili, as apparently some of the noble families there had already petitioned for an alliance between themselves and Rintala, while others had approached King Garrod for Casili's hand,"

"But wouldn't that mean that they were too busy fighting amongst themselves to plot to murder Casili on her way to the wedding?" he asked, confused.

"Apparently not. Although the two factions in the Royal Court didn't agree on whom they should seek an alliance with, neither of them wanted Voreen and Rintala to form an alliance. But whether anyone would go as far as the murder of Casili isn't known, although, as I said, Misco is of the opinion that the King is convinced they are to blame..."

"So how much time do we have left?" he asked

"Days... A week at most before King Garrod formally declares war on Castin, according to Misco."

"Let's get some air before the food arrives," suggested Domico. Helena agreed, and they went up on deck for a quick walk and some fresh air.

That evening, they sailed into Tilana and made straight for the river Nim.

The river started in the mountains to the north, little more than a small stream, but it gathered other waters as it came down from the heights, and by the time it reached Nimea, it was massive, and led straight from there to the coast. The river Nim was the main reason that both Nimea and Tilana were located where they were, as it provided an easy trade route and, of course, access to fresh water was vital for any community.

As they sailed through Tilana, small signs of mobilisation of the army were everywhere. Groups of men could be seen marching around the town, drilling with their pikes, swords and pole arms. Merchants were busy loading and unloading supplies and foodstuffs, with quartermasters taking delivery of everything from swords to wheat.

"I'm worried," said Helena. "It would appear that King Garrod has already started preparations…"

"Yes, it looks like he's already called in his levies, and those of his nobles, and is obviously already buying the supplies he needs for his campaign," said Domico.

"We really are out of time, aren't we?" she said

"Just about. It doesn't look like they have started marching yet, and it's a long way over the mountains to Castin, but we don't know what the communities on the other side of the Mountains of Voreen are doing, or how close they are to staging. I don't think we have more than a couple of days, though,"

They docked in Nimea the following evening. It was just after sunset, as they had been delayed a little by a large convoy of ships sailing down the river from Nimea towards Tilana. They were riding high in the water, so appeared to have unloaded their cargo in Nimea, and were returning to the coast empty. This was very unusual, as merchants and captains knew that sailing empty of cargo earned them no money, to say nothing of profit. It appeared to be yet more evidence of the mobilisation of the nation, with supplies being hoarded in Nimea rather than sending them off for trade elsewhere.

"We need to find somewhere to stay," said Domico as they waited for their horses to be unloaded.

"Yes, but first I'd like to see this merchant, Tomas Atos," said Helena

"I have his office address, but he's unlikely to be there at this hour," replied Domico.

"We can at least look. I feel time snapping at my heels, and we can't afford to wait for morning,"

"Right. Well, we can try," concluded Domico, trying to be conciliatory.

They mounted their now unloaded horses, and Domico led the way towards the main part of the City. It was getting dark, and the lamps lighting the street were being lit by the teams of lamplighters employed by the crown.

"I'm not that familiar with Nimea," said Domico, "but I do recall that the merchant's quarter is on the east side of the City."

Helena looked at the City as they rode through it. They mainly built it of wood, the same as Tilana, but these buildings were bigger, with many of two stories or more, although the roofs were still heavily sloped. The roads were also wider and straighter than in Faskan. Obviously, this city hadn't been built in antiquity and for defence. Most buildings also had windows on the ground floor, although they weren't large. However, the glazing in them wasn't of the best quality, with many appearing to have thick, wavy looking glass in them that distorted the view of what was within. The lamps, lighting the streets, appeared to be Device based - with glowing white crystals inside glass shrouds that were on long poles, above the height of a man sitting on a horse, and level with the second floors of the buildings.

Helena hadn't seen these sorts of devices before and was curious. "Have you seen Devices like these before?" she asked Domico, pointing to one crystal.

"Yes, but only here, and years ago in Tarshea. This used to be how Tarshea's streets were lit when I was small, before the new mechanisms were discovered. The new Devices that are used in Tarshea now are more reliable, and give a brighter light, but they are expensive, so I guess that Voreen hasn't upgraded yet. If you look closely, you'll find some of these are dimming, and will need to be replaced soon,"

Helena looked, and noticed a few crystals, as they proceeded towards the east of the City, that were dimming, and looked to be giving out a lot less light than some others.

After about an hour's ride, they approached a district that was a mix of warehouses and shops, with some offices interspersed in between.

"We need to find Atos' office," said Domico, dismounting and approaching a merchant who was just leaving one warehouse.

"Sir, can you tell me where we can find Turn Street?" he said.

"It's a couple of streets away. Go down to the end of this street, then take your first left, and then it's the third street on the right," he said, eyeing them both.

"Thank you, Sir," said Domico, mounting his horse again.

They followed the directions and found themselves on a street that was exclusively offices and homes. It wasn't a long street, and there were only about thirty buildings on it. The lamps on this street were dim, and the street felt lonely and dark, with an almost abandoned feeling. There was no-one about, not a single soul, although a dog appeared out of a small alleyway between two buildings, and barked at them before disappearing back into the darkness.

"How do we know which building we want?" asked Helena. "They don't appear to be numbered, or have names on the ones I can see from here..."

"Let's just have a slow walk along. You take this side, and I'll take that one," said Domico, dismounting. Helena also dismounted and walked her horse over to her allotted side of the street. She began a slow walk past the buildings, examining each one. Some of them did have names on them, discreetly carved into the wood above the door, so that it wasn't obvious from more than a couple of feet away.

They had proceeded about two-thirds of the way down the street when Domico suddenly said, "Over here,". Helena walked her horse over, and saw that he was standing in front of one of the larger buildings, with 'Atos' carved over a wide doorway. The building appeared to be in good repair, with carefully polished woodwork and reasonably good glass in the small window to the left of the door.

Domico banged on the door with his fist, while Helena hoped the merchant was in a back room somewhere, as nothing could be seen through the glass. However, there was no answer. Domico tried again, but once more there was no response.

"I think you're right. He's not here. I had hoped that perhaps his home was above the office or something similar," Helena said, sounding disappointed.

"We can come back first thing in the morning. Even if he was here tonight, and told us what we needed to know, we wouldn't have been able to travel anywhere else tonight, so we haven't really lost any time," replied Domico, trying to make Helena see it wasn't such a setback as she perhaps believed.

"I know. We are going round and round in circles, and I am worried. I just don't feel as if we are making any progress, despite travelling so far and covering most of the eastern part of the continent…"

"I understand Helena, but we will find the answer, and soon. I know you can do this," he said with an encouraging smile. "Now, let's find somewhere to stay, and something to eat," he said, mounting once again, and turning his horse towards the end of the street.

"Will there be somewhere close?"

"There should be. Let's look and see what's at the end of the street, and whether there is an inn or tavern close by. From my experience, merchants like somewhere close to their office to take their refreshment," he pointed out.

When they reached the end of the street and were surprised to find a small square. It contained a small statue of some merchant from the past, depicted with a rod of office in one hand and a small set of scales in the other. On the other side of the square there appeared to be an inn, with a sign hanging above the door of a barrel and hammer. Domico rode over and pointed to a wide, open set of double doors that led to a small stable. Dismounting, and walking his horse through the doors, a young stable boy appeared, tousle-haired and sleepy. Rubbing his eyes, he said, "Good evening, Sir, Mistress. Can I help you?"

"Does this inn have rooms?" asked Domico

"Yes, sir, and I'm sure that they are available. Shall I take your horses?"

"Yes please. See them brushed down, and fed with grain please, and we'll go see the Innkeeper," said Domico, taking his saddlebags, while Helena dismounted and did the same.

"Just through there, Sir," said the boy, pointing to a door that led from the stable yard into the building.

"Thank you," said Domico, handing over a small coin. He turned and led the way into the Inn.

The door led directly into the taproom, which had two rows of barrels along the right-hand side, one on top of the other, and a long bar on the left. In between were several small tables, but only one of them was occupied. The occupant of the table looked up, staring at them briefly before returning his gaze to the tabletop.

Behind the bar stood a short, thin man, whose clothing looked like it had seen better days. It was frayed and tatty, the once bright yellow tunic faded to a pale shade. The man himself looked like he hadn't had a good meal in weeks, with hollow, sunken features and dark circles under his eyes. He limped out from behind the bar and slowly made his way towards them.

"Good evening, Master, Mistress. How can I help you?"

"You have rooms?" said Domico

"Yes Master. Would you like one room or two?"

"Two please, preferably next to each other,"

"Of course Master. Please step this way," he said, limping off to a door on the other side of the room, next to the end of the bar. He opened it, revealing a short corridor, with stairs at the end leading up. He walked down the corridor and started up the stairs. Half way up, on a small landing where the stair turned to the left, he rested his leg, and gave them both a nervous smile. He continued on, once more turning to the left at a landing at the top of the stairs. In front of them was a narrow corridor, with doors on the right-hand side. He opened the first door, and gestured inside, and then opened the second door, presenting both keys to Domico.

Domico went into the first room, had a quick look and then inspected the second room. "These will be fine. How much?"

"A Silver Mark each, per night, but that also includes food. If you wish the room only, it will be one Silver Mark between you per night,"

"We'll take the food as well," said Domico, handing over two Silver Marks. "One night for now, and I'll let you know in the morning if we wish to stay longer,"

"Yes, good Master. I will see to some supper for you both," he said, limping off back down the corridor and down the stairs.

Helena, who had remained silent throughout, entered one room and had a look around. There was a surprisingly large bed, which dominated the room, an open fireplace, which was currently unlit, and a small table and chair by a window. There was no cupboard or wardrobe for her clothes, but there was a washbasin on the table, and an ewer of water for washing. She dumped her saddlebags on the bed, and sank down to sit next to them, staring at the floor.

"What's wrong?" asked Domico

"It's all slipping away from me. I can feel the time running away like an hourglass emptying its sand quicker and quicker,"

"Come on, let's get some food, then you will feel better. You're just tired and hungry and have been running around for weeks. Just take what's left of tonight to relax, eat and rest, and in the morning it will feel better. We know what the next step is, and who we need to see, which is an improvement. You will get there, I'm sure."

34

Atos

Despite a good meal at the Inn, and a long hot bath, Helena slept little that night, tossing and turning, worrying about the upcoming war and her failure to find the person responsible for the death of Casili.

She was up, and ready to visit the merchant Tomas Atos before dawn. Pacing in the taproom, she waited for Domico and breakfast, knowing that despite her pacing, Atos wouldn't be at his premises any faster.

Breakfast, and Domico arrived with the rising of the sun, and while she tried to eat, her stomach was leaden and the food tasted like sawdust in her mouth. After trying to get down a few bites, she gave up, and waited impatiently for Domico to finish his.

A short time later she hurried him out of the Inn, and over the square to Turn street. When they arrived at the right building, it was still locked, with no-one answering the pounding that Domico subjected the door to. So they waited, Helena impatiently tapping her foot when Domico could persuade her to stand still, which wasn't often.

"At this rate, you'll be exhausted before he even arrives," he tried to point out reasonably. She just looked at him in silence, saying nothing, but knowing he was right.

About half an hour later, a man of medium build came walking down the street, gazing at the two people waiting outside his premises.

"Can I help you?" he asked when he reached the building

"We are looking for Tomas Atos," Helena said, before Domico could even open his mouth.

"You've found him. Come inside, and we can talk about your needs," he said, obviously thinking that they might be buyers of his goods.

Once inside the building, Helena didn't even give him time to remove his coat. "Are you related to Greig Atos?" she blurted out as soon as the door was closed.

"Yes, he's my brother. Why?"

"I understand he purchased a Device from Mage Ripley in Portana," she said

"Possibly. He does a lot of trading for me, buying items from all over the east coast. What was this Device?"

"It stuns, using sound waves,"

As soon as she said this, she knew she had made a mistake. Tomas' face assumed a closed expression, and he took a step back, taking cover behind the shop counter.

"I do not know what you're talking about. I know nothing about a Device like that," he said. His voice had become higher, and beads of sweat burst out on his forehead. "I trade in honest goods, including some Devices, but only the common ones such as Keeping Devices or light crystals,"

"This was a prototype… Where is your brother now?"

"I don't know,"

"Oh, come on, surely you do, if he does a lot of your buying and trading," inserted Domico.

"No. He went away a couple of weeks ago, and I don't know where," insisted Tomas.

"I think you're lying," said Helena. "We can force the truth out of you if you don't cooperate,"

Tomas reached under the counter and came out with a knife. It was a wicked-looking thing, about thirty centimetres long, with one edge serrated and the other smooth, and a slight curve to the blade. Instantly, Domico stepped in front of Helena and pulled his own knife, regretting leaving his sword in his room.

He stepped forward to cut the distance to Tomas and reduce the space he had to manoeuvre to get past Domico to Helena. Tomas' eyes narrowed, and he stepped from behind the counter to lunge at Domico, but Domico was faster in stepping to the side and slicing the sleeve of Tomas' coat.

The two faced each other, crouching a little to give better balance, and as Tomas moved again, Domico stepped to the side again. Then he realised he was being pushed, herded away from the door and Helena, and turned, twisting back to place himself in front of Tomas and between him, the door, and Helena, who was shifting from foot to foot, reluctant to leave but not knowing how to intervene.

What followed looked to her like some sort of mad dance, with each man moving from foot to foot and slashing and stabbing at each other, but with neither making contact with anything but cloth. Both were now sweating, their hands busy, trying to make grabs for each other's offhand, to try and pull the other off-balance and manoeuvre themselves into a position to get a clean strike at the other. Helena danced out of the way in the background, trying to keep Domico between herself and Tomas.

No-one spoke, just emitting a grunt now and then when a strike came close, or when they almost came into contact. It was eerie. Just when Helena had decided to try to trip Tomas, or distract him in some way, he over-extended, taking just a second too long to recover from the thrust and allowing Domico to grab his knife hand and give it a vicious twist, forcing the knife out of his hand and breaking his wrist. At the same time, Domico swept Tomas' legs out from under him, and forced him face down onto the floor, kneeling on his back to keep him in place.

"Helena, why don't you lock the door, and see if there is something we can use to tie him up?" panted Domico.

Helena locked the door and rushed off behind the counter to see if there was anything stored underneath it. There was nothing there, so she opened a door at the end of the counter and found another room, this one with a chair, desk and storage cabinets. She rifled through them, eventually finding a fairly long piece of thin rope. She brought it back through to Domico, who was still kneeling on Tomas' back, holding Tomas' undamaged arm back to prevent him seeking to wrestle Domico off.

"Will this do?" she asked, moving in front of him to show him the rope.

"Yes," he replied shortly, taking the rope and tying both wrists together and looping the string down to Tomas' ankles. Tomas screamed in pain as Domico roughly handled the injured wrist.

"Are you up to interrogating him?" asked Domico once Atos was securely tied.

"I'll have to be," Helena replied. "Can you hoist him onto the counter, please?"

Domico wrestled Atos on to the top of the counter, so that he was now lying at waist height to Helena. She walked up to him and placed the heel of her right hand on his forehead. Atos flinched back with a snarl, but Domico stepped around the counter and held him in place from the back. Helena placed her hand on his forehead again and concentrated.

She closed her eyes, and pictured Tomas' forehead acting like a door, slowly opening it in her mind's eye, to reveal his thoughts and feelings behind.

In her mind, there appeared to be a thick mist, swirling around, and so dark that it blocked all sight of the memories, thoughts, and feelings.

"He's fighting me," she explained to Domico. "I think he must have had some training in this. Most people don't have the discipline necessary to focus on the block, and nothing else. Usually, once someone is trying to deliberately not think of something, it's difficult to think of anything else…" The mist continued to swirl, and as Helena placed a vision of a breeze blowing it away on it, it grew even thicker, and just swirled around even more, but keeping its heavy, dense feel, and preventing sight of anything else. She increased the pressure of the breeze, it now becoming a fuller wind, but still it didn't move.

"Yes, he's definitely had some significant training in this… Now, why would an ordinary merchant need training to avoid the touch of an interrogation from a Mage?" she mused, as she continued to try to blow away the mist. Continuing to increase the pressure, she was now projecting a full-blown gale at the mist, and while it was now streaming away, it was instantly replaced by more mist, so that as fast as she was removing it, he was creating more to fill the gap.

Helena started to breathe heavily, exerting herself and putting more and more effort into her mental picture of the doorway to his mind. She continued to push forward the gale, knowing that to stop now would mean that he could build more defences that she wouldn't be able to pierce.

Domico noted her exertion and placed his hand on Atos' broken wrist, and quickly squeezed it, feeling the bones grind together. As Atos screamed in pain, his ability to focus on the mist slipped away, and Helena was through!

In his mind, she travelled through his memories, seeing people, places, and conversations. She directed his thoughts to the Device, and saw him instructing his brother to find any unusual Devices that he could, and sharing the rumour of Mage Ripley working on something that could be deadly, directing him to visit the Mage in Portana to investigate. She also saw that Tomas was aware of Casili's proposed progress on the way to her wedding, rather than travelling by ship, and had deliberately placed one of his teamsters as drivers in her caravan.

She was about to withdraw when she saw something that was curious.

A memory surfaced where Atos had been given this shop, by someone else, and told that he must run it as if he were the owner, but occasionally he would be directed to carry out tasks, or place one of his people into a certain position. All the people that worked for him, as Teamsters and as porters, would also be referred to him. He could not hire who he wished, but in return, he could keep the profits and would have a life of relative wealth.

She tried to direct his thoughts to who this mysterious benefactor was, but somehow he could deny her the details. That it was more than one person, and felt like an organisation, with a hierarchy was obvious, but the details of who, or what they were was, once more, covered in the mist - hiding the details. Helena pushed as much as she dared, but didn't want to permanently damage his mind, so accepted defeat and withdrew.

She stepped back and took a deep breath, removing her hand from his forehead.

"What do we do with him now?" she asked Domico.

"Did you get what we need?" he asked

"Mostly. There is something else there that I need to think about, but I can't get any more from him without permanent damage to his mind, and even then, given his training, I don't think it would be reliable."

"Right, you go back to the Inn, and I'll deal with him," directed Domico

"What are you going to do?" she asked, dreading the answer, as from Domico's tone and stance, she could guess that it would not be something nice, like sorting out some care for the broken wrist...

"You don't need to know that, Helena. Go back to the Inn and I will meet you there," he said. His tone brooked no argument, so Helena nodded and left the shop.

As she made her way back to the Inn, she pondered on the true ownership of the business, and who had been directing Atos. That, coupled with the training in preventing her interrogation, hinted at something that she didn't want to even contemplate.

35

The Guild

Domico came back to the Inn about an hour later, finding Helena deep in thought in the main taproom, nursing a cup of Choo that had long gone cold.

"What did you do with Atos?" she asked when he had sat down. He waited with his reply until after he had ordered two more cups of Choo from the Innkeeper.

"He's now under guard with the City Watch. I told them he tried to kill us both when we started asking him questions about Casili's death."

"If he's as connected as I think he might be, he won't be there long," she replied.

"I'm not sure. They loved Casili in this city, so they will not be lax about guarding him," he replied. Just then, the Choo arrived, and they fell silent until the Innkeeper had moved away again.

Taking a sip of his drink, Domico said, "So, what did you discover, and what do you mean about him being 'connected'?"

"First of all, he's had some significant training in how to keep a Mage out of his head during an interrogation - that's not normal practice for a merchant - why would they need it?" she asked metaphorically. "Secondly, someone - or something - set him up as a trader some years ago. Giving him the shop, the trading connections, and directs who he employs, referring people to him who they wish him to employ. Also not normal…"

"So what do you think it means?" he asked

Helena took a drink of her Choo and considered. "I've been pondering that for the last hour, and the only conclusion that I can draw is that his business is a front for something," she said

"Do you think that rumour in Tradehome had any merit?"

"Ahh, I'd forgotten about that. That the Device was sold to the Assassins? It would explain who is behind the merchant, and would also explain the mental training to keep a Mage out of Atos' memories. But, if that's the case, then while we know the Assassins were behind Casili's death, we don't know who hired them, so are not any further forward in stopping King Garrod from declaring war against one of the other kingdoms."

"We could chase down the Teamster and see if he knows more?" suggested Domico, although not with any conviction.

"We could, but do you honestly think that he'll tell us, or let me in to his memories during an interrogation? It's much more likely that he won't know who hired the Guild of Death for this contract, even if I could force a way past his mental guards."

"So what are our options, then? As I see it, we can either chase down the Teamster, go directly to the Guild - although I doubt very much that we'll get anything but a quick death trying that - or seek to follow up on Lyton's issues with women..."

"Yes, that about sums it up. I don't know. I agree that going to the Guild itself isn't really an option. Even the prospect of war won't worry them. They have been used to start wars in the past, so we don't have any leverage with that. Which leaves us either the Teamster, or Prince Lyton... Neither are very promising, and we're just about out of time,"

"The Teamster is here in Nimea though, so we won't lose time if we seek him out straight away,"

"How do you know that?"

"I got it out of Atos while 'escorting' him to the Sheriff,"

"How?"

"He was in a lot of pain, and despite the mental training, I don't think he is an assassin himself, as he wasn't coping well with it. He was also worried about something - and based on what you've told me, I think that might be that he has outlived his usefulness to the Guild, if we now know that they use his business as a front. We could try to capitalise on that, and see what else he knows?"

"OK, it might be worth a shot. Let's see him now, and then see what he can give us to inform what we do next."

They both rose from the table and left the Inn. It wasn't a long walk to the Sheriff's office and the City Jail so they arrived less than twenty minutes after they left the Inn.

"Back already, Master Domico," said the Sergeant at the desk in the Sheriff's office.

"Indeed, I am Sergeant Jacks. This is Mage Hawke, that I told you about. Helena, this is Sergeant Jacks," he said, affecting the formal introductions.

"We'd like to speak to Tomas Atos please, Sergeant," he continued.

"Just take a seat Master Domico, Mage Hawke, and I'll check with the Sheriff," he said, stepping away from the desk and disappearing around a corner at the back of the room.

A couple of minutes later, he was back. "The Sheriff says it's alright, but we must request that one of our men is present in the room. I trust that will be acceptable?"

"Of course, Sergeant Jacks, but we request that anything said in the room remains confidential," said Helena.

"Yes Mage Hawke. I'll come in with you myself," he said with a small smile. He signalled for one of the other Watchmen to come over to the desk and took some keys out of a drawer. "This way," he said to them both.

They followed him to the back of the room and took a corridor that led along the back of the building to a small extension to the building that contained the cells. Unlike most of the buildings in Nimea, they built this building of stone - very thick grey blocks of something that looked like granite - and it gave the building a cold interior that felt as if it was never warm. Helena pulled her coat around her even tighter as they were escorted into a small square room with just a chair in it that was fixed to the floor with some large bolts. The Sergeant left the room to get Atos, returning with him a couple of minutes later.

Tomas Atos, despite it only being a couple of hours since they last saw him, appeared a different man. He had lost his colour, looking a pasty grey, and his step was slow and faltering. The room had only a small slit window, high up in the wall, so that only the sky could be seen through it, and it was nowhere near wide enough to allow a man to squeeze through, although it let some light into the room, through a heavy, distorted, glass pane.

When Atos saw Helena and Domico, he flinched, his step slowing even more so that Sergeant Jacks had to push him towards the chair, bolting him in through the use of some heavy leg irons. Tomas' broken wrist was bound up and cradled in a sling across his chest, so Sergeant Jacks only secured the other wrist to the chair, leaving the injured one free. Overall, Atos was a pitiful sight, transformed from the confident merchant of the morning.

"I know that your business is a front for the Guild of Death," said Helena, with no preamble, and noting that Sergeant Jacks' eyebrows nearly climbed off the top of his head.

"I also know that you placed an assassin in the caravan of Princess Casili," she continued. As she said so, Domico crossed to Sergeant Jacks, holding on to his elbow and murmuring "Steady!" into his ear, as he looked about ready to draw his short sword and attack Atos.

"What I want to know is, who ordered the death?"

"I can't tell you that. It's more than my life is worth," cried Atos.

"And how much do you think your life is worth now?" stated Helena flatly. "Your use to the Guild is finished, so they will either want you dead, so you can't reveal anything, or, if you're lucky, they will leave you alone, and let the Watch and the King deal with you. Neither of which will spare your life, both for the attack on us, but more importantly, for your involvement in Casili's death,"

"And we won't be gentle about it," growled Sergeant Jacks, glaring at Atos as if he was looking at some sort of monster "I'll take you apart piece by piece myself, and not a hand will be raised to stop me,"

Atos looked panicked, and Helena considered Domico's earlier point about him not being an assassin himself.

"Is your brother one of the Guild?" she asked spontaneously, following up on her thoughts.

"Of course not!" replied Atos, but not sounding very convincing.

"I think you're lying, and he is - is that how you got into this? The Guild rarely involve outsiders in anything, so there had to be some reason they picked you to act as their front in Nimea,"

"He's just a merchant, like me," he protested

"But where did he think you got the money to start the business?"

"He never asked, and I never mentioned it. He's a few years younger than me, so maybe he thinks I earned it."

"How? What did you do before you set up in business?"

"I was a factor for another merchant, conducting his business for him in Nimea,"

"And where was your brother during that time?"

"He was travelling with various merchant caravans. He was away for a few years, apart from a couple of quick visits home,"

Helena and Domico shared a look. It was awfully convenient that the brother had been 'travelling' for a few years - about the time it took to undergo the training to be an assassin - and then suddenly someone approaches his brother and sets him up in business? Too much of a coincidence, even if Tomas was fooling himself about his brother's role.

"OK, let's go back. How were you informed about placing someone in Casili's caravan?"

Atos was silent, clearly considering the ramifications of what would happen because of his exposure today. Either way, in all likelihood, he was a dead man. The question was, was there anyway that he could make a deal to survive? Or to save his brother?

"I want a deal," he stated. "I'll share what I know, in exchange for my life, and that of my brother."

"You've just said that your brother has nothing to do with this, so why does the deal include him?"

"I just don't want anything taken out on him - he isn't involved, but if what you have said about the Guild is correct, they might seek him out and I'm not taking any chances,"

"Wait here," said Sergeant Jacks, motioning for Helena and Domico to join him outside of the room.

"Is there any chance that he could lead us to whoever ordered the Princess' death?" he asked them.

"Possibly. It will depend on how much his employers share with him, or whether he has picked up more than they wanted. But either way, we've not really got anything to lose. The Guild will find a way to kill him if we don't offer him protection of some sort, and dead, he's no use to anyone, let alone us, and the King…"

"Wait here, while I speak to the Sheriff," he said, hurrying off. Domico looked at Helena and raised one eyebrow in question. She nodded. This was a deal that they should make, as getting any further forward with what they had was impossible.

A few minutes later, Sergeant Jacks returned with a large, barrel-chested man in tow. He was tall, with a shock of bright red hair and an enormous beard that seemed to start just below his eyes and continued down to his waist. How he could eat through that thing was something that Helena didn't even want to contemplate.

"Sheriff," nodded Domico, "This is Mage Hawke,"

"Mage," he nodded in return, "Jacks has brought me up to date with the interview so far. Do you think we should make this deal?" he asked.

"Yes, I think we have to. Without more information, I cannot pursue who ordered Casili's death," said Helena.

"Normally I would have to consult with the King or the Lord Chamberlain, but as you know, they are both at Tradehome… Very well. I shall agree with your recommendation, but please remember it is on your recommendation, so if our King disagrees, he will take it up with you," he said, and then walked away.

Domico, Helena and Sergeant Jacks shared a look, each nodding before they went back into the small room with Tomas Atos.

"Well?" he asked as soon as they entered the room.

"If you have some information that is valuable enough, we will spare your life and offer you, and your brother, the protection of the crown," said Helena

"If we can find your brother," added Domico

"I can direct you to where he should be."

"So, what can you tell us about Casili's death - who contracted it?" said Helena

"I can't tell you specifically who, but I know it was a Rintalan noble. The Guild didn't tell me everything, but it was my brother who was the go between for the Guild and contacted the representatives of the noble family. I was ordered to make sure that some of my people were in place in either my ships, or my caravan teamsters, so that we had both routes covered, as it wasn't known until a couple of months ago what her route to Rintala was going to be. The instruction was that under no account was she to reach Rintala."

"But why does that mean that the person who contracted her death was Rintalan?" asked Domico

"Because my brother, when he was last in Portana, was contacted by someone who worked for one of the nobles. They didn't identify which family they were from, nor did they wear a family crest, but they were informed about the marriage proposal and acceptance, just over a year ago now, before it was announced and common knowledge, and he was paid in Rintalan coin."

"The marriage wasn't announced until about six months ago, so that is early knowledge but that still doesn't mean that whoever contracted it was Rintalan - anyone can get Rintalan coin, and anyone could claim to represent one of the noble houses, so it doesn't prove it beyond doubt," objected Domico.

"My brother told me he was sure they were Rintalan, and I can only repeat what he told me," whined Tomas.

"What else can you tell us? Which of your Teamsters handled the actual death?"

"It was a man that I've had in my employ for about a year - Deltone. I placed him in the caravan and he would contact someone who would supply a substance that would kill Casili if she came into contact with it. I don't know how he did it, and I don't want to know. I was just supposed to give his name to the Royal Chamberlain who was organising the caravan, and he would do the rest."

"Where do we find this Deltone?"

"He has lodgings in Willow Street, near my warehouse close to the river docks,"

"And where do we find your brother?" asked Helena.

"He's currently staying at the Blue Swan Inn. It's also near the river docks. He thought it best if we both stayed low for a while and weren't seen together."

"Why?"

"Because ordinarily he would be out on a buying trip in Eretee at this time of year, but with the tensions because of Casili's death, that might be dangerous for a Vorainian, and he didn't want anyone who was watching me to find him, or vice versa,"

"Sounds like your brother has hung you out to dry," commented Sergeant Jacks dryly.

"No, no, it's just that sometimes it's best not to remind people we are brothers…"

"Really?" he said, becoming sarcastic. "And you want to save his life?"

"Is there anything else you can tell us?" injected Helena

"Not really. When will you move me from here to somewhere safe?"

"When we know that your information is reliable," said Domico, "in the meantime, you stay here, where we can monitor you, and have you close at hand should we need to know more."

Domico turned to Sergeant Jacks. "Can you take him back to his cell now, please, Sergeant?"

Jacks nodded and stepped forward to release Tomas from the chair, and escorted him out of the room and back to his cell.

"What now?" said Domico to Helena, once Jacks and Tomas had left the room.

"Do we go after the brother or the Teamster first?"

"The Teamster I think, as I want to know how they managed to get the venom from the Taka onto the table leg in the space of a few hours, without being seen... After all, the teamster was driving the waggon, So he was about four hours away from the Taka when it died... so he must have met with an accomplice somehow, and before Casili's tent was set up in order to put the venom on the table leg before it went into the tent. It must have been closely coordinated..."

Sergeant Jacks came back into the room. "Ah, Sergeant, can you spare some time to come with us to see the Teamster and Atos' brother? I think we will need someone to help Domico escort them back here once we've spoken to them, and the fewer who know what's going on, the better," said Helena, looking serious.

"Of course Mage Hawke. I'll just clear it with the Sheriff on the way out," he said, escorting them back to the main reception room.

They left the City Jail together, Sergeant Jacks leading the way to Willow Street. After about twenty minutes of walking, Sergeant Jacks said, "This area of the City is known as 'The Forest', because they name all the streets after types of tree. It's possibly the worst area of the City, and even us Watchmen only come here after dark in pairs, so be careful,"

They noticed the streets were getting narrower, and somehow darker, possibly because the buildings were all at least two or three stories, cutting the light and casting lots of shadows. This wouldn't be an area to explore at night, or get lost in, as the buildings all had a rough look to them, with no glass in the windows - those that even had windows - just sailcloth stretched over the openings. There was also a lot more mess on the streets, where it looked like people just threw their rubbish into the alleyways between the tall, narrow buildings.

Sergeant Jacks halted them at a corner, pointing to a building further down the street on the right, "That's the only lodging house in this street," he said, "So if Atos was telling the truth, that is where this Deltone is staying,"

"Will it have a back door? I fear he may try to run," said Domico.

"Possibly, but it will certainly have windows at the back, as I doubt that anyone with any knowledge would stay in a place with only one entry and exit," Jacks replied.

"Agreed. I suggest you go round the back and Helena and I will go in the front. You just wait and see if anyone tries to make a run for it, and grab them if they do," Jacks nodded and moved away, down a narrow alley and heading for the back of the building.

Helena and Domico waited a couple of minutes and then moved over to the entrance to the building. They entered a narrow, dingy corridor with bare wooden walls. Damp was obviously a problem, as some of the boards dividing up the space had rotted from the bottom up, and the stairs looked in danger of falling down if a heavy weight was placed on them. To their right, there was an open door, behind which could be seen an extremely fat man wedged into a chair that looked like it was slowly disappearing underneath the rolls of fat and excess skin. He was sweating heavily, despite the day being cool and the door to both his room and the street being wide open. He looked up at them and said, "Yes?"

"Deltone?" replied Domico shortly.

"Second floor. I won't take you up," he wheezed at them - obviously he was in no condition to be climbing the stairs, even if they could take his weight, which they both seriously doubted.

So they gingerly walked up the stairs on their own, Domico in the lead. On the second floor, they stepped off the stairs and stared around. There were only two doors on the floor - one at the top of the stairs and another further along the corridor, opposite the point that the stairwell rose through the floor. Domico opened the door closest to them, revealing a small bathroom that definitely needed a clean, and shook his head at Helena. He edged past her in the narrow corridor and walked to the second door. He knocked on this one and called, "Deltone? Master Atos has sent me."

There was no reply from inside the room, but sounds could be heard through the thin door and walls, so someone was definitely in the room.

Domico knocked again. "Deltone?" he called. Just then, they heard Sergeant Jacks call them, from beyond the room, in the street below - the walls really were that thin. Domico tried the door, but it wouldn't open, so he stepped back and motioned for Helena to step away from the door. He raised his right foot and kicked at the door, just next to the door handle and the door flew open - if it had had a lock, it wasn't a good one - and Domico rushed into the room, his eyes busily scanning the small room that lay beyond the door.

Opposite the door was a small window, which looked to have had some canvass material nailed across it, but it was now flapping freely on three sides. Domico cautiously stuck his head out and had a look. He could see Sergeant Jacks running back up the street towards the building, out of breath and alone.

"Gone?" Domico called to him

"Yes, sorry. He was just too fast. He leapt out of the window straight onto the roof there," he said, pointing to a much shorter building on the other side of a narrow alleyway "and was away over the roof before I had time to run around, catching him on the other side…"

"Well, come on up," said Domico, pulling his head back into the room. Jacks joined them in the room a minute or two later, and they searched the room. Unfortunately, this yielded nothing. There were no documents, personal items or anything to suggest any hint of the person who had lived there for over a year, nothing at all.

"I probably leave more information about myself in a room that I've only stayed in for a single night than this Deltone leaves in a year of living here," said Helena in frustration.

"Yes, but then you're not an assassin, trained to leave no trace, are you?" replied Domico.

"Any chance of catching him, do you think?"

"None, now that he knows someone is looking for him," said Domico. Jacks shook his head in agreement.

"Well, that just leaves us with Greig Atos, then. Where will we find the Blue Swan Inn?"

"It's not far," replied Jacks. "Let's just hope that Deltone didn't go straight there to warn Atos," he said, leaving the room and stepping gingerly down the stairs.

They arrived at the Inn a few minutes later. While its location was still within The Forest, it looked better tended, and the clientele going in and out looked to be more merchants and traders than locals, primarily because of the location at this end of The Forest being close to the warehouses, rather than the houses of local labourers and dock workers.

Domico went over to the bar and asked the barman if Greig Atos was about.

"Popular man today… You're the second to ask after him in the last half an hour. But no, he's not in at present."

"Any idea when he will be back?"

"Normally he's back about now for a late lunch, so could be any time,"

"The other person who asked after him, did he stay?"

"Nope, seemed to be in a hurry, but asked me to pass on a message."

"What was the message?"

"I'm not going to be telling you that now, am I? It was for Master Atos, not you,"

"Alright then, will you please signal me when he comes in?"

"Yes Master, I will. Now, can I get you anything?"

"Three cups of Choo please," Domico said, handing over some coins. "We'll be sitting over there," he said, pointing to an empty table.

He returned to Helena and Sergeant Jacks and pointed to the empty table. "He's not in, but someone else was looking for him a little while ago,"

"Deltone?" asked Jacks

"Probably. But he's gone and just left a message for Atos. So we'll need to wait for Atos to return. I've ordered some Choo while we wait," he said, taking a seat at the table.

A few moments later, the barman came over with three cups of Choo, placing them on the table and then walking away. The three sat, mostly in silence, awaiting the return of Greig Atos.

It was about an hour later when a tall, thin man walked through the door, and the barman left the bar to intercept him. He spoke in the newcomers' ear for a moment, and then returned to the bar, and, finally, nodded to Domico.

But just as Domico was rising to intercept the newcomer, a high-pitched sound could be heard, just at the edge of hearing, that bordered on physical pain. Helena fought past the sound, looking towards the newcomer, just as Domico keeled over. As he did, Helena noticed that everyone in the taproom was wobbling, and clutching their chests, as if in pain, including Sergeant

Jacks, and then darkness overtook her and she fell to the floor.

36

Dead end

Sound returned first. Helena could hear something, a voice, calling someone, from what sounded like a long distance away. She struggled towards the sound, reaching for it, seeking to pull herself towards it... Finally, after what seemed to be years, it resolved itself into Domico calling her name. Struggling to open her eyes, she finally managed it, and brought into focus Domico kneeling beside her, calling her name and stroking her hand.

"What happened?" she croaked out, her voice sounding loud and scratchy to her ears.

"Something knocked everyone in the Inn out. The people in the back rooms and upstairs escaped unharmed, but everyone in the taproom was unconscious for a while," he explained.

"Atos. He still has the Device, and isn't afraid to use it on a room full of people." she concluded, trying to sit up. She felt bruised and sore, as if her whole body had been clenched and rigid for some time.

"Try to stand up and walk. It will help," he said, helping her to her feet. Although Domico was holding on to her, she still stumbled the first few steps, as if her legs had forgotten how to bend and move. As she looked around, she saw Sergeant Jacks helping someone else to stand and start moving.

Domico saw her gaze moving to Jacks and said, "He's already sent a street boy for help from the Watch. They should arrive soon." She nodded and continued to try and walk. After a few moments, her walking became smoother, and her muscles seemed to remember how to work, and she felt less stiff and sore.

As she became steadier on her feet, Domico slowly let go, and went to assist one of the other people in the taproom. Helena continued to pace, getting the strength back in her legs and body. Shortly afterwards, the Sheriff arrived with several Watchmen, and they moved to help the remaining people in the taproom, while the Sheriff and Jacks came over to Helena and Domico. They sat at the table where they had previously waited.

"What happened?" asked the Sheriff

"We were waiting for Atos' brother, Greig, to return here, where it seems he has a room. A tall, thin man came in, who the barkeeper spoke to, and then there was a noise, and pain, and then the next thing, everyone was unconscious," said Jacks.

"We think it's a Device that a Mage sold him in Portana. It emits a sound that can stun its victim - person or animal - and he used it on everyone in the taproom," added Domico.

The Sheriff looked at Helena. "Can you counter it?"

"I don't know," she replied. "I have the technical specification, so if I can study that, perhaps... but we had assumed that Atos no longer had it. Now we know he does, I have to find a way to counteract its effects. It can't be allowed to stay with him to be used in this way."

"I suggest you do that next then, and Jacks and I will see what we can find out from Tomas about where his brother might go. However, it's clear that the brother is more involved in this than being just a simple trader, so we will need to consider whether we need to review the deal we made with Tomas," he concluded.

Domico and Helena nodded. "We will return to our inn, and will come and see you later, once we've studied the Device specifications. Your men might need whatever we can find out about it if they are going to be looking for Greig Atos," Domico said, standing and holding his hand out to Helena. She nodded and rose to follow him out of the Inn.

"Stupid, stupid, stupid!" Helena muttered to herself as they were walking back to their inn.

"What do you mean?" asked Domico.

"We knew Greig originally had the Device, and I've had the specification for a while, but still haven't studied it properly to figure out how to block it. It's my fault that we were caught back there, and we're lucky that he only used the 'stun' function. Everyone could have died!"

"It's not likely that anyone would be stupid enough to kill a room full of people - stunning us would be more than enough to give him time to get away to somewhere else," said Domico. "It was stupid of him to use it at all really,"

"Why? It gave him the time he needed to escape an Interrogation,"

"Yes, but it also tells us he still has the Device, and is therefore the most likely person to have killed the Taka and taken its venom to Deltone in the caravan,"

"That's true. That also proves that he is more than a 'simple' merchant, doesn't it?"

"Indeed, it does. Now, let's see these specifications and see if we can figure out how to neutralise the Device," Domico concluded. They travelled the rest of the way back to their Inn in silence.

Once back at the Inn, Helena and Domico returned to Helena's room, and Helena pulled out the specification from her saddlebags, settling down with it on the bed.

She had studied it for about an hour when there was a knock at her door. Domico rose to answer it and found Sergeant Jacks waiting in the corridor.

"He's gone to ground alright," he said without preamble. "We checked his room, and it's been cleared out. I guess that while everyone was out cold, he had time to collect his things and leave the Inn,"

"Any sign of where he might have gone?" asked Domico

"None, and his brother doesn't know. When I told him what Grieg had done, he just cried… I guess he had thought that his brother was innocent after all, but this proves he wasn't, doesn't it? I don't think we're going to get anything more out of him. He knows his brother can't be included in the deal. Have you had any luck in figuring out how to neutralise the Device?"

Domico just pointed to Helena, sat on the bed, engrossed in a piece of parchment. "Not yet," he replied, "but she's working on it."

"OK, well, I thought that you'd better know that the barkeeper is dead. The Doctor thinks that he might have had a weak heart to start with, and wasn't able to recover from whatever the Device did. So we won't be getting any information on what the message from Deltone was... I'll be at the station when you have news," Jacks replied, turning to go. Domico returned to the room and continued to wait for Helena to come up with something.

After a further half an hour, she signed and put the parchment down.

"I just can't find any weakness that we could exploit in this," she said. "The casing of the Device isn't a crystal in this case, so we can't just smash it. Nor can we get into it to disrupt the mechanism, as it's a sealed unit... What was Mage Ripley thinking? How could he possibly think it was a good idea to develop a Device that can be used in this way and that can't be turned off or permanently disrupted?"

"OK, let's just take a step back. How does this thing work?"

"Inside of the casing there is a small piece of metal that acts rather like a tuning fork. When the Device is activated, by pressing this lever on the side, a tiny metal catch strikes the 'tuning fork' and a sound vibration is created that moves out of the Device through this small amplifier into the funnel on one side. That is how the sound is 'aimed'. The sound is at such a frequency it can only just be heard, but it is strong, and powerful enough to interfere with the rhythm of the heart - human or otherwise. It is enough to stun if only emitted for a brief burst, or, if continually pressed, the sound continues for longer and can disrupt the heart so that its rhythm is changed so much that it kills the recipient."

"So we can't knock out the amplifier or the internal parts of the Device?"

"No, it's made of some sort of stone, so I doubt that even a hammer would work - that's if we could get close enough, and take it away from Atos for long enough, to hit it with a hammer..."

"So, can we interfere with the sound in some way to stop it from affecting our hearts?"

"I suppose it should be possible, but I've got no idea how,"

"We need to do something, as it looks like even in the 'stun' setting, it can kill people - especially if they have an already weakened heart,"

"Yes, I heard what Sergeant Jacks said, and who knows how many people are at risk like that…"

"Right, well let's think about that while we get something to eat." and he held his hand out to Helena to help her rise from the bed and leave the room.

They ate a meal in silence, each trying hard to come up with something that would prevent the sound waves from reaching their hearts. After they had eaten, they returned to Helena's room.

"Well? Thought of anything?" asked Domico.

"No. You?"

"I'm not an expert, but no, nothing from me either," he concluded. "So, what do we do now?"

"I'll try to get in touch with Misco. See if he knows of anything, and try to get an update on King Garrod and his declaration of war," she said, again, sitting on the bed.

37

War

Once again Helena reached out, mentally, to Misco. She found the contact easier to establish this time, as it seemed that this came easier with practice. Once she had established contact, she updated Misco on the Atos brothers, the escape of Deltone, and finally the events at the Blue Swan Inn.

"We've been examining the specifications of the Device, but can't find a way to block it. It's a sealed unit, and isn't made of crystal, so we can't just smash it - even if we could get it off Greig Atos. Can you think of a way to stop its effects? Something to block the sound waves?"

"Not off the top of my head, no, but I will think about it. In the meantime, I am recalling you to Tarshea."

"Why?"

"King Garrod won't be held any longer and is convinced that Castin is responsible for his daughter's death. The involvement of the Guild of Death won't change that, or the suspicion that it was a Rintalan noble that contracted her death. We simply don't have any proof to offer him, and it looks like you've reached a dead end. Deltone and Greig Atos have escaped,

217

and Tomas knows nothing else."

"We can look for them," offered Helena

"And what if you find Greig, with that Device that you don't know how to counter? No, I fear that we have run out of time, and war will be the result. You must leave the Kingdom and return home to Tarshea. This investigation is finished, and we have failed." With that, Misco broke contact.

Helena slumped on the bed, and Domico, seeing her expression, asked, "What's wrong?"

"We're called home. The investigation is finished. Garrod will declare war, and we must return to the Mage Order,"

"Why? It will be hard, but we could try to find Deltone or Atos,"

"Misco didn't say it, but his thoughts were open to me, and he thinks I've failed. I've let the Order down, and war will be the result," she said, fighting back the tears. "There is a Device out there that we can't counter, that could kill hundreds - no! thousands, in the hands of the assassins, each of them looking like natural causes of heart failure. More thousands will die in a pointless war, and it's all my fault!" By the end of this statement, tears were pouring down Helena's cheeks and her voice had sunk to a whisper.

"We've had this conversation before Helena," Domico said in a soft tone, and taking a seat on the side of the bed, "It's not your responsibility what others, like King Garrod, do."

"No, but if I had been able to just find out who contracted Casili's death, then he wouldn't be declaring war on an entire country!"

"True, but you have followed every lead. We've travelled across the continent, and you have used your magic to try to find answers. There isn't anything more you could have done."

"Maybe, but I still feel like I have failed, and thousands will die because of a war that I should have prevented,"

"So what do you want to do now?" he asked her

"Travel home, go back to Tarshea in disgrace and never leave the Order's grounds again!" she said, getting up off the bed and stuffing her belongings into her saddlebags.

"Helena, wait! We don't need to leave now!"

"Yes, we do. We have nothing to update the Sheriff, and I would prefer for them not to know that I have failed…"

"We need to tell them something,"

"You go then. You can tell them we haven't been able to figure out how to stop the Device, and that they have recalled us. Hopefully, they will not think I'm too much of a failure, but I can't face them," she said, with fresh tears appearing in her eyes.

"OK Helena, I'll go speak to them, but promise me you will just wait here until I return?"

"I'll wait. I wouldn't try to return without you. Anyway, I'd probably get lost and robbed trying to find the docks, as I'm that useless!"

Domico shook his head, deciding that Helena was in no mood to be rational right now, and he left the room to head to the City Jail.

He didn't look forward to the conversation with the Sheriff and Sergeant Jacks, especially as the 'deal' that they had made with Tomas Atos didn't get them any further forward at all. On top of that, they were now leaving Voreen, leaving behind a couple of assassins running loose in the capital, one of them with a weapon that could kill with no warning.

As expected, the conversation didn't go well; the Sheriff being visibly angry that not only had they no answers, but were also leaving him to pick up the pieces.

Domico informed them both that they had updated the Head of the Mage Order, who would convey the news to the King, but this was little comfort and Domico felt they had not parted on good terms.

When he got back to their inn, he noted that Helena had already packed his saddlebags and was waiting to go. So they left the Inn, collecting their horses and making their way to the River Docks to find a ship to take them back down river to Tilana and then on to Casan in Iskabar.

Helena was silent. All the way to the Docks, and, after Domico had found a ship, all the time in loading the horses and making their way to their cabin. She didn't even register the Captain, let alone greet him. It was as if she had retreated inside herself. Domico left it for now, to see if she snapped out of it later.

The following morning, Domico approached Helena and asked, "Do you want to talk about it now?"

She looked at him, her chin sinking to her chest as she looked at the floor again before whispering, "I just can't. I knew Misco should not have sent me on this Investigation. I'm just not good enough at magic, and don't have the right skills to understand something as complex as this."

"But you've been fine with the magic. There isn't anything that you have attempted that you have not been able to do, is there?" he asked gently.

"No, but perhaps if I knew more, was better at making and maintaining Devices, then we'd have found a way to counteract the one that Ripley sold to Atos,"

"Just because you can't make Devices, it doesn't automatically follow that anyone else would have been able to disrupt it, does it? Misco couldn't think of anything either, could he, and he's the head of the Order,"

"I know you're trying to be kind," she replied, "but I'm not fit to be let out on my own, and certainly not fit to be a Mage. I might have the spark, but that's not everything you need to be a Mage, and I'm obviously lacking in the rest of the things that are needed." She said miserably.

"I disagree. I probably know you better than most people in the world do, and I know, not think, but know, that you would be an excellent Mage, if only you trusted your instincts more, and believed in yourself,"

"I don't want to argue about it, Domico. I know you mean well, and are trying to help me, but I just can't take it at the moment. Please leave me alone for a bit?"

"Alright, I'll give you some time, but I won't let the conversation end like this," and with that, he got up and left the cabin.

Some time later, he came back in and found Helena still sitting on her bunk. She still had eaten nothing and hadn't changed or washed, either. She really was at rock bottom. He racked his brain to think of something to draw her out.

"Helena, you need to eat something, and I think that a wash and a change of clothing would help you feel a bit better," he said tentatively. She just looked at him listlessly.

"Come on. Come for a short walk in the air, and then we'll eat," he said, hauling her up off the bunk, and forcing her to walk to the cabin door. He manoeuvred her up the short flight of steps to the main deck and into the fresh air. Standing at the rail with her, he waited for her to look around, to take some interest in the sights of the riverbank sliding by.

Mobilisation of the people into the army was in evidence everywhere. Men were mustering in the villages, being issued weapons such as swords and pikes, and the traders were driving large herds of cattle and sheep upriver towards the capital. If Voreen was mobilising against Castin, then it would make sense for them to seek a route past Nimea into the mountains, then over them and on to the plains to the west, for the long march to the border of Castin. That would be the only route the King could take that didn't require him to either cross another Kingdom, or sail his entire army around the continent to the west coast, where they would need to attempt beach landings.

Helena stared, unseeing, at the banks sliding by, with the occasional village and farmstead to break the monotony. After some minutes, she realised what she was seeing, and once more, tears slid down her cheeks.

After a time, Domico turned to her and said, "Come, let's get something to eat," and she followed him back to the area below the main deck. Instead of leading her to the right, to go to their quarters, he led her left, to a small dining area. He seated her at one end of a long table, with bench seats bolted to the floor, and seated himself opposite.

"Well, have you thought about what I said?" he asked.

"My thoughts have been going round and round in circles... I do not know what to think any more," she replied dully.

"What more do you think you could have done?" he asked

"What makes you ask that?"

"Because if you truly believed that you had done all you could, then you wouldn't be punishing yourself this way," he said with a smile.

"I could have been more forceful with Baron Santu and Prince Lyton, and got to the bottom of that business about being with a woman,"

"And how would you have done that? They weren't exactly cooperative,"

"No, but I should have insisted,"

"Why didn't you?"

"I didn't think it was my place to force a confrontation,"

"Why?"

"I'm just me, a low-born Chandler's daughter. What right do I have to demand answers from Kings, Princes and nobles?"

"You are a Mage. You stand above everyone when investigating. The whole of the Mage Order is behind you. Why does it matter who you were born to?"

"Because it does!"

"So a Mage from a noble family is better, or more powerful than a Mage from traders or labourers? What about those born to fishers or farmers?

Are they of a lower order than those that were born to rich merchants? Are you better than those born to servants?"

"No, of course not,"

"So why do you think that a Mage born to a noble family is better than you? Are they more equipped to ask questions than you?"

"No, but…"

"There are no 'buts' Helena. Everyone who has the spark, and passes the training to be a Mage, is of the same rank. You all have the same ability to ask questions, and the Mage Order will stand behind all of you. Otherwise you are proposing that there is some unwritten caste system, and I know for a fact that Misco doesn't think like that."

"No, you're twisting what I mean,"

"Am I? Are you not telling me you're not as good as a Mage born to a noble family? That's what I'm hearing…"

"I'm just not used to mixing with that class of people. Other Mages, those born into noble families are."

"Not all of them. Some of those 'noble' families that Mages claim don't have any ancestral lands, or money, or even connections to royalty, just an old name that goes back generations. It doesn't mean that their sons and daughters are not also intimidated by nobles or royals. Sometimes they just hide it better," he said with a cynical smile.

"How do you know?"

"This isn't my first tour. You know that."

Just then, a surly, fat cook, with an incredibly stained apron straining over his bulk, approached them. He dumped two bowls of something on the table and walked away without a word. Helena, looking thoughtful, took a spoonful without thinking about it. Domico smiled. It was a start, at least.

Helena returned to her cabin, and absently washed and changed, thinking about what Domico had said.

Did she really think that she was better than some of the Mages that came from servant families, or fisherfolk? Not for a second, but wasn't that the logical extension of what she thought about Mages from noble families compared to her?

Yes, she could have been more forceful in dealing with Santu and Lyton, but would any of the other Mages done anything differently? Some of them might have, but thinking about the personalities of the Mages she knew, she doubted that all of them would have. She also knew that some of those from the noble families were unlikely to have pushed a Prince and Baron, being in awe of their rank, and having been trained from birth to be aware of the hierarchy in place in their own kingdoms and their place in it.

Perhaps Domico was right, and this wasn't about her status at birth, but just about personal confidence, she concluded.

That being so, then why was her confidence so lacking? Domico had pointed out that she had achieved all the magic she had attempted. Then she realised she was even competent at the mind-link, which not all Mages could achieve… She was adept at languages, so that wasn't a barrier. Pondering on it, she lay on her bunk and considered.

She had solved some clues in the investigation, confirming it was Taka venom, and even how it had been used. She had also managed the eavesdropping on Baron Santu and Prince Lyton to get the information about his feelings towards women, and had also been the one to force Mage Ripley to share the information about the Device.

Yes, she had made some mistakes along the way, such as not considering that Greig Atos would still have the Device, and that had been costly and dangerous - they could have died as a result. But her magic had uncovered that Atos' business had been a front for the Guild of Death, which now meant that it deprived them of one of their covers, and a source of income.

Overall, they had come a long way, metaphorically, as well as travelling across the continent. Her magic had even kept them safe from the Tontcat.

All that was left was to uncover the link between either Baron Santu or Prince Lyton and the Guild of Death. She was sure, when she considered it, that the link was there, and it was one of those two that had contracted the death of Casili. She just needed to prove it.

So, did she defy Misco and carry on with the Investigation, or did she return to Tarshea and the Mage university as ordered?

Getting up from the bed, she decided she needed to talk to Domico, and get his thoughts on what they should do. She realised she didn't know which cabin was his, but on consideration, realised that it was likely to be next to her own. Opening her door, she saw that there were only two choices, so she had a fifty / fifty chance of getting it right.

Nervously, she knocked on the door to the left of her own. This one was closer to the brief steps up to the main deck. She gambled on Domico having selected a cabin where someone would need to pass his cabin to get to hers.

She was relieved when he opened the door. He smiled, and she said, "Can we talk?" He nodded and stepped further into the small room, gesturing for her to enter.

"I take it you've been thinking about what I said?"

"Yes, and you're right about the caste system thinking. When I really considered it, I realised that I had thought that Mages from noble families were better than me. But it also horrified me that the logical extension of that would be that I thought that I was better than some others... I don't believe that at all, so perhaps you're right. I have also been thinking about what we have achieved..."

"What you have achieved, you mean. Apart from a very short couple of fights, one with a Tontcat and another with Tomas Atos, I've not done much, really."

"No, you've been the person who has guided me, both physically around the continent, but also psychologically, supporting me, and giving me confidence when I needed it. I just didn't take in what you were saying - or take it to heart, at least."

"So, what conclusion have you reached?" he asked, smiling.

"We have a choice. The only thing left to discover is the link between either Santu or Lyton and the Guild... I'm convinced that one of them is behind it, otherwise why flee to the Baron's estates? And what about the conversation I overheard with the magic? So, we either track them down and Interrogate them, or we give up and return to Tarshea as ordered."

"From the way you've said that, I gather you have a preference?" he chuckled.

"Yes. I want to finish this. I need to see Santu and Lyton again, and find that link. That will put an end to the war."

"It may only change who King Garrod declares war against, not stop it completely. You do realise that, don't you?"

"I don't think so. King Garrod would be unlikely to declare war on an entire country based on the actions of a Baron, or even a Prince, as long as his parents were not aware of his actions. The problem at the moment is that he thinks a King ordered the assassination, and that it was politically motivated. This doesn't feel like that. It's more personal."

"Are you asking me what I think about returning home, or what I think about your theory about who is responsible?"

"Both I suppose."

"I think you are right. We need to finish this, and I'll back you in doing that. The motive though... I just don't know, but I do trust your instincts, even if you are only just starting to."

"Thank you, for everything," she said with a smile. "I'll contact Misco and see if Santu and Lyton have arrived at Tradehome, and inform him that we're finishing this."

38

Misco

Helena returned to her cabin and sat on her bed, composing her thoughts. Domico followed her in and stood with his back to the door. Even in such a confined place as a ship, travelling downriver, he wasn't about to leave her alone when she would be so vulnerable.

Taking a deep breath, Helena sought to reach out to Misco. She hadn't done this while travelling before, and a stray thought intruded on whether that would make a difference. Banishing it, she once more sought to extend her mind, calling Misco's name.

After a few moments, he responded.

"Helena. I assume you are on your way back?" he said curtly. "What do you need from me? I'm rather busy."

"I need to finish this Investigation, Misco. I can't just walk away when we're so close…"

"And what makes you think you *can* finish this?" he asked testily.

"I know that there is a link between the Guild of Death and either Baron Santu or Prince Lyton. I just need to find it. Then we can present the proof to King Garrod and he'll call off the war."

"That thing about being with a woman?" he asked in surprise

"Yes," she thought back to him.

"And how will you prove it?"

"I will force them to submit to an Interrogation."

"Really? Are you up to forcing that?"

"I must be. It's the only way we will get the proof we need. This war cannot be allowed to happen."

"So you would defy me in this and refuse to return to Tarshea?"

"Yes, I must. We cannot stop now. Not only would that mean war, but the reputation of the Order would be in tatters. Our influence would be reduced and it could take years to recover."

Helena caught a whiff of a mental chuckle, "Good!" said Misco. "I was rather hoping that my demand would force you to evaluate the case, and take a stand about making sure we get to the bottom of it. You 'felt' so lost in Nimea, I needed to give you a bit of a jolt."

"What about the war?"

"It will take weeks to march the army over the mountains and to the border with Castin, so we have a little more time before people start dying, but not much, so don't waste it!"

"Have Lyton and Santu turned up in Tradehome?" she asked

"No, not yet, but they are supposed to be on their way."

"Right, I'll meet you all there then, if you can keep the Kings in place for another couple of weeks?"

"I'll stall them as much as I can. The news that you are on the way, with the solution, may help. Anything else?"

"No Misco, and thank you." She broke contact, opened her eyes, and looked at Domico. "He agreed!" she said in triumph.

"Are Lyton and Santu at Tradehome?"

"No, but they are on their way apparently, so I said we would meet them there. What's the quickest route?"

"In this tub? We'd be better off disembarking at Tilana or Portana if there is a faster ship available, and sailing to Fandar and following the river to Tradehome. But, if there isn't a faster ship, then our only option would be to disembark at Portana and then another fast ride back to Tradehome."

"Right, so let's see what ships are in port in Tilana, and if there's nothing there, we can decide at Portana."

39

Fandar

When they reached Tilana, the ship docked in order to take on more supplies and a couple of extra passengers. Domico took the opportunity to see what other ships were in port, but none of them were any faster than their current ship.

"We'll need to wait and see if there is anything else at Portana," he said to Helena when he came back on board. "It should take us about four days to sail to Portana, as this ship isn't as fast as the Wind Witch." Helena nodded and they settled in for the next few days.

During that time, Helena continued to study the specification for the Device that Greig Atos had purchased from Mage Ripley. They were up on deck, on the third afternoon, discussing the Device, when Domico turned to Helena and said, "I just can't think of any material that would stop the sound vibrations. If we could figure that out, then we could fashion some sort of shield that can be worn over the heart to stop it being affected by the Device."

"I know. The problem is finding something thick enough to stop the sound wave, but thin enough to wear and still allow movement..." said Helena, while absently turning to watch one sailor scrubbing the deck with a large sea sponge. After a few moments, what she was seeing finally registered with Helena. "What about some sort of composite shield?" she said to Domico.

"A composite of what?" he asked

"A couple of layers… Say a thin layer of stone, such as granite or slate, with a layer of sea sponge sitting behind it. Would that be too heavy, do you think?"

"If it was a thin layer, with the sponge backing it, it might work. It would certainly reduce the strength of the vibration, with little getting through the stone, and the sponge absorbing what was left."

"Let's ask Misco, as he can pass it on to Nimea through the Far-Speaking Devices at Tradehome and the Palace," Helena said, turning to return to her cabin.

She contacted Misco and explained her thinking. He agreed that it should work - certainly long enough for troops or the Watch to disable Greig Atos and remove the Device from him - assuming that they could find him. He said he would pass it on, for the attention of the Sheriff of Nimea, and suggested that if they could, Helena and Domico make themselves one each as well. "After all, we don't know that Atos has remained in Nimea. He could be on his way to Tradehome to contact Prince Lyton or Baron Santu," Misco concluded before he broke the contact.

Helena updated Domico on what Misco had said.

"Well, we can probably get the sponge easily enough while we are on board this ship, but I don't think we'll be able to find the thin slabs of stone. That will need to wait until we dock in Portana." And so they waited.

A couple of days later, they docked in Portana. Domico noted that there was a familiar ship docked further along the quayside.

"It can't be!" he gasped to Helena. "It looks like the Wind Witch. I wonder what Captain Hartan is doing here?"

"Let's find out, as soon as we're docked," Helena suggested, and as soon as they made the ship secure against the docks, they both hurried down the gangplank and made their way along the quayside to the Wind Witch.

"Captain Hartan!" called Domico as they walked alongside the vessel. "Captain Hartan!" he called again. Just then, the Captain's head appeared over the side of the ship. "Master Domico, what are you doing here?"

"I was about to ask you the same," laughed Domico

"Me? I'm on my way back to Casan. I've a full cargo for Tarshea and am leaving on the evening tide."

"Can you, once again, give us passage?" asked Helena

"Where to? I'm not changing my course. The cargo is wheat and I don't want it getting damp from a long stay in my hold…"

"Fandar," said Domico, "It wouldn't be out of your way."

"I suppose you still have horses?" he asked with a sigh.

"Yes, and we'll again need your cabin, Captain," laughed Domico.

"Usual passage fare?"

"Yes, Captain, and I'll even throw in a bonus if you can get us there quickly!"

"Quickly is what my ship does, Master Domico... OK, get yourselves and your horses here within the next hour, and we'll take you."

"Thank you Captain, we'll see you soon." said Domico, turning to hurry back along the quay. Helena quickly followed.

Back at their ship, they spoke to the Captain, a sour-looking man of few words. They confirmed they would leave the ship here, in Portana, and asked for their horses to be unloaded, then they went below to pack their bags. Shortly after, they stood on the quayside while their horses were being led down the wide gangplank to them. Helena suggested she take the horses to the Wind Witch, while Domico sought some thin slabs of stone or slate for their shields. He agreed and hurried off, while Helena led the horses to the Wind Witch to be loaded onto the vessel.

About half an hour later, Domico joined Helena in their cabin. "This cabin is starting to feel like home," said Helena with a smile. "How did you get on?"

"I found a merchant dealing in stone - primarily for decorative statues and fountains, but I was able to secure these two thin slabs," he said, producing two slabs of thin granite. They were about thirty centimetres square and about three centimetres thick. "Do you think they will work?"

"Let's add the sponge and find some way to attach them to our bodies," suggested Helena, removing a bag from under the bunk that contained several sea sponges.

They worked for about half an hour, slicing the sea sponges and arranging them like a jigsaw on one side of the slabs.
    "Do we have a way to glue them on?" asked Helena.

Domico smiled and produced a small pot from his bag. "I found this glue in the market. The Merchants use it for fixing bits of wood together for minor items. It should work." They used the sticky brown substance to attach the sponge to the slab. "We'll need to leave it to dry for a while before we see if it's worked." said Helena. "But in the meantime, we will need to think about how we can hold the whole thing in place over our body,"

"If we can drill a small hole in each of the top corners, we should be able to use a thin rope to hang them over our necks," replied Domico. "I'll speak to the Captain and see if he's got something to make the hole and some thin rope we can use," he said, getting up.

He came back a few minutes later, armed with a thin metal drill and two short pieces of thin rope. "Hopefully this will work," he said, putting the drill and rope down. "I'll wait until the glue is dry before I start. Let's see about some food in the meantime."

After they had eaten the rather plain food offered by the ship's cook, they returned to the slabs. The glue had dried, and the sponge appeared to be fixed firmly to the granite.

"You will need to be careful that the drill doesn't splinter the slab and put a crack in it," said Helena, concerned.

"Yes, I've been thinking about that. Perhaps if we keep it wet, it might stop it cracking?" he said, looking at her. Helena brought over a large beaker of water. "You drill, and I'll pour," she suggested.

A few tense minutes later, there was a hole in the top right-hand corner of one slab, and a small pool of water on the floor. "Well, that seems to have worked!" she said with a smile. "I'll get more water," she said, leaving the cabin with the large beaker in hand. She returned a few minutes later. "This is sea water, as I think it will work just as well, and we've got limited drinking water on board,"

After a short while, the other three holes were drilled and Domico attached the ropes. "Try this on," he said, holding one slab up to Helena. She slipped the rope over her head and allowed the slab to hang down from her neck, covering most of her chest area and stomach. "Yes, this covers the right area, and doesn't restrict movement too much, so let's hope that it works." Domico pulled his 'shield' on and twisted around a little. "It doesn't sit flush with the body if you move, so perhaps two more holes at the bottom, and a further piece of rope round the back, would help?"

They made the modification, seeking a couple of more lengths of rope from the Captain. "We'll need to wear these all the time once we leave the ship, won't we?" asked Helena.

"Probably, given we have no idea where Greig Atos is, and therefore where the Device is…".

"How long did the Captain say it would take to reach Fandar?"

"Three or four days, depending on the wind,"

"Nothing else to do but settle in for a few days, then."

They docked in Fandar in the early afternoon of the fourth day out from Portana, unloading the horses quickly so that the ship could return to its voyage to Casan, as the tide was already turning.

"Do you want to stay the night here, or press on for Tradehome?" asked Domico, as they led the horses along the dockside.

"We've got almost half a day left, so let's press on."

"OK, let's see if there is a barge heading up to Tradehome." He led them away from the sea docks, and towards the area known as the River Docks, which were slightly further inland, away from the sea and lining the banks of the river Fan, which started at the Lake Voreen and ran through Tradehome on its route to the sea at Fandar.

There were several large barges tied up along the river docks, so Domico looked for one that didn't appear to be overloaded with goods, and was sitting low in the water as a result.

About half way down the long queue of barges, Domico spotted one that only had a small amount of cargo tied to its long deck. He hailed the Captain to ask where, and when, she was bound.

"Tradehome," replied the Captain, "but not until tomorrow, as I'm waiting for more cargo to contracted,"

"We will pay you to leave now, if you will also take us as passengers," bargained Domico.

There followed some haggling about the price, and in the end the Captain agreed to leave, with Domico and Helena, and their horses on board, within the hour. So they both boarded the barge and settled in to a small lean-to that was the only accommodation available.

"How long will the trip to Tradehome take?" asked Helena.

"Five days," replied the Captain. "And I cannot feed you, so you will need to see to your own provisions," Domico had already expected this, and they had laid in a good supply of dried meats and cheeses, as well as a few large containers of water. "I will miss the Choo," muttered Helena to Domico as they settled in, "As will I, but speed is important and there simply isn't any way to heat water on this barge," he replied.

It felt strange to Helena to be back in Iskabar after all the travelling, and to hear her native language spoken again. The shouting and cursing of the bargemen felt strange to her ears after so long hearing the languages of Voreen and Rintala. Even Captain Hartan had been Rintalan, so it felt like months since she had spoken to anyone other than Domico in her native tongue. It took some getting used to again. She settled into the lean-to, prepared to rest and just watch the world go by for a brief spell, building her strength and determination for what, she was sure, was going to be a difficult situation in Tradehome.

40

Return to Tradehome

She was right to build her strength and take the time to recharge her energy levels. They docked in Tradehome towards the evening of the fifth day, having made good time upriver. The spring melts had already passed, and the river was getting sluggish, allowing the two men who poled the barge along to make good progress each day. The trickiest bit of the journey had been at the fork, where the River Fan joined the River Esk, which led off to Casan. At the junction, the river had become swollen, with more barges joining the flow. This formed something of a jam, with barges jostling to get past in both directions, and it took them two hours to negotiate their way past the confusion.

Helena and Domico made their way to the Inn they had stayed in before, and where they knew Misco was still staying. Their former suite wasn't available this time, but they were given rooms on the same floor as Misco. They dumped their bags in their rooms and went along to Misco's room to share the news.

Misco was just settling down to an evening meal. "Let me order something for you two as well," he said, leaving the room and waving them to a seat.

He arrived back a few minutes later, followed by a couple of serving men bearing trays of food and drink. They placed the meal on the large table and departed. Once they had gone, Misco turned to Helena and said, "Right, so what do you need to update me on since you left Portana?"

Helena outlined their journey, and the development of the 'shield' that they had developed against the Device.

"Brilliant," said Misco, examining it. "I don't know if Atos has turned up here, as I don't know what he looks like, and he certainly isn't using his own name. But I would suggest that you go along to see Baron Santu and Prince Lyton in the morning. They are staying at the Rintalan castle."

"They have arrived then?"

"Yes, but only two days ago, so they have certainly taken their time. If they set off when they said they did, they should have been here a week ago, so either they were late leaving, or they had some delays somewhere."

"And what about King Garrod? Has he formally declared war on Castin?"

"Actually no, he hasn't. I'm not sure if my efforts have persuaded him, or whether something else has happened. His kingdom still seems to be mobilising from the reports I receive from the other Mages, but so far, no-one has tried to cross the mountains with large bodies of men."

"I wonder why," said Domico aloud. "Do you think this could have been some sort of posturing?"

"No," said Misco. "He seems too committed for that, but whatever has stayed his hand, I am grateful for. Of course, it also means that both he and his wife are still here in Tradehome. If he had declared war, he would have left by now to oversee his troops and reduce the chances of being picked off by someone from Castin."

"So, is everyone here?" asked Helena

"Yes, they are. So, just in case, I want you both to be wearing your 'shields' when you leave the Inn tomorrow. Just in case your friend Atos is somewhere in the shadows."

"Where will you be?"

"Where I have been for most days since I arrived, with King Garrod and Queen Irini, trying to stop the King from doing something stupid."

"If we do manage to confront Santu and Lyton, wouldn't it be better for you to be there? We could use a witness."

"I wouldn't be classed as impartial, anyway. Many see me as too close to Voreen after the last few weeks. How were you planning on confronting them?"

"I was just going to use the interrogation magic,"

"But then there is only your word for what you see in their memories... No, with all the suspicion floating around, we'll need something else. A truth circle, perhaps?"

"I've never tried that magic. I'm not sure if I am strong enough."

"If you can manage the mind-link over the distances we've been speaking through, then I am sure you will be more than strong enough," said Misco, smiling at her. "But you will need to be rested, so I suggest you refrain from using magic to detain Santu and Lyton. Domico, you will need to make sure they are in hand, and available to appear in the circle."

"Where will we hold it?" asked Domico.

"There is a Central Hall in the town that acts as a trading centre for all the merchants that come here. It has a room that is large enough and will provide an opportunity to gather some independent witnesses. We will use that."

"When?" asked Helena.

"Let's assume the day after tomorrow. You speak to Santu and Lyton again tomorrow, and see if they will cooperate willingly. If not, we can arrange for them to be held so that they don't slip out of town and we can get them into the circle the following morning."

"Why the delay? Why not go straight to the circle tomorrow?"

"Because I will need to warn King Garrod, and King Fanton, and seek some witnesses that are not joined to either Court. I will need tomorrow to do that."

"But that will give Santu and Lyton time to try and run if they are guilty," protested Helena

"You will need to see them one at a time, and if they look like they won't cooperate, Domico will need to take them in hand and get them to the Sheriff's office here in Tradehome. He can hold them in the cells until the following day. I'll speak to him first thing to let him know what's going on."

"Seeing them one at a time might be tricky. They seem to be joined at the hip."

"You will have to manage it somehow. While I have no doubt over Domico's skills as a Guardian, I'm sure even he wouldn't want to take them on together?"

"Definitely not," said Domico, "especially if it comes to a fight, which it may if they think we are detaining them."

"Can't we enlist some troops or the Sheriff's men to help?" asked Helena

"No. They wouldn't be allowed past the gate. Each castle is classed as sovereign territory, and the Sheriff's men have no jurisdiction there. You can demand entrance for you and Domico, as a Mage and Guardian, but they wouldn't allow anyone else to accompany you."

"I guess it's up to us then," said Domico, looking grim and squaring his shoulders.

They were up early the following morning, and had arranged to have breakfast together in Misco's room. "I will arrange for the Sheriff to have a couple of men outside the Rintalan castle, just in case you need them when you come out," he said, as they were parting on their separate missions.

The Rintalan castle was on the opposite side of Tradehome, so it took them some time to walk there. They had decided against taking their horses, as they would complicate matters if they were leaving with either Santu or Prince Lyton in tow. In appearance, the castle looked much like the Vorainian one, with a large door that troops could ride out of two abreast. They knocked and waited, aware that it was early for visitors. However, within a few minutes, they were being escorted inside by a Captain of the Guard.

"I am not sure if Baron Santu will be receiving guests at this hour," he told them, as they had decided to tackle Santu first.

"Well, send someone to wake him, anyway. I want to speak to him immediately, and will accept no delay," said Helena in an uncompromising tone.

The Captain blanched and replied, "Yes, Mage Hawke. I will see to it. Please wait here," he said, pointing to a small reception room.

They waited for about half an hour before a tousled and hurriedly dressed Baron Santu walked into the room.

"Mage Hawke. I object to being summoned at this early hour. I told you all that I know when you visited my estate. What more do you wish of me?"

"I want to know about your link with the Guild of Death. Why have you been in contact with the assassins?" she said, having decided to bluff it out.

"I have not been in contact with the Guild. What on earth makes you think that I have?" he said, trying for an outraged tone of voice and expression, which, incidentally, fell short.

"I am not prepared to reveal how I know. But, will you submit to an Interrogation to prove it?" she asked bluntly.

"No, I will not. You have no right to demand it."

"I have every right, and if you refuse, it will force us to compel you,"

"You can't compel me! I am related to the King."

Helena nodded to Domico, and he drew his sword. "Right then, my Lord, you will come with us. Now." he said, levelling the sword at Baron Santu. As the Baron was unarmed, he had no choice but to agree. Helena and Domico escorted him out of the castle, with many of the servants looking on.

"That might be a problem," said Domico in a whisper to her as they approached the main gate.

"Hmm," replied Helena. "Get back here as fast as you can," However, as they stepped out of the gate, Domico saw a squad of the Sheriff's men waiting outside.

"Can you please escort the Baron to one of your cells?" he asked the Sergeant in charge. "He is not to speak to anyone, or stop off on the way,"

"Yes, Guardian," the man replied, taking hold of the Baron.

"Now, if we are quick enough, we can get to the Prince before the gossip does," Domico said, stepping back up to the gate. The same Captain admitted them, saying nothing, and Helena asked him to fetch Prince Lyton. They waited in the same reception room, and this time it took considerably longer for the Captain to return.

"The Prince is not receiving guests this morning," he told them in a flat voice.

"We are not guests. If the Prince will not come to us, then you will escort us to the Prince," said Helena, determined not to stand down.

The Captain looked panicked. "He is still in his bed. I cannot take you to his bedchamber!"

"You can, and you will. Now!" Domico drew his sword again, and pointed it at the Captain, "Unless you want to face the wrath of the Mage Order, or fight me?" he added.

They formed a small procession, walking along the corridors, with the Captain leading the way, with Domico following with his sword out, and Helena bringing up the rear. More than one person was brave enough to ask the Captain what was going on, or whether he needed help. Thinking of his own skin, the Captain told people it was all fine, and that there was no need for any assistance.

Some minutes later, they arrived at a set of ornate doors that had the royal Family Crest carved into the door, and Domico nodded to the Captain to enter. He paused, and deciding on a compromise, shouted for the Prince as he pushed open the door.

Inside, it appeared that someone had carried a warning to the Prince. He was in the process of finishing his dressing, just putting on his sword belt, with a slender rapier sheathed on it. At the call of the Captain, he spun and gestured his manservant out of the way. The Captain quickly retreated from the room.

"What do you want?" he asked

"We want to know about your link with the Guild of Death, and how that links to Princess Casili's death," stated Helena calmly.

"I have no links with the Guild. I was not responsible for her death."

"Ah, but I have proof that you were."

"What proof?"

"Your abhorrence in lying with a woman has a lot to do with it,"

"I have no idea what you are talking about. Now, leave me!"

"I'm afraid that we can't do that, your Highness. Will you submit to an Interrogation?"

"No, I absolutely will not."

"Then we must force you to comply."

"You cannot force me. My father will hear of this."

"Unless I am much mistaken, your father has already been informed," she stated, taking the gamble that Misco would already have spoken to him.

"You are mistaken. My father would not allow this. Now, leave,"

"No, you Highness, we won't. Or at least, we will leave with you."

Prince Lyton pulled out his rapier and sought to slash at Helena. But Domico was there first, with his sword blocking the move and preventing the Prince from harming her.

"You would pull a sword on a Mage?" she asked in disbelief.

"I am a Prince of Rintala. I will not be subject to the whims of the Mage Order," he shouted at her. At the same time, he disengaged his sword and tried to lunge at Domico. Helena danced out of the way, leaving Domico room to swing his sword.

A short, but nasty fight ensued, with the Prince slashing wildly at Domico, who, in contrast, remained cool. His blocks were positioned with accuracy and precision. They moved about the room, with Lyton seeking to come at Domico from different angles, looking for an opening that wasn't there. Finally, one of the Prince's lunges, seeking to pin Domico to the back of an ornate chair in front of the fireplace, was a little too far, and the Prince overbalanced. Domico augmented the slip with a quick shove from behind and Lyton ended up face down on the floor, with Domico's sword at the back of his neck.

Helena stepped forward and removed the rapier from his hand.

"Now, you will come with us. Quietly," she said, as Domico sheathed his sword and pulled the Prince to his feet.

"I'll tell you something, Helena," said Domico as they were leaving the castle with the Prince, "We need to find Atos soon, as fighting in this shield is harder than it looks!"

41

The Circle

A night in the cells at the town jail had not been kind to either Baron Santu or Prince Lyton. They had been kept separate and not allowed to speak to each other or the other inmates. Both looked like they had had little sleep, and neither had eaten much throughout their stay, despite having been kept there for just over a full day. They both appeared haggard, unkempt and in need of a wash, shave, and fresh clothing.

As they were escorted to the Central Hall building, the Prince kept his chin up, staring down his nose at his jailers, promising retribution from his father. It didn't work. The men escorting him had been personally briefed by Misco, and they were far more afraid of what an angry Mage might do to them than the King of Rintala.

Helena, Domico and Misco travelled to the Hall together. "I take it you know how to form the Circle?" Misco asked Helena.

"I know the theory, but haven't tried it before,"

"Just remember that your will needs to be strong. If you waver, even for a moment, then their minds will find a way through it, and enable them to tell a lie."

"Must I ask the questions as well as maintain the circle?"

"Yes. It is possible for another Mage to ask the questions, but I don't want it to be seen as me leading the Investigation. So in this case, I want you to do both. It should also help with your concentration, as if you are focussed on the question, as well as the answer, it will help prevent your mind from wandering or wavering."

They arrived at the Hall, and Helena took a series of deep breaths as they walked into the large room. It was quite crowded, with a group of people standing around the sides. The crowd included the Kings of Voreen, Rintala, Eretee and Castin, as well as some of the more wealthy and influential merchants from Tradehome itself.

Baron Santu and Prince Lyton were each standing on opposite sides of the room, surrounded by members of the town Watch.

Helena, centring herself, stepped forward and closed her eyes. Picturing in her mind a large circle, she made a motion with her hand and a large circle of golden light appeared at waist height in front of her. She opened her eyes and gestured for Baron Santu to be brought forward. They manoeuvred him into the circle of light, and he suddenly found, on trying to step forward, that he couldn't move.

He turned a panicked gaze to Helena and then turned to look at Prince Lyton with a stricken expression on his face. The Prince slumped, his arrogance leaving him in response to that unspoken word from his best friend.

"You are Baron Santu of Rintala?" asked Helena

"I am"

"We are here today to establish who contracted the Guild of Death to assassinate Princess Casili. Do you understand?"

"I do,"

"I have uncovered evidence that a Rintalan noble contracted the Guild, with ties to the Royal House. Was that you?"

"I did not contact the Guild," said Santu, with sweat breaking out on his brow. Helena sensed that something was missing in this statement. The Circle prevented a lie, but it didn't force the whole truth, she realised.

"Did you instruct someone to contract with the Guild on your behalf?"

There was a long moment of silence, while Santu tried to form words that wouldn't come. He realised he could not lie, and to prevaricate on this point would be a clear flag that he was guilty, anyway. "I did," he said eventually. There were some gasps from around the Hall, and some muttering broke out amongst some of King Garrod's party.

"Silence," said Misco in a hard voice, staring at people around the Hall.

"Why did you contract with the Guild?" asked Helena

"To prevent the marriage of Princess Casili to Prince Lyton," said Baron Santu.

"Why?" she asked again

There was an even longer pause before the answer came this time. His sweating had increased, and he was now trembling significantly. "Because he asked me to," this came out as a whisper. Santu clearly didn't want to admit this. It looked like he was about to collapse.

Helena wasn't in much better shape. The concentration that she needed was intense, and she felt the beginnings of a headache from the strain. Finding that she could no longer hold the circle in her mind, the light vanished and Baron Santu sank to the floor.

Misco gestured for the Watch to collect him, and they dragged him out of the room, starting the long walk back to the jail.

"Do you need a rest?" Misco asked Helena quietly.

"Just a moment or two. I don't think we can drag this out very much longer," she said, glancing towards King Garrod and King Fanton, who both looked shocked and angry.

Helena took a few deep breaths, and Domico brought her a glass of water. She drank it gratefully and then closed her eyes once more. Concentrating on the circle again, it formed, reluctantly, in the middle of the room again.

This time, they dragged Prince Lyton into the circle. He was extremely reluctant, and the Watch had to wrestle him into the light.

"Did you ask Baron Santu to contract with the Guild of Death for the murder of Princess Casili on your behalf?" This time, Helena didn't start with his name and rank. She was struggling to maintain the circle and needed this over quickly.

Lyton struggled, straining to take a step out of the light. Breaking out in a sweat, he clenched his jaw and continued to struggle, straining with all his might to break the connection of light around him. Helena closed her eyes again, concentrating hard on maintaining the circle. Lyton's mind was so strong! She felt his mental push against the barrier she had erected around his mind - the manifestation of which was the circle of light that everyone could see. It wavered for a tiny moment and then became stronger, more solid to the eyes of everyone in the room.

She pressed harder, and then harder again. Clenching her jaw and focussing on nothing but the barrier. After what felt like hours, but was, in reality only moments, the pushing stopped and Lyton slumped in the circle. Only the fact that it held him there prevented him from falling.

"Yes, I did," he responded.

"Why?"

"Because I won't marry,"

"Why?"

"Because the thought of being intimate with a woman is repugnant," he gasped as she pushed once more.

"Do you prefer men?" she asked

"No!" was the indignant reply. "The thought of being intimate with anyone is anathema to me. I won't do it,"

King Fanton now looked outraged. "I must protest Mage Misco," he shouted. "This is private!" Misco faced him down and said, "Your Majesty, we must get to the truth of the matter."

"And the need for a royal heir?" continued Helena

"Let one of my cousins ascend the throne after me. I don't care!"

"So why did you ask for Casili's hand in marriage?"

"Because my mother and father would not be stalled any longer. I had no choice but to agree to marry someone, and she was a northern barbarian, so what did it matter?"

This time, all the Kings looked stonily at the Prince. King Fanton started protesting that the view was not his, loudly, aware that the King of Voreen and the King of Castin outnumbered him in the Hall, which were both northern kingdoms.

Helena gasped at the audacity of the Prince, and the circle wavered and disappeared. However, the Prince was in no condition to flee, sinking to the floor, shaking and shivering, and sobbing. He knew they would strip him of his rank and position and would be lucky to keep his life, after embarrassing his father in such a fashion.

As they dragged him out, pandemonium erupted in the Hall, and Helena sank to the floor.

It took some time for Misco to restore order.

"We have all heard the confessions of Baron Santu and Prince Lyton here today," he stated. "King Garrod, as it was your daughter that was murdered, I shall leave you to discuss reparations with King Fanton."

"Gentlemen," he said, turning to the merchants, "This matter must remain confidential. It is not for common gossip, and if I find that someone has spoken of it outside of this Hall, then I will take action. Do I make myself understood?" The merchants nodded, shuffling feet and trying to look as if they had never dreamt of discussing the happenings of this morning.

He then turned to look at the Sheriff, "The same is true of your men, my Lord Sheriff," he said sternly. "If my men talk, you won't be the only one they need to worry about," he replied gruffly.

"Then I shall thank you all for your time, and leave you to go about your duties," he concluded. People slowly left the Hall, leaving a quiet room that felt suddenly bigger with their absence.

King Garrod and King Fanton remained behind.

"And what of the assassin?" asked King Garrod.

"It would appear that there were two of them, working in parallel, your Majesty,"

"And have you apprehended either?"

"No. One, the man who was in the caravan, named Deltone, has fled. I am sure he has returned to Tobar, given his cover is blown and he no longer has an employer."

"And the other? I assume he was the one that secured the venom and contracted with Santu?"

"Yes, Majesty. He is a man named Greig Atos. He was posing as a merchant trader. Our thinking is that he might have fled to Santu's estate, but if he is not there, then he will also have gone to Tobar."

"Then I would request that you visit the estates of the man Santu and check to see if he is there."

"Majesty, we would do so as a matter of course, anyway. We need to retrieve the Device that he used to kill the Taka, which he later turned on a room full of people in order to make his escape. However, if he is not on the estate, then we cannot pursue him to Tobar. That would be suicide for anyone I send."

"We will need to deal with the Guild," chipped in King Fanton.

"We will - eventually. But not this week, and not with just a single Mage and her Guardian," said Misco firmly. The Kings both nodded and left the Hall.

42

Retrieval

Helena and Domico took a day or two to rest before the long trip back to Brenta. Misco agreed, as they had been charging around the continent for months, and an extra day or two would not make much difference.

Now that the war had been averted, Helena felt like it was the first time that she could breathe in a very long time. So she relished the opportunity to just relax and wander round Tradehome to see the sights.

It was the height of summer now, and Tradehome, being in the southern reaches of the continent, was hot during the day. Helena and Domico hadn't really packed a great deal of clothing, so their wardrobe choices were limited. Although they could have bought more appropriate clothing within Tradehome (it was the largest centre of trade on the continent after all), they had nowhere to store the clothes when they moved on. So they continued to wear heavier clothing, and boil. This was made worse by both Misco and Domico's insistence that they both wear their 'shields' when outside of the Inn, just in case Greig Atos had come to Tradehome, rather than travelling to Brenta.

Helena was surprised at the variety of things available to buy. Some of the things she saw, she did not know what they were, or what people used them for. Her limited knowledge from her upbringing hadn't been that widely expanded at the Mage University, and in some ways she was still quite sheltered. Domico found this amusing, trying his best not to laugh, and struggling to explain some of the more exotic items. After a few embarrassing answers, she stopped asking him what things were, but she still enjoyed the brief respite from the difficulties of the last few weeks.

They decided to travel over-land to Brenta, taking the route through Suntend and Lintik, as Helena couldn't face more time confined to a small cabin on another ship or barge.

They set off on the morning of the third day following the events in the Central Hall. Misco had left the day before, needing to get back to the University and the business of the Order.

The day promised to be warm, so they wore their lightest clothing but had a slight disagreement about wearing the shields. Helena was sure she wouldn't need it yet, but Domico was adamant that she wear it, anyway. In the end, he won the argument, simply by refusing to leave the Inn until she had put it on.

They rode through the town, making their way to the Suntend Road. It was still relatively early and the activity in the town didn't really get busy until the mid-morning, so the streets were quiet.

"Do you really think that Atos will be at Brenta?" Helena asked Domico.

"Not unless he's stupid. If he is, as we think, an assassin himself, then he would be much safer returning to Tobar. Why would he go to Brenta, when we can link him with Santu?"

"He may be seeking the rest of the fee?"

259

"I would have assumed that it would all have been paid in advance,"

"Really? I'd have thought the opposite. Wouldn't it make sense to pay only a little in advance and the rest after the job is done?"

"Possibly, but he'd have had weeks after Casili's death to get the rest of the payment. Especially when we didn't arrive for a few weeks after that…"

"True. So this may be a waste of time, then?"

"Maybe, but it's not like we have anywhere else pressing to be," he said with a shrug.

When they arrived in Suntend, it was only mid-afternoon, and as they didn't have a deadline, they stopped early and relax for a few hours. It wasn't a city, or even a sizeable town. Its main reason for existence seemed to be providing provisions for people travelling to Tradehome and back again.

It was in the kingdom of Eretee, which, although one of the southern kingdoms, wasn't as well populated as Rintala, so had fewer towns and cities. It was, however, a kingdom of farms, and at this time of year, the crops were growing strong. Even more than Rintala, they had broken the landscape into regimented square and oblong fields, with irrigation trenches providing water to those areas far from the major rivers. The town itself was encircled by a high wooden palisade and a deep ditch that, at some point, had filled with water. Once inside the gates, Helena stared at the buildings. They were mostly or three stories, with stone on the ground floor and wood from the first floor up. Helena had never seen buildings constructed in this way, and wondered why they had been built in such a fashion.

Domico saw her staring. "They don't quarry stone much in these parts, as they've mostly given the land over to agriculture. It's good soil. So they build in this fashion to reduce the need for stone, but separate themselves from the 'barbarians' in the north who only use wood. It makes little sense, but it seems to work for them."

As the town seemed to exist to cater to travellers, there was an abundance of inns along the main street. Domico selected one of the larger ones and rode into its courtyard. A young man came out of a long, low building, presumably the stable, and offered to take their horses. Domico surrendered his reins and assisted Helena to dismount, leading her to the main door.

Inside, they found a large room dotted with tables and a small serving bar off to their left. There were several people at the tables, and a few serving maids moving between them, serving drinks and food. Domico escorted her over to the bar and asked the man standing behind it if they had rooms.

"We have several rooms. Good Sir. Would you wish one, two, or a small suite?"

"Tell me about the suite,"

"We have two available, Master. The first is at the front, and includes a good size sitting room, two bedrooms and a private bathing room. The second is similar, but overlooks the stables and has only one bedroom."

"Let me see the first suite and if it is good enough, we will take it."

The barman snapped his fingers at one of the serving maids and asked her to escort Helena and Domico to the suite in question. On inspection, they found it to be adequate. Each room was quite small, but clean, with fresh linen on the bed, which smelled recently aired, and clean cloths in the bathing room for washing. Domico told the maid that they would take it and asked for their saddlebags to be sent up from the stable.

"At this rate, we are going to need more funds," said Helena.

"It's fine. I got more from Misco while we were in Tradehome. Now, would my lady care for a walk about the town?"

"Yes, I'd like to stretch my legs for a bit before dinner," said Helena, removing the home-made shield.

"Oh, no you don't. You leave that on."

"But it's so heavy, and I'm sure that Atos won't be hanging around somewhere like this."

"You never know. The whole point of making these is so that if we run into him again, he can't incapacitate us and get away. So you need to leave it on, just in case he is here."

Helena looked at Domico grumpily, "You're not being reasonable. What are the chances that he is here?"

"Slim, I agree. But we Guardians can be unreasonable when it comes to making sure that our Mage is safe. That's our job… But seriously Helena, will you take my advice on this, please?"

"Oh, alright then, I'll wear the damn shield."

They left the Inn to explore the town, with no particular destination in mind. They wandered for about half an hour, and in that time covered most of the town's principal streets. Even though it was getting on toward evening, it was still quite warm, so Domico suggested they stop for a cool drink in one of the other inns.

They chose one that looked to be fairly quiet, as most of the workers in the town were now finishing their day's work, and were themselves seeking refreshment.

The Inn Domico pointed out to Helena was one of the smaller ones, off the principal streets. It was dark and cool inside, with only a few small tables in the main room, and no booths or private dining rooms as far as they could tell on entering. Helena took a seat at one table to the side of the door, while Domico went to the bar and ordered a couple of cold beers. Neither of them drank much alcohol, so he ordered small ones and carried them back to the table.

They sipped their beers, talking of nothing much and were just about to leave when a tall, thin man entered the Inn.

Domico swore and was getting to his feet when the man turned and spotted them. It was Greig Atos.

Atos quickly drew a small Device from out of his cloak, and aimed it at the table where Helena was just rising, with Domico coming fast around it towards him.

A few people at the adjacent tables suddenly went stiff and then fell unconscious to the floor. However, because of their shields, neither Helena nor Domico were rendered unconscious. Atos swore and dropped the Device, quickly pulling a sword free from under his cloak with his right hand, and pulling a short dagger free from his left boot with the other hand.

Domico kicked the table out of the way and advanced on Atos. The patrons of the Inn who had not been rendered unconscious scrambled for the door behind him, and the barkeeper hunched down behind the counter.

"Stop, Atos!" shouted Domico over the noise. "If you give yourself up, there is no reason for you to get hurt, and we know you were involved in the death of Princess Casili,"

"I don't think so, Guardian," he said with contempt. "You may have found a way of countering the Device, but you haven't beaten me yet, and that shield will slow you down. I will not let you take me back to Voreen just to face death." He backed away from the advancing Domico, raising his sword into a defensive position.

Domico continued his slow advance and circled Atos, looking for an opening. He was right, thought Domico. This shield would slow him, and Atos, as a trained assassin, would not be a poor swordsman.

Domico knew he would need to make it a quick fight, as the extra weight from the shield would tire him more quickly than would otherwise have been the case.

He therefore lunged at Atos, wanting to test his speed. Atos was indeed quick and parried the blow with little effort. Domico took the fight to him, thrusting, slashing and seeking to cut the assassin, but each time his sword was met with either the dagger or sword of the assassin. He also needed to guard himself against the dagger, as it was clear that Atos was looking for an opportunity to cut him, should his slashes or thrusts take him off balance, or leave him vulnerable to a double-handed attack from Atos.

After a few minutes, Domico was sweating, and his breathing was heavy. His grip on his sword was becoming harder to maintain, given the sweat on his arms and hands. Atos, however, still appeared cool and fit, his movements just as sharp as at the beginning of the fight. Domico knew he was losing. But there was nothing else for it but to press on and hope that the assassin made a mistake.

He didn't. The fight moved backwards and forwards across the floor of the Inn, with each of them seeking to use the tables and chairs to their advantage and putting a little space between themselves and their opponent. Domico was visibly slowing, his breathing harder, when he took a gamble and picked up a chair to throw at Atos. Instead, Atos dodged to the side, and his dagger drew a long groove down Domico's side. Domico gasped in pain as a dark red stain showed on his tunic. The slice had also done some damage to the thin rope securing the bottom of the shield to Domico's stomach. Atos stepped up his attack, using both the sword and dagger to force Domico back and up against the bar. He parried the thrusts desperately, but it wasn't enough, and Atos scored Domico's arm, with another long cut drawing even more blood and weakening him further.

Helena scurried out from behind their original table, looking for the dropped Device, but in the chaos of overturned tables and chairs, couldn't see it.

Seeing that Domico was in danger of losing the fight, she closed her eyes and concentrated on making the air around Atos dense. He was moving too much for her to be able to picture a circle enveloping him, so she struggled to define the area in which the air needed to become thick. This wasn't working, and she was beginning to panic.

Atos was closing in on Domico, and it didn't appear that Domico had much fight left in him. Helena did the only thing she could think of. She picked up one chair and threw it at Atos' back. Atos, concentrating on Domico, didn't see it coming until it was too late.

The chair hit him on his lower back and the tops of his legs. He fell forward, towards Domico, who dodged to the side and hit him on the back of his head with his sword hilt, knocking him out. Then Domico slumped to the floor, holding his side.

Helena rushed over to Domico. "You're hurt!" she said.

"Tie him up, quickly, before he wakes up," she nodded and removed her shield, taking out the ropes and using them to tie Atos' hand together. She then thought better of it, and used the second piece of rope, from round the bottom of the shield, to tie his legs together as well.

265

Turning to Domico, she said, "Let me see your side."

He raised his elbow so that she could see the cut in his tunic, now heavily stained with blood.

"We need to get this off you," she said, untying the shield.

"Find the Device first, just in case," he croaked

She stood up and started searching the floor, moving tables and chairs as she worked her way across the room. After a couple of minutes she found the Device, near the door, and picked it up and put it in her coat pocket.

Returning to Domico, she said, "We need to remove that tunic so that I can see the wound." She lifted his shield off, over his head, once she had cut the rest of the rope around his side underneath the wound.

Domico gritted his teeth as she pulled his tunic off over his head, fighting to stay conscious. Helena knelt down and examined the wound.

"I think I can knit this back together," she said with a frown.

"Then please do it, before I bleed to death!"

She closed her eyes and once more centred herself, drawing on her willpower. Opening her eyes, she imagined the sides of the wound coming together, with the muscles underneath rejoining each other. Luckily, the blade had scraped along the ribs, so it wasn't deep, but it was bleeding a lot.

Taking a cloth from the top of the bar, she wiped away some of the blood, continuing to imagine the sides of the wound closing, the bleeding slowing and then stopping as the sides came together. She concentrated hard, imagining the skin knitting itself together again, forcing each cell to attach itself back to the others on the other side of the cut.

After a few moments, it was done. A long pink scar now ran down Domico's side, but the bleeding had stopped.

"Twist, turn. Let's see if that's strong enough to hold," she told him.

Tentatively, he twisted, looking down and trying to see if the wound was about to re-open. "It's tender, but I think it will be alright," he said.

"Right, let me see your arm now."

He held out his arm, and she performed the same exercise on that. It took longer this time, as she was tired, and straining to concentrate, but eventually there was also only a thin pink scar running down his arm.

"You will need to rest, and eat plenty to build your strength back up," she told him, standing.

"And so will you, Mage Hawke. That was a lot of magic," he said, getting to his feet.

At that moment, a group of men came charging into the Inn.

"What's going on here?" shouted the man in the front. Helena and Domico looked at him, and at the state of the Inn, with its overturned tables and chairs, and Atos lying on the floor, tied up.

"I am Mage Hawke, and this is my Guardian, Domico," said Helena, stepping forward. "This man is Greig Atos. A member of the Guild of Death, who was responsible for the death of Princess Casili. We have apprehended him and will take him to Voreen to face justice."

The man bowed and introduced himself. "I am Constable Packer, Mage Hawke, and am responsible for law and order in this town. Can you prove you are a Mage, and that this man is indeed a member of the Guild?" His men moved about the Inn, checking on the people who were unconscious.

"I could prove I am a Mage, yes. As for him. I have the sworn testimony of Prince Lyton of Rintala, Atos' brother in Voreen and Misco, the Head of the Mage Order. Do you doubt their accuracy?"

"No Mage Hawke. But what I see is a tavern brawl gone mad…"

Just then, the barman popped his head up from behind the bar. Helena had forgotten that he was there, as he had stayed so quiet.

"Constable," he said, standing up and trying to pull his tunic straight. "The Mage and her man were just sitting having a drink when this man came in. They challenged him, giving him the opportunity to surrender, and telling him they knew of his part in the death. He refused to go quietly. Then he did something and some of my patrons, as you can see, were rendered unconscious… I don't think that the Mage and her Guardian had any choice but to fight him."

"Thank you Sir." Turning to Helena he said, "What did he do to make people unconscious?"

"He had a Device that a rogue Mage sold him. It was part of our mission to retrieve that Device, as it can be used to kill as well as stun,"

He looked towards a couple of his men, and one of them said, "They are out cold, Sir. They should wake soon,".

"And you have that Device now?"

"We do."

"Good. Please take it, and this man, out of my town. Tonight!" and he turned and walked out of the Inn, his men following silently.

Helena looked at Domico. "So much for a night in an Inn! But at least we can get rid of these things now," she said, using her toes to point at her discarded shield.

"Thank you for your help, Sir." said Domico, turning to the barman.

"I didn't really do anything, Guardian. Just told the Constable what had happened. He's got a mighty temper on him, and I don't think that you would want to spend a night in the cells while he calmed down."

"Well, thank you anyway."

"Helena, we will need to return to our inn and collect our things. We're also going to need an extra horse…"

They hauled Atos to his feet as he was slowly coming round. Helena untied the rope around his feet, so that he could walk. Domico used it to tie a halter around Atos' neck, so that he couldn't run away.

They frog-marched him to their inn, and Helena entered, recovering their belongings and paying the Innkeeper. She asked him about an extra horse, and he told her he had an old one in the stable that was for sale.

"He's not a quick horse mind! He's getting on a bit, and prefers a slow walk to anything faster, so if you need speed, he's not the one for you."

"No, a slow old horse would be just fine. How much do you want for him? We'll need the saddle and tack as well."

They haggled for a bit, and Helena parted with some coins. The Innkeeper followed her out to the stable and instructed the stable lads to saddle a sorry-looking bay that was in the end stall. When all three horses were saddled, Helena and the stable boys led them out into the courtyard.

"Right, Atos, get on the horse," Domico said to him, pointing to the old bay. Atos reluctantly climbed up, and Domico tied his feet to the stirrups and his hands to the pommel of the saddle. Helena held the reins while Domico mounted his own horse and then passed them over, so that he could lead Atos' horse.

Then she mounted, and they slowly made their way out of the town.

43

Delivery

The easiest way to get to Nimea from their current location was to backtrack along the road to Tradehome, and then seek to pick up a barge travelling to Lake Voreen up the River Dern. From there, they could take one of the tributary rivers from Lake Voreen towards the mountains and then back through the Tintern Pass. They decided on this route, as it would also provide some respite from watching Atos all the time, letting the barge do the work while they took turns watching him.

However, they had several days of hard-riding in order to get to the River Dern first.

That first night, they had only travelled a few miles from Suntend before they were forced to stop for the evening. They only had one tent between them, which gave rise to a discussion about what to do with Atos.

"We'll just tie him up outside the tent," suggested Domico, "but one of us will need to watch him."

"We can take turns at that, that way at least we'll both get *some* sleep. Won't it be too cold though?"

"No, I think the nights are still warm enough to prevent him from getting hypothermia or anything like that. But if not, we can always share one of our blankets with him. We want him in one piece to deliver to the King."

Atos remained silent, but watchful. He had hardly spoken a word since he woke up at the Inn, which puzzled Helena. He didn't even speak when Domico tied him to one of the trees lining the road, having already placed the tent close by.

She motioned for Domico to step away from him. "Why isn't he saying anything?" she asked him.

"He's waiting to catch up off-guard, and will then try to escape. He knows there is no point talking to us. We will not let him go, and for now, his options are limited."

"So what do we do?"

"Nothing. We just keep an eye on him, and get him to Nimea. Now, what do we have to eat?" Domico walked over to the packs, rummaging through for some food.

They ate a cold meal of dried meat, cheese, and bread, sharing some with Atos. This was distasteful to Helena, as although they did not gag him, his hands were bound, so he had to be fed a mouthful at a time.

"Be careful he doesn't bite you," warned Domico. This resulted in a nasty grin from Atos, which made Helena even more nervous at the task.

After they had all eaten something, Domico suggested Helena get some sleep, promising to wake her to take her turn to watch Atos later. Helena retired into the tent, and Domico sat down just outside the entrance, so that he could watch Atos.

It took Helena a long time to fall asleep, as she was worried about their ability to keep hold of the assassin for long enough to reach Nimea. It was just the two of them, after all. But eventually she fell asleep and was surprised when Domico woke her.

"I feel like I've only been asleep for an hour," she said, getting up out of the sleeping roll.

"I think it's about three hours to dawn, and you've been asleep for about four hours," he said with a smile.

"Is this going to work?"

"Of course. We just need to keep our wits about us, and we'll be fine. It will be easier when we get onto a barge."

"If you say so,"

"Take the Device, just in case,"

"Why?"

"If he manages to undo those ropes, you're not going to be able to fight him, so take the Device, and if you need to, use it on him,"

"And if he has a weak heart?"

"He doesn't. He wouldn't have survived the training for the Guild if he had," reasoned Domico.

"But we don't know that he is actually a member of the Guild, or just a merchant they use for contact…"

"Oh, come on Helena. Everything points to him being a full member, and he's hung his brother out to dry over it!"

"I don't like it, but I'll take it just in case," she said, emerging from the tent with the Device in her hand.

Helena sat with her back to the tent, watching Atos, who appeared to have fallen asleep, despite sitting on the roots of the tree, and being bound around his chest with his hands behind his back.

Just when Helena wished that she had something to read, and light to read it by, he opened his eyes.

"You've got it all wrong, you know," he said lazily.

"What?"

"You've got it all wrong. I'm not an assassin. I'm just a merchant, going on buying trips for my brother's business."

"Oh sure, that's why you had the Device, and tried to use it on us. Twice!"

"Yes, I had the Device, but that was only for protection. I travel through dangerous country quite a lot, and need to be able to defend myself..."

"You killed a Taka with it, and then used that Taka's venom to murder Princess Casili,"

"I killed the Taka in self-defence. But I didn't take any venom, and was certainly nowhere near the Princess."

"Your brother has already testified that you were the contact, making the deal with Baron Santu's representative to kill Casili. There is no point in you denying it."

"My brother isn't very bright. He'd say anything if he thought it would get him out of trouble,"

"Well, he's also a better man than you. You know he sought to make a deal to save your life?"

"Why would it need saving? I didn't kill anyone,"

"Of course you didn't. Now, I suggest you get some sleep. It's going to be a long trip."

"Yes, it will be a long trip, won't it?" he said with a smile that chilled Helena to the bone.

Morning came about an hour later, and Domico could be heard moving about inside the tent. He came out and helped Helena to her feet.

"My muscles have stiffened, sitting there for so long," she complained, hobbling around the camp and trying to get some feeling back in her legs.

"You walk about a bit. It'll help, and I'll sort out breakfast,"

They all ate some more bread and cheese and then were mounted again. Atos was tied to his horse's saddle and tack again, and they were off.

Two more days of this saw them to the River Dern. There were no proper docks here, merely a shallow incline leading from the river to a small village. They settled in to wait for a barge to come past, heading upriver to the Lake.

After a few hours, a large barge came into view, being poled upriver by four bulky men. The middle of the craft was piled high with bundles and boxes, all lashed down with heavy ropes. Each end had a low wooden structure that presumably houses the Captain and the workers, keeping the weather off them when they stopped for the night.

"Ho Captain!" shouted Domico as they were coming alongside. "We need urgent transport to Lake Voreen. Can you take us as passengers?"

"I could, if you can pay," responded a short, stocky man with a weather-beaten face.

"We can pay," confirmed Domico.

The Captain signalled for his men to pole the barge over to the bank.

"Your horses will not have any shelter," he said as they pulled alongside.

"That's fine. Can you provide *us* with shelter?"

"That depends on you. Will you pay my bargemen to sleep on the deck so that you may have their shed?"

"We will,"

Then the Captain noticed that Atos' hands were tied. "What's going on with him then?" he asked

"He is our prisoner,"

"Prisoner? I don't want any trouble on my barge!"

"There won't be any trouble, Captain. You have my word."

"If there is, you're off, and you won't get your money back."

"That's fine Captain. There won't be any trouble." added Helena.

A long, wide plank was run out from the barge to the bank they were standing on, and Helena led hers, then Domico's and finally Atos' horse over and on to the barge. Domico led Atos across once all the horses were loaded and tied to a small railing that ran along the middle of the barge. Domico escorted Atos to the little shed-like structure at the front of the barge. The men came and removed their blankets from it, freeing it up for Helena and Domico to use. Helena swapped places with Domico so that he could unsaddle the horses, giving them a brush down and a small bag of oats each.

At least that now they were on the barge, they could take turns watching Atos all the time, getting more sleep than they had the last few days.

Helena couldn't help thinking about her conversation with Atos. Could they have read more into his involvement than there actually was? Had his brother lied to save his own skin? She hadn't mentioned the discussion with Domico, knowing what he would think about it. He was convinced that Greig Atos was guilty, so who was right?

Her own doubts continued to bother her. She could force Atos into a circle of truth, but it was a long way to drag him - all the way to Nimea - if she was wrong...

Over and over, for the next four days of the journey, until they reached Lake Voreen, she replayed the steps they had taken so far in her head.

Tomas Atos had not believed that his brother was part of the Guild, but he had seemed naïve on that point. Was he? Or was he right and his brother was just a 'go between'? It seemed too coincidental that Greig Atos had been the one to buy that Device, and still have it with him, that had been responsible for allowing the collection of the Taka venom. He was also a skilled fighter, as his fight with Domico had proved. He was also the one that had made contact with Santu's representative.

Too many coincidences? Possibly. The only way that she would know for sure would be to use the circle again. She resolved to shelve her doubts and perform the magic for the circle when they reached Nimea.

When they arrived at Lake Voreen, they paid off the bargemen and the Captain and sought to find a vessel that was travelling across the Lake and on towards the mountains.

Being the height of summer, and with the aborted war campaign, there were plenty to choose from, so they chose one of the largest, that offered better accommodation than a shed on the deck. They moved in and again shared shifts in watching Atos.

He still had not tried to escape, and Domico was getting tense, wondering what he was up to. Both Helena's and Domico's tempers were getting frayed, with the continual need to watch Atos constantly, and little time to just relax.

After another six days, they reached the point where they needed to leave the barge and take the road for the Tintern Pass. Caravans were waiting for the barge, as they would also unload the cargo here, and Teamsters would move it over the mountains and on to Ista, Nimea and, in some cases, Tilana.

They therefore disembarked amid the chaos of unloading and sought to put some small distance between themselves and the following caravan. They did not wish to become part of it, and restricted to the short distances it would cover each day. Both were looking forward to the end of their journey and being relieved of their prisoner.

They moved easily back into the routine of taking shifts at night to guard

Atos, but it did nothing to calm tempers, with some minor flare-ups and arguments being the result.

This time the Tintern Pass was quiet. They navigated it in a single day, and with no sightings of either bandits or Rocs, for which Helena was thankful. Another five or six days would see them in Nimea and finally rid of their prisoner.

They travelled hard each day, covering as much ground as possible. Atos got surlier and surlier. He was obviously sore from being tied to his saddle and unable to adjust his seat, but he refused to mention it or complain. Both Helena and Domico also knew that he was running out of time to try to escape.

However, they were now back in his native Voreen, so they expected an attempt any day.

That attempt came on the second day out of Ista. They were moving along at a fast walk for a while, and thinking that they should see Nimea in less than a day, when suddenly Greig tried to get his horse to bolt. It didn't work. Helena was glad that they had bought such an old horse for him. It had little speed, and Domico was able to catch up quickly, reigning in the tired animal and walking it back to Helena.

"If you try that again, I will use the Device on you, and tie you over the horse for the rest of the journey. How would you like that?" he asked, looking coldly at Atos.

"It doesn't matter. I'm dead anyway if you take me back to Nimea. The King will hang me, even though I'm a simple trader., and wasn't involved in Casili's death,"

"Still playing the 'simple trader', are you? Well, it won't work on us,"

"I will have the truth from you, in front of the King," said Helena

Atos, for a moment, forgot that they tied his feet to his stirrups and tried to jump off the horse. He ended up dangling upside down alongside the belly of the animal, with one of his legs hooked over the saddle, and his hands above his head on the pommel. It was a comical sight, and Helena couldn't help but laugh.

Domico looked at her as if she'd lost her mind and dismounted to push Atos back into the saddle.

The open grassland had presented a problem in how to secure Atos at night, so they had improvised by tying him to the stakes of the tent. It wasn't as secure, but as long as one of them was watching him, he hadn't had a chance to do anything about it. Tonight would be his last opportunity, as they would arrive in Nimea the following day.

They were all aware of this, so when it came time for Helena to get some sleep, she offered to sit with Domico instead.

"I don't think I'll be able to sleep," she told him. "This has been going on so long, and I almost can't believe that it will be over tomorrow. I'll manage without sleep tonight."

"But if you are not rested, you won't be able to do the magic for the circle. Please, get some rest."

"I'll try, but wake me if he tries anything?"

"Of course."

She laid down inside the tent and closed her eyes, seeking to fall asleep, but couldn't and spent an hour tossing and turning. Just as she was finally drifting off, she heard a grunt from outside. Wondering what it was, she got out of her sleeping roll and emerged from the tent.

The sight that greeted her wasn't good. Domico was lying on the ground, out cold, and Atos was galloping away on one of their horses.

Helena quickly dived back into the tent and retrieved the Device. By the time she was back outside, he had gotten too far away for the Device to be effective.

She heaved herself up onto her own horse and galloped after him. She had never ridden bareback before, and found keeping her seat difficult, but she was slowly gaining on him.

After a few minutes she judged she was close enough for the Device to work, so she pointed it out in front of her and pressed the lever.

The horse stumbled and fell, throwing Atos to the ground. He hadn't known that she was chasing him, so had had no warning. She stopped her horse beside his body, quickly getting down to ensure that he was still alive. He was, but there would be broken bones to worry about. Then she went to check on the horse. It too was breathing, and didn't appear to have broken a leg in falling, for which she was very grateful. The horses had become friends over the last few months.

She wasn't sure what to do, though. She wouldn't be able to lift Atos on her own, and needed to get him and both horses back to the camp to check on Domico.

Just then, she heard Domico calling her name.

"Over here," she shouted

"What happened?" he shouted back. "Keep shouting and I'll follow the noise!"

"Atos must have hit you with something. Then he took your horse and ran away. I heard something and came out of the tent. I saw he had left and came after him. The Device was used to stop him, but also knocked the horse out."

"It's OK, I can find you now," said a voice out of the gloom, as Domico came into view. She was so relieved that he was up, and OK, and here... Although he had blood running down the side of his face.

"You're hurt!"

"It's nothing, just a scratch."

"Can you help me get him on to my horse?"

He nodded and between them; they draped Atos' body over the back of Helena's horse. Domico went to check on his own.

"He's OK," he said, "we just need to give him some time to wake up."

They waited a few minutes, and then his horse started stirring. Once it was on its feet, they returned to camp. Atos didn't stir for another half an hour, by which time they were back in camp, with the tent put away and ready to ride.

Atos had broken his right shoulder when he was thrown from the horse, and was in obvious pain.

They travelled through the rest of the night and arrived in Nimea about mid-morning. Moving straight to the Palace, they asked the Guard to gather Lord

Thatcher and the King, explaining who they were and who their prisoner was.

The Royal Chamberlain and the King appeared quickly, the King signalling for some of the Royal Guard to take Atos in hand and follow them.

"Mage Hawke, is this really the assassin?"

"We believe so, Your Highness. He denies it, so we will need a truth circle to confirm it, but I didn't want to do that without you witnessing it."

"Thank you. We can use that room there," he said, pointing to a small chamber just off the main Palace entrance.

The room was obviously some sort of waiting room, with chairs around the outside, but the centre was clear. Helena took a couple of deep breaths, steadying herself, and once more pictured the circle. The guards forced Atos into it, which wasn't hard, as the fight seemed to have left him since his attempted escape the night before. His broken shoulder hindered his movement considerably.

"You are Greig Atos?" she asked once he was inside.

"Yes,"

"You are a member of the Guild of Death?"

"Yes,"

"You secured the Taka venom?"

"Yes,"

"Why did you choose that method?"

"It was not the original plan, but Deltone couldn't get close enough to her to do anything direct, and we thought it would look like a heart attack."

"Why not just use the Device on her directly?"

"She was never alone, and it would have looked suspicious if a lot of people suddenly had a heart attack."

"Where is Deltone now?"

"Back in Tobar. He won't come back to the mainland for years."

"Why didn't you run there as well?"

"I was waiting to collect the second part of the payment. Santu should have paid the rest within a week of her death, but he kept moving about and I couldn't run him down. I thought he would pass through Suntend on his way home from Tradehome, but he never came."

"And your brother. Is he a member of the Guild?"

"No, he just runs the business as one of our covers,"

"Does he know you are a member?"

"No, he thinks me a simple trader, buying goods for his business."

Helena turned to the King. "Is there anything else your Majesty would like to know?"

"No," he said in a sick voice, turning away.

Helena let the circle go, and the guards came forward and seized Atos, dragging him out of the room.

"What will happen now, your Majesty?" asked Domico.

"He will hang. If I can get my hands on this Deltone, he will hang, too."

"And Kubu and Captain Hileat?" asked Helena.

"I never held them responsible. But Kubu has sought another Mistress, out of the Palace, and Hileat is back in charge of the Royal Guard."

"Thank you, your Majesty. Is there anything else you require from the Order?"

"No. Please take some rooms and rest for as long as you need. I will pass on our thanks to Misco."

44

Epilogue

Domico hurried down the corridors of the Mage University. He was late in meeting Helena for lunch. Since they had returned, they had seen little of each other, but had attempted to have lunch once a week.

He'd worked hard on the training grounds that morning, and had pulled a muscle in his leg, so was limping along as fast as his leg would allow, but he was still going to be late.

He found Helena still in the classroom, surrounded by students who were all asking questions. He leaned against the door and listened.

"But what if my will isn't strong enough to make what I want to happen, happen?" asked a boy of about fifteen.

"You need to start small, and practice a lot. The more that you practice, the stronger your will, and your imagination becomes. You can only really try, and as you all have the spark, you will absolutely be able to do it. Just practice," she said with a smile.

She spotted Domico in the doorway and smiled. "Now, be off with you all.

We're missing lunch!" she said, waving them away.

"Your class is doing well?"

"Yes, but they all think that they need to be able to do everything now, and if they can't, they are a failure. They just need more practice and a bit of confidence."

"I know someone who felt the same a year ago," he said with a laugh as they left the building and headed for one of the dining halls.

Printed in Great Britain
by Amazon

81300787R00169